THE KEEPER'S RETRIBUTION

MEG ANNE

Copyright 2019 © Meg Anne

ISBN: 978-1-7322867-5-7 (Paperback Edition)

Permission requests can be sent to Meg Anne via email: Meg@MegAnneWrites.com

Cover Art by Story Wrappers

Edited by Analisa Denny

Proofread by Dominique Laura

❀ Created with Vellum

Karma,
You are the owner of the sweetest doggie grin I've ever seen.

Kel
Dreams may be the
start of our journey, but
rarely are they the end.

Maxine

THE KEEPER'S RETRIBUTION

ELYSIA

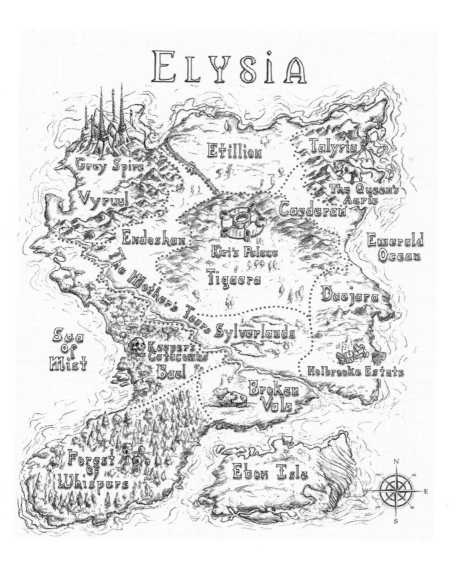

CHAPTER 1

The room lengthened and stretched until Effie felt like a great distance separated her from the others. One of the children at the Holbrooke's Estate had a toy that created a similar effect. He'd hold it up to his eyes and cackle with infectious joy as what had once been mundane transformed into something foreign and therefore incredible.

Effie did not feel incredible.

There was not a word yet created that could perfectly capture the sudden terror that had stolen her breath, made her stomach drop to her knees, and robbed her of the ability to form coherent thoughts.

She wasn't aware of anything except the sounds of her ragged breaths as she struggled to make sense of the words the Triumvirate had just uttered.

The Shadow Years.

Their spectral voices echoed in her mind, bringing about another ripple of dread. Effie blinked, and the room snapped back into focus.

It was a death sentence.

"Are you alright?" a low voice asked.

Effie jolted, her hand clutching the fabric of her tunic as she

1

attempted to catch her heart before it flew from the confines of her chest. "Mother's tits, Reyna."

The lithe female laughed softly, squeezing Effie's forearm. "I didn't mean to catch you off guard, but you haven't spoken since the hooded ones . . ." she trailed off, looking in the direction of Ronan and the Triumvirate, who were gathered in a loose semi-circle to their right.

"Told us the world was ending?" Effie offered with a tight-lipped smile.

Reyna returned it with a wry one of her own. "That's one way to put it."

Tilting her head, Effie asked, "And how else would you categorize the Chosen's greatest nightmare coming true?"

Clasping her hands in front of her, Reyna shrugged. "The Night Stalkers have no such nightmare."

Effie barely kept herself from gaping. She'd grown up with the threat of the Shadow Years. It was a legend as familiar to her as her name. One that children shared with great relish, knowing that they were safely tucked away in their beds and the horror of it would never touch them. It was hard to imagine that there were some in Elysia who hadn't heard the whispers.

"I forget sometimes that your people are from the Lost Tribes," Effie said.

Reyna nodded. "It is easy to forget about the Forsaken."

"No, that's not what I meant," Effie said, practically speaking over the dark-haired woman in her rush to explain. "I didn't mean to imply that your people are forgettable, only that our origins are different. I do not see you or the Night Stalkers as other."

Until Helena rallied the Lost Tribes, seeking them out and convincing their leaders to fight beside her and the Chosen, it had been centuries since their people had any contact at all. They referred to themselves as the Forsaken because the Chosen had exiled them for not believing in the Mother or recognizing the Kiri's right to rule.

Despite having only met them recently, Effie had always felt a certain kinship with the Forsaken, since none of their people were blessed with the Mother's magic either. Which was not to say they

2

were not powerful. The Forsaken had gifts the Chosen could never hope to replicate. Unfortunately, their ancestors did not understand that different did not mean less than. Apparently, some of the Chosen still hadn't learned the lesson.

"Let us hope our enemies forget as well; it will make them easier targets," Reyna murmured, although her eyes twinkled and her smile was kind. "Do not worry, Effie. I understood what you were trying to say. No offense taken."

Effie grinned, although her relief did little to quell the undercurrent of fear still racing through her.

The Night Stalker's leader squeezed her arm once more before asking, "So what are the Shadow Years, and why are they"—she gestured with her head—"so worried about it?"

Smile fading, Effie met Reyna's eyes. "Do your people have ghost stories?"

"Stories about the dead?" Reyna asked, her dark sculpted brows veeing over her green eyes.

"Not really. More like spooky stories that are told as entertainment."

Expression clearing, Reyna nodded. "Oh yes. We share such stories."

"The Shadow Years are such a story, or perhaps story is not the right word. It is more of a warning passed down through the generations about what would happen to the Chosen if they strayed from the path of the Mother to the extent that She abandoned them." Sighing, Effie wrapped her arms around her body, chilled despite the warmth of the room. "No one ever thought that it could be real. It was just something parents told their children to make them behave."

"Ah yes, we call such tales a *parabal*. They are the stories that contain important lessons for my people."

"Yes, exactly. The Shadow Years are one of the Chosen's *parabals*. I'm sure there are hundreds of variations of the tale, but at its heart the message is always the same: if the Shadow Years begin, then the Chosen have failed beyond redemption."

"Beyond redemption?" Reyna asked.

"They'll be wiped out."

Face grim, Reyna asked, "So your vision means—"

"Judgment is upon us."

Reyna and Effie spun toward the Triumvirate, who must have been listening in on their conversation. Effie wasn't sure if it was Smoke or one of the Mirrors that answered, but it didn't matter. She was too caught up on their word choice. Judgment implied there was still a decision that needed to be made.

Reeling with the implication, her question burst from her, "So it's not too late? There's a chance we can still stop it?"

"Your vision was the first of the markers."

Effie bit back a groan. *Leave it to the Triumvirate to answer a question without providing any actual information.* She should have known better, or at least anticipated the vague response. They might be masters of non-answers, but she was persistent. The Triumvirate might not realize it yet, but they'd met their match.

"How many markers are there?" Effie pressed.

"Dozens."

Her relief was both potent and short-lived.

"But only five must come to pass."

Mother save them. Only four more markers between the Chosen and complete annihilation. Effie gripped her hands together behind her back, trying to hide the tremors that racked them.

"Can they be stopped?" Ronan asked, picking up Effie's earlier question.

"We do not know."

"It has been decades since there's been any mention of the markers in our prophecies."

"Until now."

Effie squeezed her hands tighter, her nails digging into her skin as the memory of her vision pressed against her mind. She could still make out with perfect clarity the tendrils of corruption as they'd converged into a single being. Her lungs burned with the lack of air as she recalled how the creature sealed its mouth over hers until she'd turned into its likeness. Shuddering, Effie shoved the remnants of her vision away, not prepared to deal with any potential personal implications just yet.

Ronan's eyes were like shards of ice as he stared at the hooded faces before him. He was a warrior preparing to head into a battle he wasn't sure he could win, but he wasn't about to back down. "So what do we do now?"

"Cleanse the land as quickly as possible and pray it is enough."

Ronan and Reyna exchanged a look.

"If the Shadows are the source of the corruption, then we need to track them down. I will send word to the other realms, asking if there have been any sightings. It will give us a place to start if nothing else," Ronan said.

The Triumvirate dipped their heads in a nod.

"Should I warn them about the marker?" he asked.

"No."

"All it will do is spread fear."

"The Chosen are already on guard; it should be enough to keep them safe."

For now. The words were left unsaid, but they rang through her mind loud and clear.

Tingles raced under Effie's skin, and she rubbed her arms trying to alleviate some of the uncomfortable burn.

"Effie?" Reyna asked, missing nothing.

The Night Stalker's voice was pitched low, but it didn't prevent the men in the room from hearing. She could feel the weight of the others' stares as their unwavering attention landed on her.

"I'm fine," she hedged with a wan smile. "Just lingering side effects of the vision and too little sleep."

In reality, it was a very reasonable excuse, although Effie doubted it was the actual reason she currently felt so unsettled.

Ronan's eyes roamed over her face. "You look like you should be in bed."

Effie rolled her eyes. She knew he meant well, and had no doubt it was an accurate assessment, but no woman ever wanted to hear that she looked like a steaming pile of shit. Still, she couldn't argue the idea held appeal. Effie hadn't wanted to get out of bed in the first place, and that had been before her vision slammed into her. *Aren't they supposed to be affecting me less by now?*

"Maybe you're on to something," she said.

"I'll escort you to your room," Ronan offered.

She glanced at the Triumvirate. "Do you need anything else from me?"

"Rest, Daughter."

With a small wave at the others, she wove her arm through Ronan's and turned for the hall that would lead her back to her room.

They walked in companionable silence, and Effie enjoyed the slight reprieve from having to act like she wasn't still overwhelmed by the morning's discoveries. First there'd been the run-in with her Guardian and tutor after the prior night's series of terrible decisions, not to mention the part where she was still technically recovering from her battle with the Shadows the day before. All of that followed by yet another horrifying vision and the realization that while the war might be over, death still hunted all of them.

"Lovely," she breathed, not fully aware she'd spoken the thought aloud.

Ronan peered down at her with a raised brow. "I highly doubt you're referring to the empty hallway."

Effie smirked. "Just reflecting on the mess we've found ourselves in."

He grunted. "We've dealt with worse."

"Have we?" she stopped, turning to face him. "The Corruptor was one thing, but this . . ." she waved her arms, at a loss for words.

"Most battles feel impossible until they are over."

"Ronan, this isn't just any battle—"

"We have enemies to defeat, and we're trying to protect those we love. It is *exactly* like every other battle. You cannot give what lies ahead more power by amplifying its importance in your mind. That kind of thinking will paralyze you with fear. In battle, decisions need to be made based on instinct and speed. Fear will only slow you down."

"Fear makes you cautious."

"It's what will get you dead."

Effie crossed her arms and stared up at him, shaking her head. "I've missed you."

His eyes crinkled as he smiled. "And I you."

"It feels like months since I saw you last."

"A lot has happened since you left camp," he said, clamping a hand down on her shoulder, squeezing slightly.

Effie winced. The touch was not painful, but it caused her skin to pull where the Shadow had bitten her. Gingerly, Effie rubbed at her fresh scar, feeling icy pinpricks shoot down her back at the slight contact.

Ronan frowned. "You're injured."

She knew better than to try to lie to him. "As you said, a lot has happened."

He ran a hand over her newly shorn curls. "So it would seem. Why this change?"

"A Shadow bit me."

Ronan cursed and gently peeled her tunic back to look at the silvery scar. His expression darkened, and Effie pressed her hand over his.

"The healers fixed me up. I'm fine, Ronan. No need to worry."

Her words did little to clear the storm from his eyes.

"Effie."

Her stomach clenched before her eyes shifted to the towering figure a few feet away. "Guardian."

A quick peek showed her that Ronan wasn't any happier about his appearance than she was. The Shield's frown deepened as he stared with blatant dislike at Lucian. For some perverse reason, the knowledge filled her with glee. Finally, there was someone else around who didn't immediately cower at his feet.

She was doubly glad for Ronan's presence because it also meant she didn't have to face her Guardian alone. After last night, Effie wasn't certain she could be trusted.

"Did you need something?" she asked.

As if punishing her, Effie's eyes drank him in as she waited for his answer.

Lucian's dark eyes were unreadable under his heavy brow and thick lashes. The metallic flecks she knew to ring his pupils were barely visible in their depths.

It was impossible to ignore the pang in her chest as she recalled the feel of his stubble scraping over her skin as his lips moved against hers. Effie swallowed and struggled to tear her eyes from his mouth. Some of last night's madness must not have worked its way out of her system yet.

"I wanted to check and see if you were okay," he answered in his low rumble.

She blinked. "Oh, um. I'm alright."

He stared down at her in that unflinching way of his, and she fought the urge to squirm.

"I'm taking her to her room to rest. Triumvirate's orders," Ronan interjected.

Lucian's jaw clenched. "I'll see her to her room, Shield. She's my charge, after all," he added, throwing Ronan a pointed look.

Ronan tilted his head, returning Lucian's glower with one of his own. "Didn't seem to care about that too much when you let that monster take a chunk out of her."

Her Guardian's eyes narrowed into slits.

Effie moved fast, placing herself between them, not sure who would win if they came to blows and not eager to find out.

"Ronan," she said, pulling the red-headed man's attention back to her, "why don't you go send those requests to the other realms? The sooner we hear back, the better."

He rolled his lips together, about to argue the point.

"Please."

He lifted his gaze to stare at Lucian over her head. He didn't speak, but the threat was evident in the harsh lines of his face.

"I'll check on you later, Effie," he said, moving back the way they'd just come.

Alone now, Effie realized her palm was pressed firmly against

Lucian's hard chest. Heat crept into her cheeks, and she dropped her hand. She knew they'd end up alone together eventually, she just hadn't expected it to happen quite so soon.

It was hard to meet his eyes, so she stared at a spot in the middle of his forehead instead. *Should an immortal have such a heavy crease between their brows?* Maybe immortality couldn't completely counteract all of Lucian's time spent scowling.

Effie's lips twitched. *Serves him right.*

"I heard about your vision."

It took a second for his words to sink in, but when they did, her face scrunched in confusion. "In the five minutes since I left them?"

"The Triumvirate have an efficient way of communicating."

It was true they could speak directly into someone's mind, but Effie had always thought it required the person to at least be somewhat close to them physically. Then she remembered how the Triumvirate had been able to announce to all of the Keepers that Elysia was under attack. So maybe she didn't know much of anything at all about what the Triumvirate could or couldn't do.

"Mmm," she hummed noncommittally.

"Effie?"

"Hmm?"

"Why won't you look at me?"

Her eyes snapped to his. "I am looking at you."

One side of his mouth curled in a mocking smile, but his eyes were serious. "Are you okay?"

"Why does everybody keep asking me that?"

His thumb brushed lightly over her cheekbone, just beneath the purple smudges she'd noticed in the mirror before trudging out of her room that morning.

"It might have something to do with the fact that you almost bled out yesterday. Or it could just be because despite your best efforts to the contrary, people care about you."

The words were meant to provoke her temper, and any other time it might have worked, but his voice was soft and his eyes more concerned than she'd ever seen. He'd been worried about her.

9

Some of her tension ebbed, and Effie took a deep breath, deciding to take a risk and tell him the truth. "I feel like I've been trampled by a pack of Daejaran wolves, and that's just emotionally. I probably look better than I feel, truth be told."

Creases bracketed his mouth as he frowned.

"Lucian, about last night . . ."

If his gaze was intense before it was molten now.

Effie tried not to cringe as her stomach twisted itself in knots. The words needed to be said so that things could go back to some semblance of normal between them, but she'd rather clean the floor with her tongue than have this conversation.

"I-I'm sorry, that I . . . put you in that situation. You were right, I was drunk and not thinking clearly. It was a mistake." The words left her in a single breath, her cheeks burning by the time she was finished speaking.

His expression hadn't changed, his eyes still pinning her in place. "And what happened after? Was that a mistake too?"

"After?" she asked, her voice high and chest tight.

"After you left me."

He barely spoke above a whisper, but she flinched.

"It's not like Kieran made it seem. I mean, yes, I went to his room, but I changed my mind before . . . before I made a mistake I couldn't fix," she finished lamely.

Perhaps she didn't owe him an explanation. She was a grown woman, after all. Who she decided to take to bed was really none of his business, but it was important to her that he understood what had—and *hadn't*—happened.

Lucian's eyes burned as he stared at her. "I see."

"I was hurt—"

Lucian recoiled as if she'd struck him.

"—and I just wanted to—"

"Effie, stop, it's okay."

"—feel what it was like—"

"You don't have to explain," he tried again, this time lifting his hands and gently grabbing the sides of her arms.

"—to be wanted."

Before she finished speaking, he'd wrapped his arms around her and pulled her roughly against him. One of his hands cupped her head and the other banded across her back.

Effie froze, stunned by his reaction. *Lucian is . . . hugging me.*

He rested his cheek against the top of her head and held her. She could hear the thundering beat of his heart; it was a twin to her own. It took a full breath before she relaxed against him, tentatively wrapping her arms around his waist.

"Perhaps this time I am the one that owes you an apology," he rumbled above her.

"Lucian—"

"Shhh," he whispered. "Now it's my turn."

Effie clamped her lips together.

"I shouldn't have let you leave with things unresolved between us. If nothing else, I should have saw you back safely to your room. I am your Guardian; your well-being is my priority."

She shrank into herself. *Mother take me, he feels guilty because he believes he failed in his duty.*

"But Effie?"

"Hmm?" she asked, praying her voice sounded steady.

Lucian shifted, the hand cupping her head releasing her so that his fingers could run along her cheek and gently tilt up her chin. "Don't ever think I didn't want you."

Her heart stuttered, and she forgot how to breathe. All she could see was the naked desire shining in his eyes. He blinked and the moment was lost, his feelings tucked away behind his carefully crafted façade.

Effie sucked in a ragged breath, feeling like she'd been running for hours.

"I'm sorry for my part in causing you pain. It was never my intention."

"Mine either," she whispered.

Lucian held her a moment longer, before moving both hands back to her arms and taking a small step backward.

She shivered, her body instantly missing his heat.

"Does that help?" he asked.

"Help with what?" she asked, feeling like she'd lost the thread of their conversation.

"Ease some of the Daejaran wolf trampling?"

Effie snickered. Lucian was trying to make a joke. A sweet one, at that. As she reflected on his question, she was pleasantly surprised to find that their talk had done much to ease some of the previous night's sting. The pressure that had settled in the vicinity of her chest had fled, allowing her to take her first easy breath all morning.

"Yes," she admitted, smiling shyly.

"Good," he said, returning her smile with one of his own. "Let's get you back to your room, then, so you may rest."

He gestured for her to precede him down the hall. Effie turned and had only gone a few steps before he spoke again.

"Maybe this time you'll follow one of my orders."

Effie stared at Lucian, her eyes wide before she tilted her head back and laughed. "No promises."

CHAPTER 2

*E*ffie rolled and stretched, feeling fully rested for the first time since coming to the citadel. Still mildly disorientated from sleep, it took a moment for her to realize the orbs of enchanted light flickering around her chamber were the bright gold of morning and not the soft amber of afternoon or early evening.

Bolting upright, she shoved the blankets from her legs and scrambled out of bed.

Mother's tits, I slept through the whole damn day. Why didn't anyone come for me?

She rubbed her eyes and shuffled around her room, pulling on whichever clothes she stumbled upon first. She paused in front of her mirror only long enough to ensure that she looked mostly presentable and to run her fingers through her wild curls. *At least I don't have to waste time worrying about what to do with my hair.*

Biting her lip, she scanned her room trying to remember where she'd tossed her boots the day before. Generally, Effie made a point to put everything back in its place, but she'd been more exhausted than even she'd realized and didn't have the energy to manage more than haphazardly flinging her clothes about the room.

Spotting one curling lace peeking out from under her bed, Effie sighed and dropped to her hands and knees, crawling beneath it to retrieve them.

The first boot was easy enough to find, requiring her to only slap it out from below the bed, but the second proved more difficult. She must have used a bit more force when she kicked it off. Effie was having trouble making out much of anything in the dark shadows, and so she had to rely on touch to try and locate her boot's twin. She batted her arm around, fingertips straining as she searched.

No luck.

Cursing, Effie scooched a bit further under the bed, her head and most of her torso fully cloaked in the dim light.

"Ah-ha! Found you, you little—"

"My, what a delectable sight," a muffled voice drawled from somewhere behind her.

Effie let out a garbled scream, her head bashing into the wooden bed frame as she jumped. "Elder's gnarled knob!"

There was a snort and then a wheezing laugh.

She pushed herself back and stood, the lost boot dangling from her fingers forgotten as she rubbed the back of her head and glared at Kieran. He was red-faced with laughter, tears of mirth streaming from his eyes.

"Wh-what did you just say?" he choked out.

"What are you doing in my room?" she demanded.

Wiping away a few tears, Kieran shook his head. "Not so fast. First, tell me how you came about such a colorful phrase."

Crossing her arms, Effie debated about whether she could get away with kicking him in the shin. "It's not like I had much time to think about it. It just slipped out."

"Indeed," Kieran murmured, shoulders still shaking with the last of his laughter.

"You can leave now," she said, looking pointedly at him and then the door.

After a final snicker, Kieran said, "I did knock, you just didn't hear me. Now I know why," he added with a lascivious waggle of his eyebrows.

"How did you take my lack of answer as an invitation to come in? Doesn't that defeat the purpose of knocking in the first place?"

"I was checking to make sure you were still alive. You've been asleep for almost a full day."

"After the way you treated me yesterday, I have trouble believing you're concerned about my well-being."

"After the way I treated *you*?" he sputtered.

Anger was swiftly replacing embarrassment as Effie recalled the horrible things he'd said to her in front of Lucian and Kael. "You practically labeled me a whore in front of the Guardians, Kieran. How would you classify that treatment?"

There wasn't a trace of laughter left on Kieran's face. "Perhaps it was not my finest moment, but I was upset. Can you blame me? I'd just learned I was Lucian's sloppy seconds."

Sharp ringing filled her ears, and Effie's jaw dropped. "He told you?"

Kieran's brows lowered over glittering green eyes. "He didn't have to. It was all over your face when you looked at him. I inferred it easily enough, and you just confirmed it."

"It's none of your business what I choose to do or with *whom*."

"It is when I am the runner-up. Effie, you know how I feel about you. How could you do that to me?"

Effie tried to rein back her emotion, recognizing that there was the smallest vein of truth to his words. She hadn't treated him fairly, but it did not give him the right to bully her because of it.

"Kieran, I wasn't in my right mind. I'm sorry if I hurt you—"

"Because that makes it better." Kieran snorted. "To think I was here to tell you I forgive you—"

"Forgive me?" she sputtered.

"You led me on."

"Everyone has the right to change their mind," she spat out, any hint of understanding vanishing.

"So you'll spread your legs for the Guardian, but not me?"

Crack.

Effie's palm stung with the force of the slap.

15

Kieran's hand lifted to his cheek and then his lip. He glanced down at the blood staining his fingers and then back up at Effie. He took a step forward, but she stood her ground, tilting her chin up.

There was a blur of movement and Kieran flew away from her, his body crashing into the bookcase on the other side of her room.

"You'd dare raise your hand against a woman?" Lucian growled, already across the room leaning over him.

"I wasn't going to hit her," Kieran groaned, pushing himself up.

Lucian fisted his hand in Kieran's tunic, pulling him to his feet. "That's not what it looked like."

Kieran twisted his head and spat out a mouthful of blood. "You always make a habit of spying on your charge when she's in her room?"

Effie was shocked he had the balls to goad him. Lucian was fury incarnate, his lips peeled back over his teeth in a deadly snarl and his eyes on fire with savage promise. He pulled the fabric of Kieran's tunic taut and lifted him higher until the tips of his boots scraped over her floor.

"You listen, and you listen well, *princeling*. You so much as look at her wrong and I will rip your spine out through your mouth." Twisting, he shoved Kieran toward the door. "Get out."

Kieran paused only long enough to shoot Effie a dark look. "This isn't over."

Raising a brow, Effie glanced between Kieran and her Guardian. "Seems over to me."

Jaw clenched, Kieran made for the door. Lucian tracked each step like a predator preparing for the hunt.

Seeking to distract him, Effie stepped into his line of vision. "I had the situation under control."

He looked at her with wild eyes, his nostrils flaring. "He was going to hurt you."

Effie tilted her head, finally realizing just how little control Lucian had over himself. "If I recall correctly, I'm the one that landed the first and only blow."

Lucian's lips curled in a cruel smile. "Good."

Something dark and bloodthirsty deep within her appreciated the violence that was still rolling off him in waves. Violence that, while not directed at her, had built because of a perceived threat to her. It made her feel protected in a way that wasn't familiar.

Not ready to look at the new feelings too closely, Effie decided to try to diffuse his remaining anger.

"He didn't touch me," she added softly.

A shudder racked Lucian's body as he processed her words, and his gaze dropped as he took a deep breath. "It's the only reason he's still alive."

Silence stretched between them as Effie gave Lucian the space to regain control. When he looked at her again, his eyes had lost their predatory gleam.

"Are you alright?"

She lifted a shoulder. "They were just words. I've heard worse."

Lucian nodded and then frowned. "I wasn't spying."

It took a second for Effie to follow the shift in conversation. "I didn't think you were."

"The door was open. I was coming to fetch you. We've already received word of other attacks."

Effie took a long breath. *Right.* Time to focus on something more important than wounded male egos. There was a realm to save.

"Well, what are we waiting for?"

Lucian's eyes dropped to her bare feet.

She rolled her eyes, and bent to snatch her boots off the floor.

Lucian was smirking as he watched her lace them.

"What?"

He shook his head.

"*What?*" she demanded, standing with her hands on her hips.

"I was just thinking that you must have something against shoes. You never seem to be wearing them."

Effie bit back a smile. "I'll have you know this is only the second time you've seen me without my shoes on."

"Fourth."

"Fourth?"

"You're forgetting when I found you in the pub."

"Right, then and now. That's two."

"And the next morning . . . and the other night in the hallway."

Effie groaned. "Fine, four times. That's not exactly a habit."

"Sure seems like it."

"Lucian," she groaned, picking up a pillow and waving it threateningly.

He smiled, the first full smile of his she'd ever seen. It was transformational. His eyes crinkled, and the small metallic flecks shimmered with his mirth. If possible, his bottom lip looked even fuller as it curved up, and a hidden dimple flashed high in his cheek.

Robbed of her ability to speak, Effie blinked at him. *He's beautiful.* She'd been attracted to him before, but the strength of her reaction to him now was . . . unexpected.

"What?" he asked, eyeing her warily.

Effie shook her head, nowhere near ready to repeat that little revelation to him. "Nothing, let's go."

He stared at her a moment longer before nodding. "After you."

It wasn't until she walked past him and out into the hall that she realized she wasn't the only one with a habit.

"Is there some reason you're always making me walk in front of you?"

For a second, she didn't think he was going to answer, but then a slow grin spread across his face, warming her insides.

"I like the view," he said in his low growl.

Her stomach clenched, and her heart flipped in her chest. *Mother's tits.*

Effie stumbled as she turned back around and picked up the pace. Lucian's laughter followed her the entire way.

CHAPTER 3

*A*ny fragment of levity fled as soon as Effie stepped across the threshold of the Triumvirate's inner sanctum. The room could have doubled as a tomb, not one person speaking as they waited for the last of the summoned guests to arrive.

As she took her place beside Ronan and Reyna, Effie ignored Kieran as he glowered at her from the far right of the room. She cast them a brief smile before glancing up at the lone figure standing atop the raised dais.

A ripple of unease slid down her spine. It was the first time one of the Triumvirate had removed their hoods since she joined them. She'd almost forgotten how eerie it was to be stared down by a man that had black sockets in place of eyes.

Needing something to focus on that was less disturbing—which instantly ruled out his cracked lips and the cord of black that stitched them shut—Effie shifted her eyes up to the top of his bald head. The deep navy runes that were inked there seemed to pulse and shift along the pale white skin. Effie blinked, and the markings settled back into place.

It was hard to reconcile the memory of Smoke and his brief

glimmers of humanity with the *being* standing before her. Although, the person on the dais could be any one of the Triumvirate's three members. It's not like there was a way to tell them apart unless they were using their personal voices while speaking telepathically.

Swallowing, Effie focused on the dark red wall behind him, but it did little to ease her unrest while she waited for him to speak.

The sanctum was painted the same deep scarlet as the Triumvirate's robes. In contrast, the bone-white skin of his gaunt face practically shone against the vibrant color. Effie couldn't shake the image of a skull bobbing in a sea of blood. The similarity to her visions was more than enough to distress her.

Lucian chose that moment to stand next to her. He did not touch her in any way, but the sheer force of his presence commanded Effie to look up and acknowledge him. Her Guardian gave her a long searching look, a deep crease forming between his brows as he frowned.

A side door Effie hadn't noticed creaked open, interrupting whatever she might have said to him.

Kael stepped across the threshold, two men in blue robes trailing behind him. It took less than a heartbeat for Effie to recognize the delegates from Sylverlands. They both had long, pale blond hair and silver eyes, trademark features of the Sylvanese people. One was slightly taller than the other, although neither of the men came close to Ronan or Lucian's towering size. That did not diminish the aura of quiet confidence they exuded. These were men that were used to others obeying them without question.

"Zane Sylver, heir to the Sylvanese throne, and his consort, Xander," Kael intoned.

Effie's brows lifted slightly. She hadn't realized Zane was the Sylvanese heir. They must be worried about the Shadow attacks if he came personally.

The men bowed their heads a fraction of an inch.

"We appreciate you replying to us so quickly," Ronan said as they straightened. "And being willing to meet with us here while the Kiri is away."

"It is a privilege to be welcomed to the citadel, despite the unfortunate circumstances. I have long wondered about the Keepers and the information contained within these walls," Zane said.

"When we have dealt with the matter at hand, you are more than welcome to return."

Zane and Xander flinched, not accustomed to the Triumvirate's ability to mind speak. Not that Effie blamed them. It was uncomfortably personal, especially when coming from a being that looked like a walking nightmare.

Pressing her lips together, she dipped her chin to hide her smile. Out of the corner of her eye, she noticed Lucian do the same.

"You honor me. Thank you," the heir said with another bow.

"Please relay to the others what you disclosed in your missive."

"A little less than a fortnight ago, three of our raiders discovered one of the lakes was covered in unfamiliar algae. It is rare for any of our lakes to become polluted, and algae of any kind is always investigated to ensure that no harm comes to the fish and other wildlife that live in our waters. We didn't need extensive testing to tell that this was no natural growth. It was foul smelling and a gray color peppered with black. Not a day later, fish began to float to the surface. At first, we thought they had died, but when our fishermen cast their nets . . ." Zane paused to clear his throat, as if he was unsure how to verbalize what came next.

Xander's hand snaked out to squeeze Zane's.

The Sylvanese heir nodded as if acknowledging some silent exchange, and continued. "They were not dead. It was a trap. As soon as the nets landed in the boats, the fish began to snap, their teeth razor sharp and dripping with some kind of venom the same color as the algae. We lost seven of our men that day. Those not killed outright died later, succumbing to whatever poison was transmitted from the bites."

Effie sucked in a breath. Not surprised by the news so much as stunned that the corruption spread so quickly.

"The lake has been dammed to stop the spread of corruption, but whatever the algae comes into contact with rots and decays. We have started to drain the nearby lakes so that they cannot be tainted, although there's no telling how long such a solution will work if the rest of the land becomes infected as well," Zane finished, his golden skin flushed with emotion.

The Sylverlands had been named for the metallic hue of their water, which was so pristine it was rumored to be infused with liquid silver. For one of their lakes to become corrupted must feel like the worst kind of attack. Not just on their land, but on the very essence of who they were as a people.

"Have there been any Shadow sightings, either prior to the discovery at the lake, or after?" Ronan asked.

"A few days prior," Zane said, shifting to face the red-haired warrior. "A hunting party thought they saw someone spying on them, but when they went to investigate, there was nothing to be found. They did not realize what they had seen. It wasn't until they reported the odd shape of its limbs and fingers that Xander and I put the rest together. Until we received your message, we didn't realize the two events might be connected." Zane shrugged. "The sighting was just before the announcement of Rowena's death. We assumed, perhaps naïvely, that her abominations would die with her, so we focused instead on mitigating the spread of the algae."

"Do not be too hard on yourself. No one thought that the creatures would survive her death," Ronan said.

Zane dipped his head in thanks.

"You will go to Sylverlands. See what you can learn about the nature of the corruption. Check the lakes as well as the area where the Shadow was spotted. Report back with your findings."

"All of us?" Effie asked, her eyes darting to Kieran before shooting back to the dais.

"Is that a problem, Daughter?"

Blushing, Effie shook her head.

The Guardians made sense; they were trained for such tasks and had centuries of experience to back them. Plus, they were the Triumvirate's eyes, going where they could not and sharing what they found. Ronan and Reyna were also highly skilled fighters and diplomats in their own right. As for her, Effie was the one whose visions had pointed them down this path in the first place. Perhaps any new discovery would trigger additional insights. But what purpose did Kieran's presence serve?

Effie wished she knew if Smoke was the one standing before her. Then she might risk asking. She would also dare to ask had she been alone with any member of the Triumvirate, but not in front of the others.

"When do we leave?" Reyna asked.

"As soon as possible," Lucian responded. "Go grab what you need for an overnight visit and report back to the main archive. Once we're all gathered, we'll travel by Kaelpas stone to avoid delays."

Kael gestured for the Sylvanese men to follow him back through the side door. Zane paused after a few steps and turned back toward the dais. "Thank you."

At the Keeper's inquisitive head tilt, the Sylvanese heir elaborated.

"For offering aid. It is rare for any of the Keepers to involve themselves in such matters. We appreciate your guidance at such a trying time."

"The Keepers do not hold themselves apart because they do not care. Oftentimes to intervene in any way risks interfering with what must come to pass."

"So what has changed?" Xander asked.

Zane shot his consort a look filled with censure, as if his impudence might make the Keeper reconsider.

Effie wasn't sure who was more surprised when he actually answered.

"We find ourselves on the verge of something so horrific that to not be involved only guarantees our destruction."

Goosebumps raced down her arms. She'd known as much from their discussion the day before, but to hear it stated so bluntly, especially from a man who rarely offered up anything less than vague half-truths . . . it was sobering.

The color drained from the faces of the Sylvanese men as they processed his words.

"But you can help us stop it?" Xander asked, voice hoarse.

"That remains to be Seen." With a slight bow, he turned and left the sanctum, effectively putting an end to the conversation and any further questions.

CHAPTER 4

*S*ylverlands' beauty would have been enough to take Effie's breath away, if she'd recovered enough of it to have any to lose. Travel by Kaelpas stone was notoriously disorienting. She considered it a sign of progress that she'd remained upright with the contents of her stomach intact, even though she was covered in cold sweat and her knees felt wobbly.

Ronan grinned at her. "Timmins damn near shit himself the last time we made him travel by stone."

Effie gasped in shock before snorting with laughter. Timmins was the Kiri's Advisor. He was a master of protocol and all-around know-it-all, at least when it came to propriety. The thought of him losing control in any fashion was enough to bring some color back into her cheeks.

"Poor guy," Effie murmured fondly. Timmins had a grandfatherly air she'd always found endearing. She hoped he hadn't suffered too badly.

Squeezing her shoulder, Ronan stepped around her and moved to stand beside Reyna, who was positioned further down the hill. As always, the Night Stalker looked completely unruffled.

Effie turned away from her friends and back to the incredible view before her. They'd arrived on top of a small hill overlooking a massive lake. The water was so pure the reflection of the sky gave the impression that the world had tilted upside down. If not for the random ripple in the otherwise smooth surface of the water, one might imagine they were walking amongst the clouds themselves.

A stone castle was nestled behind a couple of hills along the horizon. Deep navy blue flags with silver waves emblazoned in the center blew gently in the breeze. The climate was cooler here, lacking the oppressive humidity of Bael's jungle. Effie wrapped her cloak more tightly around her shoulders, thankful for the extra layer of warmth.

It was a serene picture; one that made it easy to forget why they were here. Death lurked in the shadows, and it was coming for them all.

Effie gave a start when a voice began speaking just behind her.

"I thought the benefit of the Kaelpas stones was that we didn't have to travel further upon arrival."

"Don't," Effie snapped, not bothering to face the intruder.

"Don't what?" Kieran asked.

"Act like nothing happened," she hissed, incensed that he'd try and pretend otherwise.

"You're the one who slapped me."

Eyes flying wide with incredulity, Effie spun toward him.

"At least you're looking at me," he said lightly, a self-mocking smile ghosting across his mouth.

Scowling at him, Effie crossed her arms. "And what is it exactly that you want me to see?"

"I'm not your enemy, Effie."

Insults built inside her mind, ready for her to unleash them. Instead, she bit the inside of her cheek and stared at him in silence. Kieran had always shown a knack for manipulating her responses. He knew what would shock her into laughter, or force her temper to rise. She was tired of being his puppet, even if she'd always been an unwilling one.

When the silence stretched, his eyes hardened, looking like two foggy pieces of green glass. A vein pulsed in his temple. Leaning closer, he dropped his voice. "Why are you so determined to believe the worst of me?"

"For one who insists they care for me, you certainly have an odd way of showing it."

"How can you say that? I've done nothing but come to your defense and support your decisions since you got here."

Effie would have laughed if it wasn't so obvious he believed what he was saying. "I must have missed that between the times you were busy sulking when you didn't get your way or besmirching my name in front of others," she said dryly.

"I already apologized for that," he insisted, taking a step closer to her.

Effie took a hurried step back. "Did you?"

Kieran nodded, golden strands of his hair lifting in the wind. "This morning."

"Funny, I don't remember that part."

"I told you it wasn't my finest moment—"

"You consider that an apology?"

Kieran's mouth snapped shut. Hurt and frustration were at war in his eyes. He looked away from her. "Effie . . ."

"I'm not sure this is the time or place for you to finish that sentence, Kieran. Just give me some space."

Kieran's hands clenched into fists, his knuckles turning white.

"Let's get a move on," Lucian called, waving them over.

Letting out a breath she wasn't aware she'd been holding, Effie brushed past Kieran and quickly walked back to the others.

There was no missing the banked anger in her Guardian's eyes as she approached. Lucian had clearly witnessed her and Kieran's exchange. Idly she wondered why he hadn't interjected sooner. Especially after the threat he'd issued that morning.

Maybe he wanted to give you a chance to fight your own battle.

Effie peeked up at her Guardian, startled to find him returning her stare. Tentatively, she stretched out her fingers, letting the back of them rub against the side of his arm. His muscles jumped in response to her light touch.

"I'm fine," she whispered.

Lucian grunted, stepping past her to speak with their Sylvanese guides.

Effie's shoulders started to droop, thinking perhaps she'd misread the reason he'd been staring at her so intently, when Lucian discretely brushed his fingers along her arm. He didn't look at her, didn't acknowledge the action in any way, but the fact that he echoed her own brief touch must have meant something. Effie just wasn't sure what it was.

"Is he the one keeping you up at night?" Reyna asked in her low husky voice.

Effie groaned. That was the last thing she needed. People speculating about her relationship with Lucian.

"Or maybe it's that one?" Reyna asked, her eyes landing purposefully on Kieran, who had walked down the hill to speak with Kael.

Cheeks burning, Effie shook her head. "It's not what it looks like."

Reyna's eyes were glittering with merriment. "Of course it is. Once we're finished with today's hunt, you and I have lots of catching up to do."

"I don't think it's fair how much you're enjoying my misery," Effie muttered.

"Oh, sweetheart. That's not misery. What you're feeling is the thrill of the chase." Leaning closer, she whispered, "The real question is which one are you chasing?"

"Neither!" Effie sputtered.

Reyna's grin grew, and she leaned over to bump Effie with her shoulder. "The only person you're fooling with those lies is yourself."

Effie shook her head, which only caused Reyna to laugh.

Even in a moment of unguarded glee, the Night Stalker looked formidable. She'd found time to paint black whorls on her face before they'd left the citadel. Her people always used such markings when they were about to step into battle. The bold stripes and curls around her already intense green eyes only made them look fiercer, reminding

Effie of a large jungle cat peering out at its prey just before pouncing. Reyna may be beautiful, but she was also deadly.

Thank the Mother she was fighting on their side.

"Come on," Reyna said, linking her arm through Effie's. "The sooner we finish up here, the sooner you can fill me in."

Effie sighed, knowing nothing she could say would save her now.

KIERAN WATCHED the two women stride toward the small copse of trees at the bottom of their landing site. Anger simmered within, causing his eye to twitch.

The morning had not gone according to plan. Not at all.

Somehow they'd ended up fighting when all he'd meant to do was smooth things over between them with a few soft words. The next thing he knew, Lucian had him dangling by the neck like he was some sort of naughty puppy.

Eyes narrowing to slits, he glared at the Guardian. Let the smug bastard think he'd won for now. By the time Kieran was finished with him, he'd be begging for help with his mortality problem. Help Kieran would more than willingly provide.

Teeth clenched, Kieran turned once more to the problem at hand.

Never had he thought things would end with the girl from his dreams fleeing from him. It was rare for a woman to look at him with anything less than adoration in her eyes, but the last few times Effie's wide, cornflower blues were aimed at him, they were filled with mistrust and perhaps even a bit of disdain.

How did I manage to fuck things up so royally?

Kieran had yet to meet a woman he couldn't turn to putty with a flirtatious wink or a few seductive words. Effie was proving a harder conquest than anticipated. He couldn't rely on just his charm to win her over. Not that she was completely immune to him; the way she'd melted into his body when he'd kissed her had proven that. Unfortunately, it didn't seem likely he'd get close enough for her to willingly submit to more of his kisses anytime soon.

He needed to change her perception of him, and fast. One heroic act was all he needed for her to see him in a new light. A single moment to prove that he was a man of worth and upstanding moral character.

Kieran smirked. He had just the opportunity in mind. So what if he was going to create the chaos she needed rescuing from? No one ever said he had to fight fair. A smart man knew that the odds always needed to be stacked in his favor if he was playing for keeps.

Just a few more pieces needed to fall into place, and then he could repair the damage between them. His Effie was a sweet girl with a kind heart. She would forgive him, and then she would come to him willingly. For good.

Lips curling in a dark smile, Kieran watched Effie nod in response to whatever the Night Stalker said. *Soon, little one.*

Let the games begin.

⌁

"THEY SPOTTED HIM JUST OVER HERE," Xander said, pointing between two trees with silvery bark and leaves so dark they almost looked blue.

Ducking her head, Effie stepped under a low-hanging branch and scanned the leaf-strewn path for a sign of anything that didn't seem to belong. Hard to know what that could be when it was the first time she'd been there. *I guess you don't need to be overly familiar with something to sense a general wrongness about it.*

Today's errand almost reminded her of their scouting trips in the jungle in that regard, except for the absence of insects and the abundance of sky overhead. The trees were much sparser in Sylverlands, merely dotting the landscape instead of covering it. Instead of a forest like Bael or Vyruul, Sylverlands lent itself to long stretches of flat land broken up by the occasional hill or lake. The more open area explained why the Sylvanese scouts would have noticed a figure moving through the trees from a distance, but not how it managed to elude them.

Kael and Lucian were talking in hushed voices, their heads bowed together and faces grim. No matter how hard she strained to hear them, Effie couldn't make out a single word, much to her chagrin.

Ronan stood with his arms crossed, Reyna at his side, her hands hovering just above the blades sheathed at her hips. Xander and Zane stepped back, allowing Lucian to kneel beside the two trees they'd just indicated. Kael moved to stand beside Kieran, their entire group falling silent as Lucian lifted his hand. Closing his eyes, Lucian pressed the palm of his hand against the tree on his right.

Muscles taut with tension, Lucian remained bowed beside the trees. All Effie could see was the slight expansion in his back as he inhaled.

She wasn't certain what Lucian was doing, or what he expected to find, but a tingling awareness hummed within her. It almost felt like the start of a vision, but it was a subtler sensation. More an insistent tug for her to pay attention than a complete overtaking of her mind.

Trusting the instinct she didn't quite understand, Effie followed suit. She closed her eyes and breathed in deeply from her nose. Focusing only on her breathing, she repeated the technique. She wasn't Helena, with her powers of Spirit and Earth, who would be able to discern a living thing's essence just by concentrating on it, but she had come face-to-face with the Shadows. Effie knew what it felt like to be amongst them.

The way the tiny hairs on the back of her neck would stand on end.

How her blood would ice and cause goosebumps to erupt down her limbs.

The metallic taste of terror in her mouth.

Shuddering, Effie's hand spasmed against the rough bark. Yes, she knew exactly what it would feel like if something of the Shadows was left behind.

It only took a few heartbeats for Effie to know with absolute certainty that they would not find a trace of the Shadows' perversion here. Eyes fluttering open, she blinked against the bright light and refocused on the others, the hum of knowing no longer present.

Lucian had risen while she'd been busy with her own attempt at an investigation. He now faced their loose semicircle, his eyes still closed and his lips slightly parted as he searched for answers the rest of them couldn't find. Effie wasn't certain what kind of magic the Guardians possessed, outside of their immortality and considerable skill in battle, but she had a feeling she was about to witness it.

Effie's breath caught in her throat as Lucian opened his eyes.

The tiny bronze flecks that had always caught her attention had expanded to the point that none of the deep umber was left. Upon closer inspection, Effie realized that the brilliant bronze was the only color present in them at all. Gone were his pupils and whites of his eyes, replaced entirely by the brilliant pulsating light.

Wonder filled her. The only other person she knew whose eyes changed when they accessed their magic was Helena. She could only assume for the Guardian's to do the same spoke of incredible and rare power.

"Are you seeing this?" Ronan asked in a low voice, leaning over to speak in her ear.

Wordlessly, Effie nodded her head.

"Know what it means?"

"No," she breathed, eyes never leaving Lucian's face.

It was hard to tell where exactly Lucian looked as he scanned their surroundings, but she could feel the moment his attention landed on her. Energy zinged through her body, running through her like a current.

Seconds passed and he didn't look away, the force of her body's reaction building with each consecutive beat of her heart. It was like being hot and cold at the same time. Her skin was flushed, warming from the inside out, but goosebumps rose to the surface. Her nipples tightened into hard peaks and heat began to pool in her belly.

It was impossible to fully comprehend what was happening to her. Effie would have said she was aroused, but it was not desire causing her body to respond. It was much simpler and incredibly more complex than that, an awareness of self she'd never experienced before. She could feel the blood flowing through her veins, the infinitesimal growth of her hair and nails, the movement of air through her lungs. Every living, microscopic part of her had come into crystalized focus, and she was feeling every single piece all at once.

The soft breeze was almost painful as it blew over her skin. The sensation was too intense, like the feeling of a fingernail scraping over a sunburn. Just when she thought she couldn't survive another second, the feeling started to subside.

He'd been looking at her for less than a minute, but it felt like lifetimes had passed by the time Lucian finally shifted his focus.

"Did you feel that?" she asked Ronan a bit breathlessly.

"No," Ronan said slowly, his thick brows furrowing. "What?"

Biting her lip, Effie shook her head. "I'm not sure. Maybe I imagined it." She risked a glance at her friend, wondering if he picked up on her lie. Ronan had an ear for the truth that was uncanny, but if he'd sensed her fabrication, he chose to let it go.

Effie let her eyes return to Lucian. She had more than a few questions for her Guardian the next time they were alone. First on the list was finding out what in the Mother's name he'd just done to her.

Lucian blinked, his eyes returning to normal.

Kael stepped forward. "Anything?"

"No, not a trace."

The Guardians exchanged frowns before turning back to their Sylvanese guides.

"Will you show us to the lake now?" Kael asked.

"Yes, of course," Zane replied, glancing up at the sky. "It's a bit of a walk from here, but we should make it with enough time to get to the keep before sundown. If you'll follow me."

In silence, their small group converged behind the blond men, following them down a winding path. It was a pleasant enough walk; the sun warm on her back while the cool breeze kept the heat from being unbearable. At least, until the smell of rotting flesh hit her nose.

Effie tried not to gag as her eyes watered, the stench of decay so overpowering she soon had to use her cloak to shield the bottom half of her face. Around her, others did the same. Only Lucian appeared unaffected.

Xander turned back to them, his face apologetic. "We should have warned you it's a bit ripe."

33

"A bit, he says," Ronan muttered. "I've walked among battlefields that smelled better."

Effie snickered.

"You laugh, but men shit themselves when they die. You don't understand how a stench can attach itself to something until you've had to wash the stink of war off your leathers."

Giving him a droll look, Effie asked, "Who do you think did the wash at the estate? If you ever need tips on getting a blood stain out, I'm your girl."

Ronan gave her an appraising look. "I'll keep that in mind."

They took a few more steps when Effie added, "But if you shit your pants, you're on your own."

She heard Ronan's breath hitch and smiled to herself as she continued on. He was still laughing by the time she caught up to Lucian.

"What's that about?" Lucian asked.

"Laundry."

The Guardian raised a brow.

"Nearly there now," Xander called. "It's just around the next bend."

"I didn't realize laundry could be so amusing," Lucian said after a beat, glancing down at her.

Effie grinned, seeing through his carefully bland statement. "Are you prying, Guardian?"

Lucian glowered. "I don't pry, fledgling. I observe and comment."

"Call it what you will."

Sighing, Lucian shook his head. "You're impossible."

Somehow the way he said it made it sound like a compliment.

Smiling, she opened her mouth to goad him further, just as they came around the last hill and stopped dead.

CHAPTER 5

"*M*other's tits," Ronan swore.

Between one step and the next, they'd left the quiet beauty of Sylverlands behind and stumbled upon . . . hell.

There was no other word for the wasteland before them. Nor was there need for tricks or magical abilities to suss out signs of corruption. The Shadows' taint had spread far and wide, their destruction unmistakable.

The lake was more of a swamp, the water murky and rank. No signs of life moved beneath its surface, although there were large bubbles that would burst at infrequent intervals, releasing more of their foul smell into the air.

Outside of the water, the land was dry and cracked, mutilated carcasses of what had once lived within scattered around. The soil beneath them appeared leeched of any kind of nutrients. What was left of the lush grass was brittle, the few spikes looking like they would slice through her fingers if she tried to touch them.

"It grows worse every day," Xander said, his voice pained.

"Is it spreading?" Lucian asked.

Swallowing, Xander nodded.

"Is there anything we can do to stop it?" Effie asked Lucian in a low voice.

And by *we*, Effie really meant Lucian. Her power was useless here.

Lucian's frown deepened. "Not without risking corruption ourselves."

Too big a risk.

"We need Helena," she murmured, eyes darting to Ronan. "Is there any way to contact her?"

"She and her Mate did not leave word of where they were going, but I have an idea. I will try to get a message to her once we get to the keep."

The thought of having to leave the ruin in front of them alone to fester and grow did not sit easy, but it was the only avenue available to them.

Her eyes sought out the Sylvanese heir. "I'm sorry there's not more that we can do."

"Coming here is a good start. I hope that it helps you find and eliminate the source." He gave her a small smile, but it didn't quite reach his eyes. What was happening to his land was affecting him deeply.

Sighing, Xander said, "We should start heading back. It's probably not good to remain here longer than necessary."

Lucian and Kael nodded their agreement.

"I would keep your people away from here for now. Other than to mark any new developments, they should not come into contact of any kind with the tainted land," Lucian said.

"It will be done," Xander promised.

"We will be back once we know how to eliminate and hopefully reverse the effects," Lucian added, his expression fierce.

Something like hope flared in Zane's silver eyes. "We would be most grateful."

With a curt nod, Lucian turned, his hand briefly resting on Effie's lower back. With a gentle press of his fingers against her, he signaled for her to start moving.

As she turned, Effie caught a glimpse of the expression on Kieran's face, and her steps faltered. His gaze was zeroed in on the spot where Lucian touched her, his face filled with disgust and unmistakable malevolence.

She shivered, drawing both Lucian and Kieran's attention.

Her tutor's expression cleared, and he spun away, stalking back along the path.

Lucian lifted a brow, silently asking what was wrong.

Effie shook her head, not having an answer, but the feeling of unease wouldn't leave. Whether triggered by the corrupted lake, or the darkness of Kieran's expression, she wasn't sure, but a feeling of premonition swelled. It grew with each step, until a single refrain echoed inside her.

A storm was coming. One they couldn't outrun.

DINNER WAS A SOMBER AFFAIR. The large hall was obviously meant for entertaining, its raised dais likely for live entertainment of some kind. There was no entertainment tonight.

There were maybe twenty people in total, the Keepers' small group joined by a handful of the Sylvanese court. The clatter of silverware on dishes and their hushed voices were lost in the giant space, giving the illusion of silence.

The heir had invited the Guardians to sit at his table, but there was not enough room for the others, so Effie, Reyna, and Ronan sat across from them at another table made out of silvery wood. Kieran had been absent since they returned to the keep, and she had no clue if he'd be joining them or taking his meal elsewhere.

Nor did she care.

Effie pushed her food around her plate, unable to take more than a bite or two. The succulent clams and cream sauce over a bed of noodles should have been appetizing, but she couldn't seem to make herself eat it.

"Eating works better when you actually put the food in your mouth," Reyna murmured beside her.

"Is that how it's supposed to work?" Effie replied, looking up.

Reyna's smile grew. "I have it on good authority."

Wrinkling her nose, Effie explained, "My stomach is still too unsettled for such rich food."

"Your body is still recovering; you need to eat something. Want me to see if they can bring you some broth?"

The Sylvanese ate a primarily seafood and grain diet. Effie had a hunch their broth would be similarly made, and the thought of anything fishy made her gag.

"No, but thank you for asking."

Reyna frowned. "I'm not the only one that noticed, you know."

"What do you mean?" Effie asked, her brows dipping in confusion.

The Night Stalker used her chin to gesture to the table parallel to theirs where Lucian sat with Kael and members of the Sylvanese court.

"Your Guardian keeps glancing over here and frowning."

"Is that all?" Effie laughed. "All Lucian ever does is frown. Don't read too much into it."

Reyna hummed.

Setting her fork down, Effie turned to face Reyna fully. "Okay, what's *that* supposed to mean?"

A small smile played across Reyna's clean face. "He does more than frown."

"Oh, and when in the short time you've been here have you had a chance to witness that miracle?" Effie asked, genuinely curious.

She'd only seen Lucian's rare half-smiles a handful of times, and a true smile once. Otherwise it was all broody glowers and dark scowls.

"When he looks at you."

Effie snorted. "I doubt that."

Reyna's eyes glowed with amusement. "You should bed that man, and soon, lest he start setting the rest of us on fire with the smoldering looks he sends your way when you aren't paying attention."

Effie sputtered, not sure how to begin responding to that statement. Or what to think about the warmth that unfurled low in her stomach at Reyna's assessment.

Reyna laughed, the husky sound catching the attention of Ronan, who sat on her other side, and a few other males seated along their table.

"Speak for yourself," Effie murmured, missing none of the heat in her friend's eyes as he stared at the Night Stalker.

Reyna's smile was pure alpha female as she replied, "I'm working on it. True prizes require a proper hunt."

Effie let out a startled laugh. "Does *he* know that?"

Reyna lifted her shoulder in a shrug. "The ground has been laid and things are progressing nicely."

Effie chuckled, loving the thought of big, badass Ronan being pursued. He'd had his heart broken by his longtime lover and deserved to be with someone who could truly appreciate him.

"If you hurt him, there's more than one person you're going to have to answer to," Effie murmured, not hiding the slight edge to her voice.

Reyna's eyebrows lifted. "Warning received, Keeper."

Effie nodded, letting her smile return.

"So is the reason you keep your Guardian at bay because you're harboring feelings for the blond one?" Reyna asked, after taking a bite of her food.

Cheeks burning, Effie scanned the dining room, ensuring that no one, especially a certain blond tutor, had overheard the question. Thankfully, Kieran was still nowhere to be found, and the others were all focused elsewhere.

"Not quite," Effie gritted out.

"Explain," Reyna ordered, washing her food down with some berry cider.

"It's . . ." she paused, searching for a word, and finally sighed, "complicated."

Reyna's intense gaze said she wasn't letting Effie off that easily.

"Kieran thinks himself in love with me. He's made it abundantly clear that our futures are interwoven and we will end up together. He's been . . . single-minded in his pursuit of me," she explained, her voice low.

"And this is a problem because you do not return his feelings?" Reyna guessed, taking another sip.

Effie shrugged. "He's handsome enough, even kind sometimes, but—"

"But a certain dark-eyed Guardian has caught your attention?"

The flush that crept up her neck gave her away.

"So if he's the one that you really want, what's holding you back?" Reyna asked, not beating around the bush.

"I came to the citadel to learn how to interpret my visions and help end the war. I shouldn't be distracted by *either* of them. Besides, Darrin—"

"Is dead," Reyna said bluntly. "You are not. No one expects you to live your life in mourning for the man, Effie. Least of all him. He'd want you to find happiness. Especially with none of us knowing how long we might have left."

Effie's mouth fell closed and some of the weight she hadn't realized she'd been carrying eased. Reyna's permission helped wipe out the guilt that had plagued her since her drunken liaisons. It had felt like a betrayal of Darrin's sacrifice to want anyone, especially for that one moment with Kieran when he'd felt like a stand-in for the man she'd once loved.

No one would ever replace Darrin. He would always be her first love, and if he was alive, they'd probably still be together. But he wasn't. Just as she wasn't the same girl she'd been when they first met. With all that had happened leading up to and after his death, she was another woman entirely now. It only made sense that she needed a different kind of partner. Darrin was perfect for who she used to be, but not even he would have been a match for who she'd become. Whoever she gave her heart to now would have to be strong enough to help her on this journey without growing to resent her evolution.

Taking a sip of her punch—she was staying far away from anything with alcohol for the foreseeable future—Effie admitted, "Even if I still entertained the idea of pursuing something with Kieran, I could never be with him. He's too caught up on who he thinks I am and doesn't see the real me. It would never work. I'd be a constant disappointment to him."

"And Lucian?" Reyna asked.

Effie glanced at her Guardian, whose head lifted as if he sensed her eyes on him. They stared at each other for one heartbeat, two . . . and then his lips curled in a slow smile she found herself shyly returning.

"He sees right through me," Effie murmured, dragging her eyes back to Reyna. "And he doesn't hesitate to call me out on my nonsense. He pushes me, but also knows when to give me space to try something on my own, even if he knows I might fail."

"So what are you doing still sitting over here talking to me?"

Eyes dropping to her lap, Effie stared at her hands. "It would never work between us."

"Why not?"

"He's immortal, for one, not to mention sworn to the Triumvirate."

"I fail to see how immortality is an issue. So he lives longer than you? I doubt it's the first time he's done so. Besides, that is true of almost all couples."

Effie's stomach clenched at the thought of Lucian with another.

Reyna's voice was thoughtful as she continued, "As for the second concern, last I heard, he was *your* Guardian."

Effie looked up. "He's made no vows to me."

"Perhaps not directly, but he's claimed you as his all the same. From what I know of the Brotherhood, they do not do so lightly. Their duty is their life."

"I don't want to be his *duty*," Effie muttered, making a face.

Reyna laughed. "What do you want to be then, Effie?"

His.

The thought shocked her with the amount of longing it brought to the surface. Until now she hadn't considered her feelings anything more than misplaced attraction, a side effect of everything else she was going through. Uncomfortable at times, but easily dealt with and overcome. Now she wasn't so sure.

Somewhere between his subtle touches, lingering glances, and the way he'd reacted when he thought Kieran might have hurt her, something had shifted. Mere attraction had turned into something much more complicated and unyielding.

It made no sense; Lucian was nothing like the man she envisioned the few times she'd allowed herself to dream of a future. Effie always thought she'd end up with someone gentle. A man that would hold her tenderly and offer sweet words of praise when she made him dinner.

Nothing about that scenario fit Lucian . . . or her, if she was being honest with herself. Not anymore.

"Effie?" Reyna prompted.

"It doesn't matter," she said finally.

"Yes, it does," Reyna insisted, placing her hand over Effie's. "It matters very much. You have just as much right to have what you want as the rest of us. Maybe more."

Effie blinked, wondering how much Reyna knew about her past.

"What's holding you back?" Reyna whispered, her green eyes kind.

"I couldn't stand the rejection. Not from him. Not again." She hadn't meant to say the words out loud, the raw honesty hinting at more than she was ready to share.

Reyna was quiet for a minute as she considered what Effie had revealed. "I've only known the Guardian a short time, but I know with certainty he is a man of honor. If he turned you down, it is only because his honor compelled him to do so."

Lucian had said as much when he'd pulled away from her. He hadn't wanted to take advantage of her altered state of mind. Hope began to flicker in her chest as Effie stole another glance at Lucian. *Is that really the only reason he stopped me?*

Effie's breath hitched as she studied his face. He still hadn't shaved, the light beard softening some of the hard angles of his face. It wasn't enough to disguise the aura of violence that always surrounded him. All he was doing was eating dinner and he was still the most formidable man she'd ever laid eyes on.

That was saying something considering who her friends were.

Effie was fooling herself believing she'd ever be satisfied with a gentle, soft-spoken man. She was far too drawn to warriors and their strength. The way they unapologetically protected those they considered theirs, even from themselves. For her, the kind of safety they offered was potent. She'd spent far too long hiding from those who would harm her.

Lucian frowned at whatever Kael said, and Effie looked away before he could catch her staring at him again.

Reyna gave her another knowing smile, and Effie couldn't help but wonder if she was right. If the circumstances had been different . . . would Lucian have given in?

CHAPTER 6

*E*ffie woke early, eager to return to the citadel and share what
they had learned. She'd been granted accommodations far
grander than any she'd had before, being treated as both a member of
the Kiri's court and a Keeper in her own right.

It was odd. She still wasn't quite used to her new station, but Effie
wasn't going to complain about sleeping on an actual mattress or with
a soft blanket. Not after years of being made to sleep on the floor with
little more than damp rags to cover herself.

Granted, that was a long time ago, but one never really forgets to
appreciate little comforts when they've had to live without.

She took a final glance around the chamber. It was filled with
expensive blue and silver furnishings. Her eyes lingered on the
numerous antiques lining the shelves. Gilded picture frames, miniature,
highly detailed figurines, a music box with an intricate mosaic on the
top, and a pale white bust of some woman who must have been
important to warrant such a tribute. And that was just what she could
identify from here.

Mother, it would take hours to properly dust all those trinkets.
Effie's nose tickled just thinking about dealing with the arduous task. A

year ago, she would have been the one responsible for it. *I suppose being a Keeper isn't all bad, considering.*

With a soft laugh, she shook her head and tightened the straps of her bag. Satisfied she wasn't forgetting anything, Effie pulled open the door, freezing momentarily when she spotted Kael waiting for her outside.

"Good morning."

He flashed her his dimpled grin. "Morning."

"Do you often wait outside my door?" she asked, only half-joking.

Kael shook his head. "Lucian didn't feel comfortable leaving you unguarded in an unfamiliar place."

"Were you here all night?" she asked, thinking it wasn't fair he should look so good after a night without sleep.

"No. I replaced Lucian sometime around dawn. He wanted to check in with the Triumvirate before we returned."

Effie hadn't known that either of the Guardians had been posted there. She felt oddly touched by their concern.

"Is this something you two do often?"

"There's no need at the citadel. No place in all the realms is more protected. Why?" he asked, his grin filled with mischief. "You doing things in your room you're embarrassed about being overheard?"

Effie was quick to shake her head. "No, I save my humiliation for more public places. Pubs. Hallways. Dining halls."

Kael chuckled. "Thanks for that."

She fell into step beside him, their banter light as they moved through the keep.

"Any more visions?" he asked, as they came upon the main staircase.

"No. Not since we left the citadel."

Kael nodded, as if anticipating the answer.

"Kael, would you mind if I asked you something about your powers?"

He matched her hushed tone, his eyes teasing. "They aren't a secret, little warrior. There's no need to whisper."

"So little is widely known about the Brotherhood, I wasn't sure it would be polite to ask."

Kael shrugged. "There are few secrets between the Brotherhood and the Keepers. What do you want to know?"

"Well . . . is that something all of you can do? That thing with your eyes?" she asked.

"Is it the Guardians you want to know about or a certain one in particular?" he asked, his grin widening.

Not him too. The last thing she wanted was another person invested in her interest in Lucian. There'd been far too much of that already.

"It just made me realize I don't really know what you guys can do, outside of, you know . . . killing things."

Kael laughed. "Yes, I can do that too, although Lucian's gift is stronger than mine."

"What was he doing?"

"Inspecting the essence of the area, trying to see if he could find the presence of any corruption that would still be invisible to mortal eyes."

"I'm not sure I understand."

"Guardians have the ability to see the true form of all living things. It's what allows us to see the strands that tie all life together, and if we want, to transform them. If there had been sign of corruption, he'd have seen it like a stain on whatever he was looking at."

"Transform them how?"

"Well, Lucian is the best of us. He can create things on the spot, practically weaving them out of thin air."

"Like weapons?" Effie asked, recalling how she'd thought his weapon had been made of smoke during the angcerta fight.

"Exactly."

"And you can't?"

Kael shrugged. "I can, but it takes me far longer, and much more concentration. It's not a skill I'm able to use mid-battle, as he does."

"I see," Effie murmured. "Is that all?"

"Is that not impressive enough?" Kael teased.

Effie blushed. "Sorry, I didn't mean to—"

Kael stopped her. "No need to apologize. We are also the only beings in Elysia capable of creating portals—and hiding them."

Effie's mind was racing with this new information. The Guardians were much more powerful than she'd realized. Their abilities weren't only tied to the battlefield. They could actually manipulate and transform the world around them, even to the extent they could hide things in plain sight. And those were just the tricks she knew about. With magic such as that, there was no telling what else the Guardians could do.

Awe tore through her as she realized they might just be the three most powerful beings in Elysia, the depth of their power even eclipsing Helena's.

"You're . . . you're the ones responsible for the illusion hiding the citadel," she said, a bit in shock.

Kael nodded.

"How?" she asked, wonder causing her voice to sound breathless.

"Once you can see the threads of life, it's easy to tie them together. To create a portal requires the strands of two separate places to be joined. If the weaver wishes to obscure the presence of a portal, they can craft an illusion by willing the strands to appear as something new. It's almost the same as outright transformation, except when tied to a portal, whatever they've created exists only on the surface. It's a mirage, if you will. After that, it's as simple as placing one foot in front of another."

Effie shook her head, laughing a little at the absurdity of his comment. "Simple, right."

Kael laughed at her and shrugged. "You asked."

"And the immortality?"

"It's part of the package. In order to receive the power, our essence is transformed. Although only the strongest of us have the ability to perform the transformation; it's the most complex of our magic. It's why we are the Guardians of the realms. With our power comes the responsibility of protecting those that cannot protect themselves. At least until we find our true purpose."

"True purpose?" she asked.

48

Kael's answer was interrupted by Ronan and Reyna walking toward them.

"Sleep well?" Ronan asked, his gaze raking over her.

Effie nodded. "You?"

Ronan grunted. "I learned a long time ago how to get a proper night's sleep no matter where I am."

Kael nodded in understanding. "The life of a warrior."

"Aye."

Reyna rolled her eyes. "His mattress was made of feathers. He slept like a babe."

"And how do you know what his mattress was made of?" Effie teased.

"Because I was plucking feathers from his hair when we were walking down here," she replied matter-of-factly.

"Mmhmm," Effie said, not buying the story for a second.

Ronan shook his head as Reyna held out a hand filled with downy white feathers.

"Fair point, well made," Effie said, impressed by either Reyna's foresight or her self-control.

Kieran was the next to join them, his sage green eyes guarded and hair unkempt. It was unusual for the ex-prince to appear anything less than perfect. Right now, he looked like he spent the night trying to sleep on a bed of rocks. Even his clothes were mussed, like he'd slept in them.

He offered a nod in response to the other's greetings, and then settled his gaze on her. Effie turned away before he could speak to her, not in the mood for another one of his misguided attempts to apologize. It was too early, and they had other things to worry about.

Zane and Xander wandered in.

"We wanted to make sure we saw you off," Xander said, his voice husky with sleep.

Ronan clasped forearms with the other man. "We appreciate your hospitality."

"We appreciate the Kiri sending her Shield in her absence, and the Keepers, of course," Zane said, gesturing to Effie, Kael, and Kieran.

"Lady Reyna, it was a pleasure to meet you. I look forward to our people getting to know each other during better times."

Reyna nodded. "The Night Stalkers will be begging to visit once they hear of Sylverlands' beauty."

Zane placed a hand over his chest and bowed low. "Let us hope we can restore her to her former glory."

Murmurs of agreement met his words before the group fell silent.

"Leave it to our fearless leader to be late," Kieran muttered snidely behind Effie.

"I was the first to arrive," Lucian replied, strolling toward their group from a door to their left. "I used the extra time to check in with the Triumvirate."

Kieran's cheeks flamed scarlet, but he did not comment further.

"Word of an attack from another realm came in. We're to head there before returning to the citadel," Lucian continued.

A heavy silence settled over their group as they processed the news. While they'd anticipated there might be more evidence of Shadow attacks across the realm, Effie didn't think any of them really expected to discover two separate occurrences in the span of as many days. Or maybe they were just trying to cling to the naïve hope that things weren't nearly as bad as they seemed.

"Which realm?" Ronan asked, adjusting the straps of his weapon harness.

"Caederan. Khouman has already been notified of our arrival."

Effie smiled slightly at the mention of the Caederan delegate. She'd met him only briefly, but Khouman and his partner Tinka were hard to forget. The Caederans were short in stature, smaller even than she was. They really would look like children beside Ronan and the two Guardians' hulking height.

She found herself looking forward to seeing them again. If nothing else, it would be nice not to have to look up while talking with somebody.

"May the Mother bless your endeavors and keep you safe," Zane said with a small bow.

"You as well," Effie murmured.

Zane gave her a small smile in response, and with a final wave, he took his consort's hand and the two men left the room.

"We ready to go?" Lucian asked.

They nodded.

Turning to Kael, he said, "We'll have to travel in two groups. My stone has less charge than I thought."

"Will you be able to make it to Caederan and then back to the citadel?" Kael asked.

Lucian nodded. "I can bring one other with me."

Kieran snorted. "Convenient."

Her Guardian ignored him, but Effie saw a muscle in his jaw twitch.

"Why don't we all go with Kael?" Ronan asked, clearly not liking the thought of splitting up.

Kael pulled a Kaelpas stone the size of her smallest fingernail out from a pouch tied to his belt. "Lucian's is bigger than mine," he said with an exaggerated frown.

Effie laughed. "I was told once size didn't matter."

Kael winked at her. "Unfortunately, it does when it comes to Kaelpas stones. I only carry this one in case of emergencies. It's big enough for a handful of short trips, or one long journey. Honestly, it's never been an issue since there's usually no more than three of us going out to scout. But with a larger group like this, we'll want to be careful. More people means a stronger drain on the stone. More drain means less distance. And if Lucian's is low on charge, splitting up instead of all going together ensures that we'll have enough power to make it back to the citadel."

"Uh," Ronan murmured, looking mildly concerned, "we're going to make it there in one piece, right?"

"I haven't lost anyone yet," Kael said with another grin. "You'll be safe with me."

Ronan gave the Guardian a look that said he didn't feel remotely reassured.

Lucian cleared his throat, pulling their attention back to him.

Kael was still grinning when he rolled his eyes at Lucian. "Alright. Take Effie, the others will come with me."

Lucian gave Kael a look like there was never any question who his plus one would be.

Chuckling, Kael faced his group. "Move in tight. From what I remember of Caederan, those cliffs are narrow. We don't want anyone plummeting to their death upon arrival."

Kieran shot Lucian and Effie a dark look as he placed his hand on Kael's shoulder. Ronan had his hand on Reyna's waist. She, in turn, was touching Kael's wrist. Once Kael checked everyone was connected, he gave Lucian a nod and the group vanished from sight.

"Did the Triumvirate tell you what to expect when we get there?" Effie asked, taking a step closer to Lucian.

Lucian's dark eyes were unreadable as he replied, "Sounded like more of the same, except they had survivors."

"Oh," she breathed, a sense of foreboding turning her blood to ice.

Nothing about that sounded like a good thing.

Lucian held his hand out to her, palm up.

Without hesitation, Effie placed her hand in his, trying to ignore the burn of his skin where it pressed against hers.

"Thank you," she said, before he could use the stone and transport them.

"As much as I prefer your thanks to your insults, what exactly did I do?" he asked, one side of his mouth lifting in an amused smile. A mouth that was no longer obscured by his beard, she noticed.

Lucian had found time to shave, and Effie couldn't stop staring at his full lips.

"Standing guard last night," she mumbled, more than a little distracted.

His eyes widened ever so slightly. "I have to say, I expected a bit of push back from you on that. Especially after how hard you fought against having a guard in the first place."

Effie shrugged, biting the inside of her cheek as she thought of how to respond. "It wasn't you I was fighting against as much as circumstances being so outside of my control. Everything is changing so fast, and some days I can't make heads or tails of what my power is trying to tell me. The visions are bad enough, but now these random premonitions . . ." she trailed off as Lucian scowled.

"What premonitions?" he snapped.

Effie was taken aback by the censure in his voice. "Like I told you before . . . the feeling that you shouldn't go into the jungle alone. That I needed to be with you. And just now," she admitted before he could grill her, "when you mentioned the survivors."

"That's why you fought me so hard?" he asked, his voice a little softer than before.

Effie nodded. "I just didn't realize what was happening at the time. I still don't," she admitted. "Not really."

"What are these premonitions like?"

"It feels like the start of a vision, but not as intense. Sometimes, like just now when you mentioned the survivors, it's a buzzing under my skin. Almost as if it's a call to pay attention to whatever's happening around me. More often though, like all those times I fought against you going into the jungle alone, it starts as tension in my neck and shoulders. If I ignore the warning, the pressure grows until it feels like a weight burying itself in my lungs, making it nearly impossible to breathe."

"Hmm," Lucian murmured, his eyes scanning her face. "And you had this feeling now?"

Effie nodded.

"Just the buzzing? None of the pressure?" he asked, looking thoughtful.

"Yes," she confirmed, wondering where he was going with this.

Lucian gave a short nod. "We'll be on guard, then. There's something about these survivors that your power wants you to pay attention to."

"What would you have said if I told you I had felt the pressure?"

"That I was taking you back to the citadel immediately."

"What? Why?"

"From the distinctions you made, and the times you've mentioned these feelings, the pressure seems to sense danger. I'd gladly risk your wrath to keep you safe."

Warmth expanded in her chest at his confession. "What if I fought you? Insisted I should be there?"

Lucian surprised her by smiling. "You mean like every other time I try to do something in your best interest that you disagree with?"

"Exactly." She laughed because that's exactly how things had been between them from the start.

"It depends."

"On?"

"How compelling your argument was."

"I must not make very compelling arguments," she muttered, thinking of all the times he'd gotten his way.

Lucian brushed his thumb along the back of her hand, squeezing it gently. "You'd be surprised how often I give in to you. It's not in my nature to yield once I set a path."

"So why do you?" she whispered, her chest tight as she waited for his answer.

"Because you ask me to."

The simplicity of his answer stunned her, but there was nothing simple about the way he was looking at her. The bronze flecks in his eyes were glowing with the intensity of his gaze. Effie's mouth went dry.

"Oh," she said, because she couldn't think of what else to say.

"No one else dares to defy me the way you do." As if sensing her confusion, Lucian leaned down until his lips brushed against her ear. "I think I like it."

Effie gasped when he activated the Kaelpas stone, robbing her of the ability to reply. Or breathe.

CHAPTER 7

*E*ffie's knees buckled and she threw an arm out to keep herself from falling, Kael's warning about toppling over the edge of a cliff still ringing loudly in her ears.

Please don't let me fall. Don't let me fall.

Her hand slammed into something hard, before fingers closed around her arm in a bruising grip.

Looking up, her eyes found Lucian's. His lips barely moved so she didn't realize he was speaking until the words reached her ears.

"I've got you."

Heart somersaulting in her chest, Effie straightened.

"There you are! What took you so long?" Ronan boomed.

Effie risked a glance at the others, expecting to be met with a combination of dark stares and knowing smiles. As for the first, Kieran had his back to her so she couldn't tell what he thought of their delay. Reyna's face was a mask, the Night Stalker wholly focused on their reason for being here. Kael had a slight smile on his face, but that wasn't unusual for him. He almost always looked like he was laughing at some secret joke the rest of them weren't in on.

"The heir returned to ask me one last question before we left," Lucian lied smoothly.

Ronan's eyes narrowed, but he didn't comment. He glanced at Effie, as if personally assuring himself of her safety, before nodding.

Realizing her hand was still pressed against Lucian's chest, Effie slowly lowered it.

Lucian's lips twitched in a smile that was gone just as quickly as it appeared.

Steady now, she was able to take in their surroundings. Where Sylverlands was rolling hills and glittering lakes, Caederan was sweeping vistas overlooking a sunken valley to the south and cloud-shrouded mountains to the north.

Their group had arrived on a cliff—much more spacious than Kael led them to believe—on the southern side of Caederan's lone mountain. Despite being placed at the base of a vast mountain range, only one of the mountains fell within the boundaries of their land. The Caederans' main town was situated on the mountain itself, while the rest of its inhabitants were scattered in the valley below.

Northeast of Tigaera—the capital of Elysia and home to the Kiri and her Circle—Caederan was all that separated the rest of the Chosen from the closed realm of Talyria, the land that belonged to the massive winged felines known as Talyrians.

For centuries, none that ventured into the mountainous territory returned. It was rumored the Talyrian queen destroyed all interlopers. While the exact method of her execution—teeth or fire—had long been under debate, all agreed it was done to protect the land . . . and their secret. The Talyrians had been thought extinct.

Until one returned.

"All here?" a voice boomed as the top of a dark head appeared out of a nearby cave.

"Khouman," Ronan greeted, extending his hand.

The top of Khouman's head barely reached the bottom of Effie's rib cage as he strode past her to shake Ronan's hand. For such a small man, he had a powerful voice and build. A barrel-like chest and heavily muscled arms were covered in visible scars that he wore with pride. His long, braided beard hung half-way to his chest and had a few tinkling bells woven into its length. He wore the deep orange and reds of his people, colors that were selected to mimic the fiery sunsets unique to their realm.

"Welcome to Caederan," he intoned, dark eyes sweeping over them as if searching for someone.

"Helena is away at the moment. I'm afraid you're stuck with me in her stead," Ronan said, answering the unspoken question.

"Then you will have to do," Khouman replied with something that resembled a smile. It was a little too close to a grimace for the joke to land true. "Since this is not a friendly visit, would you mind if we skipped the formalities and I take you to the site directly? Our people are terrified and would appreciate some answers."

"Not at all," Lucian said, speaking for the first time.

The little man eyed him skeptically before giving him his back and staring expectantly at Ronan.

Kieran didn't bother to disguise his snicker.

For her part, Effie had to bite down hard on the inside of her cheek to keep from smiling. No one showed Lucian outright disrespect. Ever.

Well, except for her.

She could feel Lucian go still beside her, his pride demanding he address the insult. They weren't going to get any answers if Lucian accidentally murdered their guide, so she shifted her weight. The move allowing the side of her body to brush against his.

Answering tingles raced along the rest of her as he shifted his focus to her. A silent question burned in his eyes.

Effie gave him a small smile and whispered, "You said you liked it."

There was a sharp intake of breath and the bronze flecks in Lucian's eyes blazed as he stared at her for an endless moment. Effie watched as Lucian forced himself to relax. His fists uncurled and tension around his mouth softened. The muscles in his jaw clenched and unclenched as he released the breath he'd been holding.

Finally, the expression in his eyes shifted, the bronze fading.

Feeling like she'd just tamed a wild animal, Effie couldn't stop the smile from stretching across her face. Realizing the others had already started walking away while they'd been distracted, she started moving.

Lucian's voice stopped her dead.

"When it's you."

She twisted, looking back at him over her shoulder, not sure she'd heard him correctly.

"Only you."

Those words from his lips, in context or not, were beyond potent. Especially when he was looking at her with that banked heat in his eyes.

An answering heat gathered between her legs. A disinterested Lucian had been distracting enough, but one that said things like *that* while looking like he was about to devour her?

Mother's tits, I'm in trouble.

"You coming?" Kael called, breaking the moment.

"Yeah," Lucian answered, his eyes never moving from her. With a nod, he gestured for her to walk ahead of him.

Remembering what he'd said the other day, Effie added a little more roll to her hips than usual as she walked away.

Lucian let out a strangled groan.

Effie chuckled the entire way down the path. At least she wasn't the only one suffering.

KHOUMAN LED them to a different cave about a thirty-minute walk from where they'd arrived.

The view below was spectacular, the land coming to life as the sun rose higher in the sky, and the path they walked was wide enough for five of them to walk shoulder to shoulder if they wished.

Carved into the mountains were several caves. From what she remembered of the handful of history lessons she'd been allowed to attend, the Caederans had discovered a way to access the water trapped within their mountain. She'd yet to see anything that hinted at how.

"Where's the town?" Effie asked.

Khouman spared her a glance but did not slow. "Most of these caves are connected by a series of tunnels. Follow any tunnel long enough it will spit you out in the heart of the mountain."

Frowning, Effie tried to make sense of the answer.

"Their town was built inside the mountain itself," Kael explained in a soft voice.

Understanding dawned and Effie's curiosity bloomed. *What a sight that must be; an entire city hidden within the heart of a mountain.*

Just ahead of her, Khouman came to a stop. Shoulders stiff, he waved a hand at the cave entrance beside him. "No use trying to explain it," he muttered. "You'll see for yourselves soon enough."

Lucian took the lead, stepping into the dim cavern closely followed by Ronan and Kael. Effie and Reyna followed with Kieran bringing up the rear.

With each step, the now familiar buzz built beneath Effie's skin. Her gift was warning her.

Torches blazed along the dark walls leading them deeper into the cave. It was impossible to tell where they were going, the path winding and narrowing at times so that only one of them could pass through.

Effie shivered as her fingertips skimmed the damp surface. It was entirely too similar to her recent visions of a cave of blood filled with floating corpses. Swallowing back a wave of nausea, she prayed that's not what was waiting for them below.

The path dipped down, growing darker despite the flickering lights. Effie tried not to let her imagination run wild. Whatever had happened here, it couldn't be any worse than what they'd found in Sylverlands.

It didn't take long for the smell of wet earth to be replaced with rot and decay. *We must be close now.* The thought was proven true when Effie followed Reyna into a large empty expanse. The space was awash in torchlight, but almost more eerie with the shadows flickering along the back wall.

Something about the wall seemed odd, like it was further away than it should have been, given where the reddish-brown floor stopped. Moving closer, Effie noticed that the platform they stood on overlooked another space below.

She knew without even seeing it, that whatever they were here for waited down there.

Lucian stood at the edge of their platform, his hands on his hips and his gaze fixed on something beneath him. Beside him, Ronan reached for his weapon, but his hands were frozen just above it, as if he wasn't entirely aware of the instinctual response to a perceived threat.

Whatever they were seeing couldn't be good if it caused two such strong men to react that way.

The buzzing was almost painful in its intensity as Effie moved to Kael's side. The Guardian's expression was grim as he studied the area beneath them.

Sucking in a deep breath, Effie looked. The harsh buzz was now a roar in her ears. She had been wrong. It *was* worse than Sylverlands.

So much worse.

Shiny black vines covered with dripping thorns twisted up the sides of the cavern and crisscrossed along the floor. Noxious liquid spilled from the jagged stems, leaving pale silver tracks snaking down stalks as thick as her leg. The trails glittered in the torchlight. It should have been beautiful. Perhaps it would have been, if not for the bodies trapped within them.

Everywhere Effie looked, she found more tormented Caederans.

Mouths frozen open in soundless screams.

Bloody holes in place of eyes.

Fingers grasping vines where they were wrapped around broken necks, worn to the bone from a failed attempt to get free.

She didn't realize she was trembling until Kael's warm hand wrapped around hers.

How was this possible? How could the land devolve so quickly? Especially here, where it was tucked so far away.

"They tried to stop it," Effie whispered, her voice echoing down the cave.

"They were dead as soon as they set foot down there," Khouman said, his voice hollow. "At first, it was just a few random growths along the wall. My people thought to cut them down, but as soon as they touched 'em, the vines began to triple in size, thrashing and splashing that foul liquid all about. Their screams . . ." he trailed off, gulping. "Their screams echoed so loud we could hear it in town."

"If you were in town, how do you know what happened?" Ronan asked.

"They weren't all dead when we got here."

Bile burned in the back of her throat as she imagined how horrific it must be to see the twitching bodies of her friends and family trapped by the vines.

"The liquid . . . I've never seen anything like it. It paralyzed them only long enough to trap them. But when it wore off . . . it's like the cursed things feed off the screams. The more they struggled, the faster they grew."

"How long ago did this happen?" Lucian asked, body rigid with tension.

"We don't know when exactly it started. The growth could have been lying in wait for weeks for all we know, maybe longer. We don't come down here that often. It's one of the few caverns without any access to a well so there's no point."

Ronan's eyes sharpened on his face. "You think it could have been a trap?"

Khouman shrugged. "I don't know what to think."

"So when did you discover it?" Lucian pressed.

"The screams began weeks ago. We've lost over thirty men and women down here. We removed the ladders and forbid anyone from going down there. It was a death sentence and only seemed to make matters worse. Some—" his voice caught, and he shot them a look so filled with pain it gutted her.

"Khouman?" Effie prompted, when he didn't finish the sentence.

Clearing his throat, Khouman forced himself to continue. "Some folks have formed additional scouting parties since the war. We thought things were starting to return to normal, but now . . ."

"Now?" Effie whispered as the buzzing became so relentless she felt like something was actually crawling beneath her skin.

Khouman was saved from answering by a wet snarl. He turned his face to the cavern below.

"See for yourself," he said, his voice broken.

There was another snarl. It seemed to be emanating from a dark corner the torches didn't reach. Squinting, Effie stared into the darkness as the sound of her racing heart filled her ears.

A long, low growl began to reverberate off the walls, followed by two shuffling steps. Far below them one of the Caederans twisted her face up to the light and let out a shriek of rage.

Effie couldn't stop the horrified gasp that left her lips.

Mother no. Not Tinka.

CHAPTER 8

*T*here was little left of the woman Effie remembered in the pale creature stumbling out of the darkness. Tinka's lustrous black curls hung in dirty clumps around a gaunt face. If not for the familiar bells dangling limply from a few tangled patches, or the distinctive necklace hanging from her neck, Tinka would have been unrecognizable.

All of her feminine curves were gone, as if her body had consumed itself and only left behind a sack of skin to hang off the frame of her bones. She might have even been mistaken for a child, except that her head was too large for the otherwise tiny body. Even so, she would have still looked almost human, if not for the slithering black lines in her eyes.

Tinka was turning into a Shadow.

Effie shuddered.

"You said there were survivors?" Ronan asked, turning away from the shrieking woman. "Do they know what caused this?"

"There were," Khouman replied, any remaining life within him extinguished after confronting what was left of his wife.

"H-how?" Effie asked, tearing her gaze away from the creature below and back to their guide.

Khouman took a deep breath. It was like watching a man try and will himself back together. Her heart broke for him. It must be the worst kind of torture having to witness the woman he loved turn into that thing and be completely helpless to stop it.

"One of our scouting parties, a group of about ten, returned a few weeks ago. They mentioned fighting off a group of Shadows near the Eastern border, and that they sustained injuries, but nothing their assigned healer couldn't handle. I never thought . . ."

"How many are left?" Ronan asked.

"Just T—just her."

"What happened to the others?" Reyna asked.

"They turned on each other."

Ronan rested a large hand on Khouman's shoulder. "Perhaps you should start at the beginning."

Nodding, Khouman stared down at a spot on the floor. "Caederan is a peaceful realm, but we've always had scouts. It's how we tracked the movements of the packs that live nearby and make sure that none of our caves get breached by them. Once the war started, we increased the size of our scouting parties, and focused more on our borders than the caves."

Khouman sighed, looking so worn down that a gust of wind could knock him over. "Each group would go out for about a week before returning and sending the next group. We all take turns, you see, to share the burden of being away from home. Well, the group returned like usual and they seemed fine, until . . ."

When Khouman didn't resume his retelling, Lucian stepped forward. "Until?"

Blinking a few times, Khouman refocused. "Until the fighting started. First, it was just Jinx and Cal. Those two were little better than drunks on a good day. Always rough 'round the edges. No one thought anything of them acting up. But then Laurel and Wylmar started up. They're married, see, and have been going through a bit of a rough patch. Wyl never lifted a hand against her, but they fought ugly more often than not. A couple days after they came home, Wyl came barreling out of their house, a dagger hanging out of his thigh. He was completely crazed, practically foaming at the mouth. When we could calm him down enough to ask what happened, we learned that Laurel stabbed him for asking when dinner would be ready. The only thing that kept him from slitting her throat was he couldn't get the blade free before she ran off." Khouman looked at each of them, his bafflement evident in his wide-eyed stare.

"What about the others?" Ronan asked, his stance stiff, as if he already knew what was coming.

Khouman shrugged. "More of the same. As the days went by, it was clear no one from the party were themselves. The first couple of incidents were odd in a way, but not completely out of character. But once the others started up it was obvious something more than just a Shadow attack must have happened out there. By then, it was too late to question any of them. One by one, they changed before our eyes. All of them turned—even old Marge, the healer."

Khouman sucked in a breath, his voice thick with emotion. "Tink was the last to turn. Tink is—was—such an amazing woman. Strong and kind. Would never hurt a fly unless it was to save someone. When she returned to me, I thanked the Mother for keeping her safe, but then I started to notice the changes in her, too. A savagery so out of place with her gentle heart. And not just her . . ." he said, his voice growing stronger. "It was the same with all of them. Small things at first. Surges of temper out of place for the situation. A new proclivity toward violence."

Effie scratched at her arms, the incessant buzzing growing more uncomfortable as Khouman spoke.

Lucian shot her a look, his frown deepening as he noticed her fingers raking over her skin.

The small man looked so lost. Like he couldn't believe what he'd seen. The terror of it still held him firmly in its clutches.

"After Marge attacked Kevlyn, we knew we couldn't risk keeping them in town with us anymore," he said.

"Kevlyn?" Ronan asked. "Another party member?"

"Her grandson," Khouman replied.

The story was bad enough already, but for the woman to harm her own grandchild . . . Effie wasn't sure she needed to hear the rest.

"Once that happened, we knew that we couldn't risk harm coming to the rest of our children, you see?" Khouman said as if begging for their understanding, or perhaps it was their forgiveness.

"Of course not," Effie murmured.

His dark eyes met hers, anguish on full display. "We brought them here."

Effie tried to keep her face from showing the horror she felt at the admission. The verdict wasn't just exile; it was death.

"Did the vines . . ." Reyna started to ask, glancing over her shoulder.

Khouman shook his head. "No. The vines didn't attack them like we expected. They walked freely."

"Come again?" Kieran said, pushing off the wall he'd been leaning against.

Khouman shrugged. "We were just as confused by it as you. After weeks of destroying every poor soul that went down there, the damn things didn't so much as wriggle once."

Lucian's eyes were burning bronze as he unleashed his power and turned to look down into the pit.

"Lucian?" she asked.

"They're the same," he said, not facing their group.

"What do you mean?" Khouman demanded.

"At their core. Whatever corruption has tainted them is the same. It's why what was left of your scouting party moved freely. The vines recognize them."

When Lucian faced them again, his eyes were dark umber once more.

"That's to be expected," Kael said, his hand running over his face. "But it doesn't help us get any closer to finding the source."

"No," Lucian agreed. "Not without survivors to tell us what happened."

"So whatever is harming the land, it can harm us too?" Ronan clarified.

Lucian nodded. "Seems that way."

"Has the corruption spread outside of this cave?" Kael asked.

"Not as far as we can tell. It seems confined, at least for now," Khouman answered.

Effie frowned. They were missing something. The buzzing that hadn't dulled since entering the cavern transformed, turning into a familiar tingle that worked its way up the back of her neck.

A startled gasp left her as Effie's vision took hold.

The last thing she saw was Lucian lunge toward her as she started to fall.

In every direction the world was black. Wind raged around her, causing her hair to whip her face. Each new lash broke the skin, leaving trails of sticky blood in its wake.

The world tilted, and she started to fall back as the sense of weightlessness took over. Her mouth opened in a scream that was lost to the wind; her arms windmilled and her legs kicked into the nothingness.

Pain exploded through her body as she crashed into a wall of glass. Thousands of tiny shards flew up, filling the emptiness above her with fragmented reflections of herself. Instead of mirroring her reality, each bloody shard revealed something more terrifying than the last.

In the first, Effie was screaming, her body curled in on itself as her nails tore through her skin.

Another had Effie rocking back and forth staring vacantly into the air.

Then there was one where she was laughing manically as she ripped out a man's throat with her teeth.

It wasn't until she saw the image of her broken and tortured corpse that Effie slammed her eyes closed. As she did, the shards rained down upon her, feeling like daggers as they sliced open more of her skin.

Blood began to pour from her ruined body until she was drowning in the now familiar sea of blood.

She tried to open her eyes, knowing that she wouldn't be alone here, but she was blind.

Drowning, surrounded in darkness, Effie could only scream when the monsters came for her. There was no knowing how many there were, but it felt like dozens of hands moved over her, twisting and pulling until she was torn apart.

When they were done, there was nothing left of her but the sounds of her screams.

CHAPTER 9

*L*ucian's heart stopped as he watched Effie's body teeter backward. He hadn't realized she'd been standing so close to the edge.

Time froze, the ripple of Effie's cloak the only movement for one fractured moment as her eyes met his. There was no trace of fear there, she had no clue how much danger she was in.

Springing forward, Lucian roared her name, his fingers outstretched as he grasped for her.

Her limbs spasmed, the vision fully taking control as she started to fall.

Panic he hadn't felt since he was a child took hold. He wasn't going to reach her in time.

Time had slowed to a crawl, each second stretching out until it felt like an hour. He could see everything as it was happening, but he was helpless to stop it.

Lucian's fingers skimmed the air where she'd been standing, mere inches away from her body as it continued to fall. Her feet were barely touching the edge, the heels of her boots sliding backward off of it.

Already the vines were coming to life, the scrape of their stalks moving against each other as they unfurled, ready for their next meal.

No. They couldn't have her.

With another savage bellow, Lucian took a lurching step, stretching his arm until he felt the burn of muscles tearing. When his fingers grazed the supple leather of her chest piece, he could have wept with relief.

The cool metal of one of the garment's buckles slid against his skin, and Lucian closed his fist, holding onto the strip of leather with everything in him.

His relief was short-lived as his momentum continued to propel him forward. Eyes flaring wide, he tried to counter the motion by pulling Effie back, using her slight weight to slow his movement.

It wasn't enough.

He continued forward, his stomach rolling as his feet skidded along the ground.

Almost as one, two hands wrapped around him, their grasp stronger than iron. One around his free arm, the other on his shoulder.

"Not so fast, Brother," Kael said.

Lucian came to a grinding halt, Effie half-suspended over the ledge, held up only by the fist wrapped around her buckle.

"Mother's tits," Ronan swore as he and Kael pulled Lucian farther back from the edge.

Lucian barely heard the other's frantic voices as they crowded around him. Their words were drowned out, their presence entirely forgotten as he dropped to his knees. The only thing that existed for him right now was her. That he'd come so close to losing her.

Pressing his back against the wall of the cave, he cocooned Effie's much smaller body in his.

It had been close. Too close.

Adrenaline caused his body to shake as he wrapped his arms around her.

"I've got you," he whispered against the cool skin of her forehead. He hoped wherever Effie was, she could hear him. That she would come back to him.

He wouldn't feel quite human again until he could see her eyes twinkling with impudent laughter. Or see one of her smirking grins as she called him a bossy asshole.

Anything to affirm he hadn't lost her.

Lucian's heart continued to slam against his chest as he held onto her. The whole thing happened in under a minute, but Lucian was still breathing hard. Each ragged breath coming out in a harsh pant.

Taking a deep breath, he watched as tremors continued to rack Effie's limbs, her vision unaffected by her brush with death.

It was another full minute before she grew still, her eyes slowly opening.

"Lucian?" she asked, her voice faint. "How did you get over here so fast?"

A shudder tore through him. He almost hadn't been fast enough. All he could see was her, the delicate pulse fluttering in her neck, the bright blue eyes blinking up at him, the soft pink flush returning to her cheeks.

He'd almost lost her.

With a low groan, Lucian dropped his lips to hers in a desperate kiss. He cupped her cheek in the palm of his hand, his fingers splaying in her soft curls as he pulled her closer.

Effie's breath washed over him before she was kissing him back, her body arching into his. Each press of her lips against his was just as frantic.

It wasn't enough.

Needing more, Lucian changed his angle. He slid his tongue along the seam of her lips, taking the bottom one between his teeth and biting down before gently sucking on it.

Her lips parted on a wordless gasp, and he slid his tongue against hers, needing to taste her. Lucian's heart continued to race, his need driving him as their tongues tangled together.

It still wasn't enough. Lucian feared nothing would be.

She was inside him now, laying claim to part of him he'd never given to anyone else.

Never had a simple kiss affected him like this. Effie was sweeter than honey, more intoxicating than Daejaran wine. He'd never tire of tasting her.

His hand moved over her cheek, sliding down the side of her neck to rest on the exposed skin just below her throat. Her heart was beating hard beneath his palm, and Lucian would have moved it lower, continuing his exploration of her tempting body . . . if not for the distant sound of someone clearing their throat.

Remembering they weren't alone, Lucian tore his lips away. His was still shaking when he pressed his forehead to hers, although this time perhaps not from fear.

Her eyes were dazed when they met his, her cheeks flushed. "What was that for?"

Brushing his thumb over her lips, Lucian's voice was rough when he replied, "Don't ever do that again."

"Have a vision?" she asked. "I can't exactly control those."

His arms tightened around her without conscious thought as he shook his head. "No, almost die."

∼

"OH," Effie said, swallowing.

Her vision was momentarily forgotten as she studied her Guardian. He looked wild, his chest rising and falling in rapid breaths and his eyes equal parts bronze and umber. She could tell he wasn't totally back in control. Whatever had happened while she was under had terrified him. It clearly wasn't a feeling he was used to.

"You almost fell off the edge," he told her.

"But you caught me," she said, resting her hand against his cheek, sensing that he needed the reminder.

"Barely," he whispered, the confession guttural.

And there it was. Lucian wasn't used to coming anywhere close to what he considered failure. It had cost him something, those moments of uncertainty. No wonder he looked like he was on the brink.

"I'm right here; I'm safe," she promised.

Closing his eyes, Lucian took a deep breath before relaxing his hold on her.

If not for the shuffling of the others beside them, Effie might have stayed put awhile longer. Coming to in Lucian's arms—his worried eyes raking over her face—wasn't something she'd ever forget. It took more effort than it should to force herself to stand and move away from him.

He moved with her, holding his hand out to help her rise. She had to fight back a smile when he didn't let her go.

Her Guardian wasn't quite okay just yet. Effie wasn't about to complain. Holding his hand did just as much to soothe her as it comforted him.

"Are you alright?" Ronan asked, once they were both upright and facing their small group.

Licking her lips, eyes darting to Lucian a final time, she nodded. "Yes."

"Gave us quite a scare, little warrior," Kael said, his dark skin ashen.

"I'm sorry, I seem to be doing that a lot lately. I wasn't expecting a vision to be triggered."

"Of course you weren't," Ronan said, shooting Kael a censorious glance.

"I should have warned you to stand back from the edge," Khouman said, the small man looking a bit shell-shocked.

"Never seen a Keeper in the throes of a vision?" she asked, offering him a small smile.

He shook his head, the small bells in his beard tinkling.

"What did you See?" Ronan asked.

Ice danced down her spine at the memory of her vision, cooling some of the fire Lucian's kiss had set off inside of her. This vision felt different from the others; darker somehow. Her Guardian insisted that Keepers never had visions about themselves, but Effie couldn't shake the feeling that this one was personal.

"Nothing new," she lied. "It can wait."

Lucian's hand tightened around hers. "You sure?"

She nodded, knowing she would make a point to tell him about it as soon as they were alone. "Yes. We should finish dealing with . . ." she trailed off, suddenly realizing who was missing. "Where's Kieran?"

Kael and Ronan glanced around, clearly surprised to find he had vanished.

"He stormed off while you two were *indisposed*," Reyna informed them, her eyes glittering with amusement.

As soon as they were alone Reyna was going to grill her. Effie knew it as certainly as she knew her name.

"And you didn't think to stop him?" Ronan gritted out.

Reyna shrugged. "Why bother? How far is he going to get?"

Kael let out a low groan. "As far as he wants. He took my Kaelpas stone with him."

CHAPTER 10

*T*ension permeated the cave as the implications of Kieran's selfishness took hold. The glower on Lucian's face told her that Kieran would receive an earful once he was found. As for the rest of them, with Lucian's stone low on charge, only two people would be able to return to the citadel as planned. The others would have to stay behind and wait for someone to return with a fresh stone.

Assuming of course there was a stone available.

As far as Effie knew, the Guardians were the only ones at the citadel who regularly had access to the stones. If anyone else used them, she wasn't aware of it. Since time or powerful magic was required to recharge a stone, most Keepers relied on more traditional means of travel.

Effie glanced at Ronan. "Do you still have your stone?"

Ronan scowled. "Not on me. Not that it would do us any good if I did. I left it at the citadel to be refilled."

"Oh!" Effie said, causing the others to snap their attention back to her. "I have the stone Helena gave me. It's in my room at the citadel. Whoever goes back can use it to return for the rest."

She was guessing that Kael and Lucian would return first, since they would need to report their findings to the Triumvirate. Afterward, they could come back for her, Ronan, and Reyna.

Some of the tension in the cave ebbed as the others realized they would not be stuck idle or having to face weeks of travel to return to Bael.

"Alright, that problem is resolved for now. What are we going to do about Tinka?" Ronan asked.

Tinka let out a low growl at the sound of her name.

"Can she understand us?" Effie asked.

Khouman shrugged. "I hope not. I can't bear to believe anything of her is still trapped inside that *thing*."

Effie's mind was racing. If Tinka was still in there somewhere, perhaps they could find a way to save her. Her eyes marked her as a Shadow, but which version? The mindless fanatic that was little more than an animal, or the sentient one still capable of accessing its power? Tinka was the only Shadow Effie knew about that hadn't been created by Rowena, so it was possible she was something else entirely.

Maybe there was a way to find out . . .

"Lucian?" Effie asked.

Her Guardian shifted to face her. "What are you thinking?"

"Does Tinka's essence match the Shadows we came across in the jungle?"

Khouman flinched, his eyes dropping to the ground.

The bronze flecks in Lucian's eyes seemed alight with inner fire as he considered her question. "Similar, not identical," he answered thoughtfully, scrubbing his free hand along his jaw.

"Different source?" Kael asked, picking up on the direction of Lucian's thoughts.

Ronan and Effie exchanged confused looks. They were having a bit more trouble connecting the dots.

"It's possible," Lucian said. "But I don't think that's the reason."

"Speak plainly," Ronan demanded, arms crossed over his chest.

"The corruption appears like a black stain blotting out life's natural light. In reality, it is far more than just a stain. It is a parasite, consuming its host until it perverts it entirely. In this way, the corruption is the same everywhere we have found it," Lucian explained.

"So, if the corruption acts the same regardless of the source, how are Tinka and the Shadows different?" Reyna asked.

Lucian's lips pulled down in a frown. "Not an easy answer, I'm afraid."

"Try," Ronan said, his tone making it clear this was not a suggestion.

Lucian's eyes narrowed, obviously not appreciating being given orders by someone he still considered an outsider. He remained silent as he considered how to respond to Ronan's question. With a shake of his head, Lucian finally answered. "It is almost impossible to explain the essence of life to one who cannot experience it."

Effie gave his hand an encouraging squeeze.

Closing his eyes, Lucian returned her gesture. His lips lifted slightly as she stared up at him. Letting out a long sigh, Lucian began talking.

"When I peel back the layers of a living thing to look into its essence, I always see the same thing. Glowing, interwoven strands that vibrate with the force of what powers them. The stronger the being, the purer their soul, the more intense the glow and the more powerful the vibration. This is true no matter the species. Sometimes the smallest creatures glow the brightest," Lucian said.

Effie sucked in a breath as Lucian speared her with a look, his slight grin growing until he looked back at the others. He paused for a second, his eyes resting on each of them to ensure they were still following. After a few nods, he continued.

"These vibrations are unique, although the more similar the beings, the more alike the vibrations."

"Sort of like a song, right? We are all different instruments but the notes are the same?" Effie asked.

Kael grinned at her, his dimples flashing. "Exactly. Using your metaphor, humans would all be drums but a tree might be a wind instrument."

Ronan and Reyna nodded to show they understood. Khouman's

expression was distant as he stared with furrowed brows down into the cavern below.

"Despite the differences in their vibrations," Lucian said, picking up his explanation, "every living being is in harmony. The corruption is a break in the harmony. A dissonance, if you will."

"Someone's singing off-key," Ronan muttered.

Kael snickered. "That's one way to put it."

Reyna shushed them. "Let him finish."

Despite the levity of the others, Lucian looked somber as he said, "The dissonance I sense in the woman, is not the same as when I looked within the Shadows . . . *yet*."

Effie's heart sank at his assessment.

Lucian continued, "My assumption is the difference between them is only temporary. I would have to look at her again once her transformation was complete to know for sure."

Silence filled the cave. Not even Tinka, who had been snarling and shuffling below during the entire exchange, made a sound.

Effie was the first to speak. She tried to phrase her next question carefully, still clinging to what was left of her mostly shredded theory, but not wanting to give Khouman false hope. "But, if Tinka *is* different, is it possible that she will not become like the rest of them? That we can reverse this?"

"It is more likely that she is still in the midst of transition," Kael said, giving Effie an apologetic frown.

"So there's nothing you can do for her?" Khouman asked.

"We do not yet have a way to undo the corruption. It is unlikely we will be able to help her in time," Lucian said.

His expression was unreadable and his voice firm, but Effie could feel the tension rolling off of him. Lucian was used to having all the answers and always being in control. For both to elude him now . . . it was wearing on him.

"Then I have one final request before you go," Khouman said, his gruff voice thick with emotion.

"Anything," Ronan promised.

"Kill her. Please."

"Khouman—" Effie started.

"Please, I beg you. I cannot bear to let her suffer this way. She would never have wanted to become this. I would do it myself, but—"

Tears brimmed in Effie's eyes, her heart breaking for the man.

"Are you sure?" Lucian asked, his deep voice softer than Effie had heard him use it with anyone but her.

Khouman nodded, a lone tear leaving a dusty trail down his cheek. "We've already said our goodbyes."

"It will be done," Reyna promised, moving closer and dropping to her knee beside the Caederan man.

Khouman released a shaky breath. "My thanks, lady. I-I think I'll wait outside, if you don't mind. I'll see you to town once it's . . . over." He didn't wait for them to reply, turning and walking back down the torch-lit pathway.

"Reyna, you can't really mean that," Effie sputtered once he was gone.

She raised a dark brow. "Why wouldn't I? She is an abomination, a threat to all of us. I eliminate threats."

"Sure, but—" Effie protested.

"But this monster has a name?" Reyna asked, her voice gentle.

Effie's chest hurt as she turned to the men, hoping one of them might agree with her. Not even Lucian, whose dark eyes burned when they met hers, was on her side.

"It's murder," she insisted.

"There is mercy in death," Reyna replied. "As well as peace. Does she not deserve both?"

"Of course she does—"

"This is a kindness, Effie, I promise," Reyna said.

Even if a more rational part of Effie agreed with her, it still felt wrong. "But what if we find a way to save her a week from now? Couldn't we just take her back with us? Wait for Helena to get back . . . or maybe the Triumvirate know of a way . . ."

"Effie."

It was Lucian's voice that finally broke through her rambling pleas. She shook her head, not wanting to hear what he was about to say.

"You know that she would only be a danger to us. We cannot risk it," he said.

"We have to at least try," she said, her voice raw.

"It's too late, little warrior," Kael said, lifting his hand to place it on her shoulder.

Effie flinched away.

"I'm sorry," he said.

This time when he wrapped his arm around her shoulder Effie let him.

It was one thing to put down a creature that was trying to kill her. It was something else when it was someone she knew, even if they'd only crossed paths a handful of times.

Reyna and Ronan moved back to the edge, peering down into the depths. They spoke in low voices, but the cave amplified their words so it was as if they were speaking right next to her.

"Without the ladders to climb down, we will need to bring her to us," Reyna said.

"Thanks to the vines, we couldn't risk it even with the ladders," Ronan reminded her. Sighing, he added, "I don't have enough ability in Air to fly her up."

"A rope would do," Reyna murmured, her eyes calculating.

Ronan speared her with a dry look. "I must have left my spare rope in my other pants."

"I can help with that," Lucian said, joining them.

Ronan lifted a brow. "How's that?"

Lucian answered by pulling his cloak off his shoulders. His hands blurred as his eyes began to glow with bronze light. Effie's eyes could barely track the movement of his fingers as he transformed the cloak into a long strand of rope.

When he was done, Lucian held the rope out to Ronan.

Ronan grunted. "Well, that's just fucking useful."

Her Guardian shrugged, and Reyna snagged the rope from his hands before Ronan even reached for it.

Effie might have also been impressed by the display of Lucian's power, but her stomach was tied in knots. "Are you sure this is the only way?"

She was speaking to Kael, and her voice was barely more than a whisper, but Lucian whipped his head around to face her. He looked torn. Effie could see the war raging in his eyes. His duty was demanding he take care of the threat, but it also pushed him to ensure she was alright.

Kael squeezed her, dipping his head down. "You know it is. He would never agree to this otherwise. Lucian wouldn't kill someone he could save."

Lucian's gaze still boring into hers, Effie swallowed and gave a small nod. It seemed to be all he needed. He turned away, refocusing on Reyna who had begun looping the rope and was preparing to toss it down.

"You sure you know what you're doing?" Ronan asked.

Reyna glared at him. "Do you think this is the first time a Night Stalker has had to raise something from the ground?"

Since her people lived amongst the trees, Effie supposed Reyna probably was the most qualified for the task of bringing Tinka up.

"My aim is perfect," Reyna continued, as she began to twirl the lasso she'd created above her head.

Ronan smirked. "Don't I know it."

Wholly focused on her task, Reyna didn't bother replying. She released the lasso in her right hand, her arm swinging across her body while still holding the rest of the coiled rope in her left hand.

There was an enraged shriek and the rope began to buck in Reyna's hand. Ronan moved quickly, stepping behind Reyna to help pull it in.

Effie didn't have a clear view of what was happening in the cavern, but the sound of unfurling vines was unmistakable. "Watch out!" she cried, seeing the tip of one begin to writhe in the air.

Lucian's sword was in his hand before she was finished speaking. Swinging the blade, he cleaved the vine in two, the squirming tip falling back into the pit as silver liquid began spewing out of the other half.

The top of Tinka's head cleared the edge of their platform as more vines began to snake upwards, stretching toward them. They were growing fast, swelling in size as they reached for their next meal.

Tinka was tearing at the rope around her waist, squirming frantically as she tried to break free, her shrieks bouncing off the walls.

The foul liquid began to pool on the ground as Lucian dispatched more of the vines.

"Don't let it touch you!" Effie called out.

A part of her itched to join the fight against the vines, but Lucian was moving so fast she knew she'd only be in his way. Besides, her dagger wasn't exactly an ideal weapon as it would force her into close proximity to those razor-sharp thorns.

Eyes bouncing between the two separate fights, she sucked in a breath as Tinka lunged at Reyna, her hands outstretched as she tried to claw the woman holding onto the other end of her lead.

Letting go of the rope, Reyna launched three daggers in rapid succession. Two landed in Tinka's chest, the third in her throat. Tinka dropped to her knees, her tiny body sagging as blood spurted from her mouth. It wasn't quite the black ichor the rest of the Shadows had, but it was darker than anything Effie had ever seen come from a human.

Swallowing, her eyes fell closed.

"You don't have to watch this," Kael said in her ear.

"Yes, I do. If I'm going to stand here and agree to this, I at least owe it to Tinka to see it through."

"Why?"

"Because if it was me in her place, I would want to know that I had someone there who cared at the end."

She could feel Kael's dark green eyes on her, but she didn't look at him. Instead, when her eyes opened, she watched as Reyna unsheathed the long blade at her back and swung it in one fluid move, completing the kill. With a sick thud, Tinka's head landed on the ground beside the rest of her spasming body.

Effie swallowed hard, her hands balling into fists. It was the only physical reaction she allowed herself. "May the Mother carry you home," she whispered, turning away.

Lucian began moving away from the edge. "We should get out of here before these things get big enough to climb over the edge," he said.

Effie couldn't agree more. She wanted to get as far away from what happened here as she could. Without another word, she started running. Footsteps echoed around her as the others followed suit.

Khouman looked relieved as they spilled out of the cave. "It's done, then?"

Lucian nodded.

Khouman's eyes fell closed, and his lips began to move with silent words.

"Your people should stay out of the cave until we learn how to deal with the vines permanently," Lucian said once he was done.

Khouman nodded. "I'll make sure of it."

"Alright, then," Lucian said, "we should get back to the citadel. It will probably be a couple of hours before I make it back to collect the others. I don't want to impose on your hospitality, but I know they haven't had a chance to eat today."

Effie's stomach rolled. Food was the last thing on her mind, but it was sweet of him to think to ask.

"Of course. It's the least I can do."

Lucian turned to her expectantly. "You ready?"

"Me?" Effie asked, her eyes shooting to Kael, whose lips were pressed together like he was fighting a smile.

Lucian crossed his arms, brow quirking with challenge. "You spent the better part of the last month bitching at me every time I so much as hinted at leaving the citadel without you, now you want me to leave you behind?"

Effie was about to protest, especially since she just explained to him about her premonitions, when she caught on to what he was doing.

Lucian didn't let his guard down around anyone, which made him a hard man to get to know. On the surface he was a broody bastard, and he knew how to play up that persona. It kept others at arm's length and prevented them from looking too closely.

To them, the Guardian was just being the same jackass he always was, but Effie knew him better now. She had seen past his mask. He was offering her a distraction, trying to cheer her up after what had gone down inside the cave by making himself a scapegoat so she had somewhere to channel her churning emotions.

How long had he been doing just that? Playing the role she needed him to in an attempt to help her process all of the changes in her world?

"I'd be happy to accompany you, if you think that's what's best, Guardian," she said, visibly shocking him with her answer.

"That might be the first time you've ever agreed to one of my suggestions without having something to say about it," Lucian said as she moved into place beside him.

"I told you I could be reasonable."

"Hmm," Lucian murmured, his eyes unreadable. "I think it's more likely you hit your head while we were in the cave."

Biting back a laugh, Effie shrugged. "If that's what you need to believe."

Lucian shook his head. "I don't trust new, agreeable Effie. What have you done with my fledgling?" he asked, the slight twitch of his lips giving him away.

"I need to keep you on your toes, Lucian. Can't have you feeling too sure of yourself."

"Why not?" he asked, amused.

"Where's the fun in that?"

Lucian sighed, pulling the Kaelpas stone out of its pouch. "Come on, then."

"You sure you believe it's me?"

"Oh, it's you alright. Only my Effie could be cheeky enough to find a way to make agreeing with me a method of undermining me at the same time."

Effie bit the inside of her cheek, surprised at how much lighter she felt after exchanging a few teasing words with her Guardian. She had to give the man credit; sometimes it did feel as if he knew exactly what she needed.

84

Lucian wrapped his fingers around hers. "I'll meet you back here in three hours," he called over her head.

Effie didn't even have a chance to wave goodbye to her friends before Lucian activated the stone and transported them back to the citadel.

CHAPTER 11

*L*ucian's grip on her hand was the only thing that kept Effie upright as her feet made contact with solid ground once more. No matter how many times she'd done it, the Kaelpas stone still affected her.

"How do you make it look so easy?" she panted, trying hard not to gag as bile worked its way up her throat.

"You'll have to be more specific."

Effie shot him a baleful look. "You look like you just took a stroll through the garden, and I'm probably some lovely shade of green while my stomach attempts to climb out of my throat. So what's the secret?"

Lucian let out a bark of laughter. "I can assure you, you're not green."

"You aren't going to tell me, are you?"

He brushed a damp curl off of her face, his finger lingering to stroke her cheek. "If there was a secret, I would tell you."

"That would be a first."

Some of the laughter faded from his eyes. "There are many things that I am bound from revealing to anyone. Secrets I've kept for longer than you've been alive. Even if I could tell you, many of them aren't mine to share. But I promise you, Effie, I take no enjoyment in leaving you in the dark."

"I know," she whispered. And she did. It was right there in his eyes. If Lucian was closed off, it was only because he had to be.

Swallowing, unsteady now for reasons that had nothing to do with the Kaelpas stone, she let her fingers slide from his and looked around the unfamiliar room.

It was a cross between some kind of study and a storage room. Weapons and books dominated nearly every free surface, including the walls. Three massive padded chairs—which could easily have been mistaken for thrones anywhere else—were in the center. The room was made to be lived in, the furnishings well-worn but comfortable.

"Where are we?" Effie asked as her fingers brushed the velvety blanket resting on the back of the nearest chair.

"The Hall of Guardians."

Effie's brows raised. "Sounds important—and off limits."

Lucian shrugged. "It's a glorified barracks for my brothers and I. We come here when we need privacy."

Heat flooded her cheeks at the thought of what she and Lucian could do with a bit of privacy, and she turned away, not wanting him to see the direction her thoughts had taken.

Noticing four black doors encircling the room, Effie asked, "So, you what? Come here to read?"

"More like to sleep." Lucian gestured to the door on his left. "That's my room. Kael is across from me," he said, pointing to the door on his right. "You haven't spent much time with our other brother, but his room is just there."

Effie's eyes were still glued to the door he'd identified as his. Curiosity ate at her. What would she find if she peeked inside?

"What about that one?" Effie asked, turning her back to his room to try to remove the temptation to ask to see it.

"That is the exit. It will take me directly to the Triumvirate's quarters, which is where I am heading now. Wait for me here, this shouldn't take long, and then we can go get the stone from your room and return for the others."

"You don't want me to come with you? Tell them what I Saw?" she asked, more surprised he'd willingly leave her in such a private space than disappointed he would be seeing the trio without her.

Lucian's lips lifted. "Ah, there she is. I knew your blanket acceptance wouldn't last long."

Effie rolled her eyes but fought her own smile.

"As for your vision, I am sure they will be eager to know what you Saw. I wouldn't be surprised if they summoned you."

"Are *you* eager?" she asked, wondering why he hadn't brought her vision up before now.

"You said it wasn't anything new," he replied, brow lifting. "Was that a lie?"

"Well, no . . ."

He shrugged. "Then I can wait. Besides, I'm not really the one you're supposed to be sharing your visions with."

"Are we still clinging to that nonsense? You can't honestly be telling me it's still expected I filter my visions through Kieran after everything that's happened. Besides, when has something as silly as a rule stopped me?"

Lucian laughed. "I expect nothing less from you. If you Saw something you thought I needed to know, you would have told me by now. I will never push you to reveal something before you are ready. As for Kieran, we're in agreement. The Triumvirate need to know what he's done. His actions the last few days have made it clear he cannot be trusted where you are concerned. We'll see about finding someone else to work with you."

Effie briefly wondered if Kieran would face any sort of formal discipline for his actions in the cave. It wasn't like he had broken an official rule, but he had left two of their Guardians in a potentially sticky situation. The Triumvirate wouldn't be pleased about it.

"Will I get a say in who tutors me this time?" she asked, returning her thoughts to their conversation.

Lucian's lips quirked. "Doubtful."

"I figured as much. You're all a bunch of control freaks."

Her Guardian shrugged. "Guilty."

Sighing, Effie settled into the nearest chair. "Alright then, better not keep them waiting."

Lucian nodded and started for the door. He paused with his hand on the knob. "I'd bring you with me if I could. The Triumvirate operate under layers of formality and ceremony. A breach in protocol is not tolerated—by anyone."

"Not even you?" she teased.

"Especially not me."

Effie was surprised by the admission. Lucian seemed untouchable. It was hard to picture him answering to anyone other than himself.

"They do love to hoard their secrets," Effie murmured, picking up a heavy book from the table beside her.

Lucian snickered. "That they do."

The unexpected irreverence in his tone made her look up. "Not a fan?"

"Let's just say things would be a lot easier without all of the fanfare."

Effie could only imagine how exhausting it must be to work for three such beings. "I don't envy you."

Chuckling, Lucian opened the door. "Alright, I'll be back. Make yourself at home."

Effie lasted all of three seconds before she sprang out of the chair and crept toward Lucian's room. It was his own fault. He had to know she was going to snoop if he left her alone. He'd practically goaded her into it by telling her to be at home.

She didn't hesitate as she opened the door and pushed inside, his scent immediately enveloping her. Effie closed her eyes, savoring the smell. It was like standing outside at night in the rain: clean, dark, and a little earthy. It was utterly masculine and wholly Lucian.

You don't have much time . . . a more rational part of her brain reminded her. Effie's eyes flew open. Unless she wanted to get caught snooping, she'd better make this fast.

As far as rooms went, it was fairly nondescript. There were no personal touches scattered around to indicate that it was his sanctuary.

If not for the delicious smell of him, Effie would have thought Lucian never used the room.

The bed was neatly made, a red blanket folded at the foot of it. A large chest, similar to hers, was filled with folded clothes. Not so much as a quill sat on his desk and its accompanying chair was tucked beneath it. There wasn't even a rug on the floor to add a bit of warmth to the space. It was completely lacking in deep, dark secrets.

Effie fought back a wave of disappointment. *How underwhelming.*

There was a door to the right of the space that was partially open. Effie pushed open the door, expecting to find more of the same. What she was not expecting was the black tiled bathing chamber, which was easily bigger than the one she had to share with the other female Keepers.

"Not fair," she whispered in awe, her voice echoing around her.

As she stepped inside, hidden orbs sprang to life, illuminating the room with a soft glow. Unlike the rest of his room, this was a space he clearly used. Everything about it screamed relaxation. There was a deep tub set into the floor, large enough for three or four people, with benches carved into the sides. Thick red candles lined the tub, most held in place by hardened pools of wax.

Effie had to force herself to look away from the tub before the image of a naked Lucian—submerged in water and surrounded by candlelight—made her combust.

A recessed section of the back wall caught her eye. Effie moved closer, trying to figure out what Lucian used the space for. She stumbled when the floor dipped, not noticing the cubicle was slightly lower than the rest of the ground. Squinting, she bent over, noticing small holes evenly spaced along the bottom.

"Huh, what are those for?" she wondered, using the wall to push herself back up.

As she did, her hand moved over a silver square she hadn't noticed. Effie shrieked as warm water began to fall from the ceiling. She was drenched in an instant, her stunned brain struggling to make sense of what just happened. When it finally caught up, she slapped at the silver square until the water stopped.

"Mother's tits," she groaned, shoving her damp hair back.

She was sopping wet. There'd be no hiding her snooping now. Even if she managed to make it back to her room and change before Lucian returned, the wet trail she'd leave behind would give her away.

Effie froze at the sound of low chuckles. *No. Please, no.* Lifting her head slowly, she cringed at the sight of Lucian standing in the doorway, arms crossed as he leaned against the door frame.

Shivering a little as the cooler air touched her wet skin, Effie lifted her chin. "Back so soon?"

"I forgot something," Lucian said, still laughing.

Effie nodded as if she should have expected as much.

"Find what you were looking for?" he asked.

"Not quite," she said, stepping out of the cubicle and slipping a little as her wet boots slid over the tile.

Lucian laughed harder as she struggled to catch her balance.

"That's an interesting um . . . what do you call that thing?"

"A shower."

"Right. So, are you going to find me a towel or just stand there luxuriating in my misery?" she asked, taking another careful step forward.

Without looking, Lucian reached over to a shelf she hadn't noticed on the other side of the door and held up a plush towel between two fingers. "You're going to have to come and get it."

"You can be a real bastard; you know that?" Effie grumbled, slipping once more.

Lucian grinned. "Only seems fair to make you suffer a little for being nosey."

She couldn't even argue the point. In his place, she'd do the same. "You could try to be the bigger person and just help me out."

"Where's the fun in that?" he said, throwing her earlier words back at her.

Effie glared at him. "You're evil."

"I'm not the one who needs the towel."

After two more steps, which were more accurately graceless slides across the tiled floor, Effie looked over at him. "Lucian?"

"Yes, Effie?" he replied, his eyes crinkling with silent laughter.

"You might not want to be still standing there by the time I make it over. There's a good chance I'm going to kick you."

Shaking his head, Lucian pushed off the wall and strode forward. "Don't ever say I didn't do something for you," he muttered, using the edge of the towel to wipe some of the water drops from her cheek.

She blinked, looking up into his face, feeling a little breathless at the warmth in his eyes. If he kept looking at her like that she wouldn't be responsible for her actions. Snatching the towel from his hand, Effie started to run it over her hair to hide what the tender gesture was doing to her.

"I think I've got it from here. You can go now."

"And miss you try to figure out how to get out of this? Not on your life."

"The Triumvirate are waiting for you," she reminded him.

Lucian sighed loudly, and Effie risked peeking out at him from behind her towel.

"That is quite possibly the only thing you could have said to get me to leave."

"I know," she replied, throwing him a cheeky grin.

He shook his head, his smile still warm. "If I have to miss the aftermath of your little transgression then it just means I'll have to think up another way to repay you."

"You're welcome to use my bathing chamber whenever you want, but you might give the other ladies a heart attack."

"That's not quite what I had in mind."

"Oh no?" she asked, running the towel along her arms, trying to soak up as much of the water as she could. "What do you have in mind?"

Lucian gave her one of his enigmatic half-smiles. "I guess you'll just have to wait and see."

CHAPTER 12

*K*ieran slammed another heavy tome onto the table, his fury thrumming through him like a second heartbeat. Teeth clenched, he frantically flipped through the pages searching for the annotation he'd found a few days earlier.

Nothing about these records was straightforward. Few, if any of them, were dated or labeled in a way that made logical sense. Instead, they seemed to be grouped by topic, sometimes with footnotes indicating that a prophecy might also appear elsewhere as it could be inferred in another manner.

He'd still yet to find a single volume that was comprised of prophecies explicitly about the Shadow Years, but he had discovered a reference to a marker. It would have to suffice.

"Where is it?" he growled, practically tearing the pages out in his haste.

Sucking in a frustrated breath, Kieran forced himself to slow down. He couldn't afford for anyone to know he'd been in here. Thankfully, the Triumvirate likely thought he was still traipsing around with that band of fools. He wouldn't be missed for at least another hour or two. He had time.

Running a finger down another page, Kieran let out a triumphant whoop. "There it is."

'AND BEASTS WILL FALL, *the docile becoming fiends in their quest for blood.*
    Peaceful no more, the prey become the hunters;
    upon the threshold of day, where life and death meet, converging into one.
    <u>*Let it be a mark of the end, a herald of destruction.*</u>
    None will be safe when the gentlest amongst us are lost.'

KIERAN WOULD HAVE MISSED it initially, if not for the bold lines beneath the reference to the mark. Scrawled in the margin, was another note:

CONNECTION TO *TMJ* PROPHECY? *Ref. 274-00249*

HE HAD no clue what the numbers meant, or the letters TMJ. His best guess was that the numbers were associated with another book, which contained the prophecy in question. He needed to find that prophecy, but in the meantime, this passage would serve. It was certainly vague enough that it gave him room to maneuver, and after what he'd seen in Bael, he knew exactly what he needed to do.

Lifting his knapsack from the ground where he'd dropped it, Kieran pulled out the glittering purple stone.

Now to bait the trap.

CHAPTER 13

*E*ffie walked beside Lucian, hoping she at least looked mostly put together. Her curls were still damp, but she'd managed to pull on a fresh pair of pants and a light blue tunic before the summons came.

Lucian had been oddly reserved since coming to fetch her. Well, not odd for the old Lucian, the one whose dark scowls and brooding silences had filled many of their first interactions. But it was a far cry from the playful banter they'd shared less than an hour earlier.

His meeting must not have gone well. The thought sobered her; it didn't bode well for her own.

They came to a halt outside the door to the Triumvirate's sanctum.

"Here?" she asked.

Lucian nodded, and Effie frowned, wondering if their use of their formal chamber held any significance. Previously, whenever she'd met with the Triumvirate alone, it had always happened somewhere in the archives. Or the healing wing.

"They're waiting for you," Lucian said when she made no move to go inside.

"You're not coming?" she asked.

He shook his head. "I need to go back and collect the others.

97

Besides, I was not the one who was summoned. No one invites themselves to one of the Triumvirates meetings. Protocol, remember?"

Effie made a face. It wasn't that she feared the Triumvirate. Not really. Her conversations with Smoke had shown her that they could be kind, but she'd gotten used to Lucian's steady presence beside her.

"Something wrong?" Lucian asked, picking up on her unease.

Feigning a breeziness she didn't feel, Effie smiled. "No, nothing. I'll see you when you get back?"

"You're bound to eventually," he said.

Effie's eyes narrowed at the non-committal answer. "You're as good at giving vague non-answers as they are."

"Guess it was bound to rub off on me after centuries of being amongst them," he said, a small smirk ghosting his lips.

Effie sighed. "One of your less attractive qualities, to be sure."

"Your statement implies you find some of my *qualities* quite attractive."

Effie could feel the heat creeping into her cheeks. "Don't you have somewhere to be?"

"Don't you? You're the one standing here stalling and telling me how attractive you think I am."

"I did *not* say anything resembling that."

Lucian ran his knuckle over her burning cheek. "Sure you did, fledgling."

Her heart sped up at the touch and any half-hearted protest died in her throat.

"I'll see you later, Effie," he murmured before wandering back down the hall.

"Bye," she whispered to his retreating back.

Alone once more, Effie faced the arched doors with a grimace. She couldn't put this off any longer. Steeling her shoulders, she took a deep breath and walked inside.

"Daughter."

Effie gave the two robed figures a little wave. "Just the two of you?"

Mirror One tilted his head. *"Does that bother you?"*

She gave a quick shake of her head. "No, I just thought all three of you would be here. So which one of you is absent? Smoke?"

She guessed his name, only because he had a tendency to stand front and center whenever he was with the others, while the Mirrors always stood side by side. It was hardly a perfect science, but it helped her when she could pretend she knew which of them she spoke with.

The odd rush of wind she'd come to associate with their amusement flowed through the chamber.

"With the telepathic link we share, the three of us are always present no matter how many physical forms you see before you."

"That must be . . . loud," Effie said, trying to imagine her mind being constantly invaded by others' thoughts. "So, you can hear everything . . . all the time?"

Was anything she'd said to Smoke kept between them or had the Mirrors been listening in the entire time? The thought stung.

The Mirrors shrugged, avoiding the question. She really should know better than bothering to ask direct questions by now.

"It is convenient."

"And allows us to go where needed."

"Of course," she murmured. "So I suppose you wanted to ask me about our findings?"

"We know about the Shadow-touched."

Effie straightened at the unfamiliar term. *Are they referring to the land . . . or what happened to Tinka?* They didn't give her time to ask.

"You had another vision," Mirror Two prompted.

"I did." *Let's see how they like it.*

"Care to discuss it?"

The question was a courtesy. They weren't actually asking.

Effie shuddered as the memory of hands tearing her apart filled her mind. Any futile desire she might have had to try and fight against telling them what they wanted to know fled. The two men standing before her might be the only people in all of Elysia who knew what her vision meant.

"Before I do, may I ask you a question?"

"You may always ask, Daughter."

"Can you at least promise to try to answer this one?" she pleaded, trying to keep any note of aggression from her voice. This was a genuine request; she didn't want them to ignore it out of hand.

The Mirrors nodded in unison.

"Is it true that Keepers never have visions about themselves?"

"Never in our history."

"Then why is it I keep seeing myself in my visions?"

"Seeing yourself how?"

"You're familiar with my last few visions." It was a statement because she knew that they would have Seen everything when Smoke pulled the visions from her mind. "The objects in my visions are continuing to interact with me personally."

"Yes, but the visions are not about you."

"They have been warnings about the Shadows."

Effie shook her head. "That's not how it feels. Especially this most recent one. The Shadows weren't just attacking me. They tore me apart. I was falling through the sky until I landed in glass, shattering it. The shards filled the sky, reflecting thousands of terrible images—each one of them mine. Then they fell, shredding me and leaving me blind as I drowned in a pool of my own blood. How is that *not* personal?"

"Our visions come to us in metaphor."

"You need to seek out the truth trapped within."

Maybe that was the case for most visions, but this time Effie was certain they were wrong. Today's vision wasn't about the Shadow attacks, or at least it wasn't *just* about the attacks. The images it contained might very well be metaphors, but somehow they directly related to her. There was no other subject contained within her vision outside of the faceless monsters that destroyed her.

"With all due respect, I'm telling you my truth. This is what I sense when I replay the images from my vision."

The robed figures remained silent for several heartbeats while they considered her words. As the silence continued to stretch, Effie wondered if they were carrying on a private conversation.

Mirror One held up his hand, the navy rune in its center standing out in sharp contrast to the pale skin. *"Perhaps if you showed us?"*

Effie shrank back. Knowing that the member of the Triumvirate that touched her could relive every experience she'd ever had left her feeling vulnerable in a way she didn't like. Some memories were too personal to share. Especially some of the more recent ones.

She didn't feel as comfortable with the other two members of the Triumvirate touching her. It didn't matter if Smoke could telecast her every thought to the others as he was experiencing it, or however their connection worked. At least with Smoke it didn't feel like an invasion when she opened herself up to him. Maybe it was because he made a point to speak to her directly, and it had created some sort of bond between them. Whatever the reason, the other two felt like strangers by comparison.

Unsure how she could express her reservation, especially after allowing this very thing on multiple other occasions, Effie glanced between them.

"Daughter?" Mirror One prompted as his hand started to fall.

"What don't you want us to See?" Mirror Two asked.

"It's not that I'm hiding anything, I promise. I would just feel more comfortable if Smoke was the one to access my vision, if you really feel it's necessary."

There was a rustle of fabric as Mirror Two stepped forward. *"I'm right here,"* he said, switching to the smoke and campfire voice that was uniquely Smoke's.

"Why did you let me believe—" Effie trailed off, realizing it didn't matter. It had been her assumption that Smoke wasn't among them. No one had misled her except herself. "Well there go the nicknames," she said with a little sigh.

He stepped off the dais, closing the distance between them until Effie could no longer see Mirror One behind Smoke's hooded frame.

"May I?" he asked.

Taking a deep breath, Effie dipped her chin in a nod. She closed her eyes as he lifted his hand, but before he could touch her, the door crashed open. Kieran stumbled in, long hair wild and his eyes bloodshot.

"You dare set foot in our sanctum uninvited?"

A loud crack of thunder shook the room, punctuating the accusation and underscoring the speaker's anger.

Effie didn't know which member of the Triumvirate spoke, but she'd never heard any of the Triumvirate use such a darkly menacing voice. It was thrilling in a way that confused her.

"Pardon the interruption, but this couldn't wait. I've had a dream."

Effie gaped at Kieran, his earlier misdeeds forgotten in the face of his obvious fear.

"What did you See?"

Visible shudders racked Kieran's body as he struggled to catch his breath. "There's been another attack."

"Where?"

"In the jungle. I—I can't make sense of it. There's so much blood."

"Did you See what happened?"

"No, just the aftermath."

"Could you find your way there?"

Kieran nodded. "Yes, I think so. It happened near the waterfall."

"So close," Effie whispered, dread pooling in her belly.

Kieran didn't so much as look at her. His attention was wholly focused on the Triumvirate.

"You will take the Guardians there."

"Of course."

"What can I do?" Effie asked.

"Go with them. See if it triggers anything from your visions."

Swallowing, she nodded. "I need to grab my weapons."

"I'll meet you in the portal room," Kieran said.

"The others will be back soon. Wait for them."

Effie nodded absently, her mind already filled with what could be out there. Adrenaline coursed through her veins, urging her to act. If the attack had just happened, then the source of the corruption could still be out there. This might be their chance to get some answers.

Smoke grasped Effie's wrist, pulling her attention back to his hooded face. *"I mean it, Daughter. Do not leave without the others. Stay by their side. No one is to wander off on their own."*

Effie detected a note of fear in his voice. "Did you See something like this in a vision? Have you been waiting for this to happen?" she asked, trying to guess what could make one of the Triumvirate afraid.

Not even with the situation in Sylverlands had they expressed any outward sign of agitation.

"It is only a matter of time before more of the markers come to pass."

"How do you know this will be a marker?"

"I don't."

"Then why . . ." Effie trailed off, eyes narrowing in concern.

"It is a suspicion. One I sorely hope is unfounded."

Effie nodded. "Alright. I will make sure we stick together."

Finally, Smoke let go of her, and Effie started to race out of the room.

"Daughter—"

Skidding to a stop, she glanced back over her shoulder.

"Be careful."

The finality of the words and the heaviness with which he uttered them made Effie shiver with apprehension. Why did she have the feeling he knew exactly what awaited them, and that there was a chance not all of them were going to make it back?

CHAPTER 14

Somehow she was the last to arrive.

"Sorry," Effie murmured, moving to stand beside Ronan.

"Do you know what this is about?" he asked in a low voice.

"There's been another attack," she whispered.

"Here?"

Effie nodded.

"Something about this doesn't sit right." Deep lines bracketed Ronan's mouth as he frowned. "If it's the Shadows, there's no sense to their movement. At first, it seemed like they were moving out from Vyruul in a wave, which is in line with the other attack sites and is keeping with the theory that they were fleeing. Why would they double back now?"

"To cause as much chaos as possible?" Effie guessed.

"Perhaps," Ronan murmured, eyes troubled.

If anything, Ronan echoing Smoke's warnings had Effie more on edge. Needing to see if Lucian was giving off any outward sign of concern, Effie moved her eyes to where he was standing with Kael and Kieran. None of them were smiling, but of the three, only Kieran seemed afraid.

The knowledge helped steady her. If Lucian wasn't worried, then perhaps things weren't quite as bad as they seemed.

Peeling himself away from the others, Lucian moved over to her.

"Any premonitions?" he asked in a low voice.

Effie's brows veed as she performed a mental check. Her internal warning system was oddly silent. If she was walking into danger, shouldn't that infernal buzzing be screaming at her?

"No, nothing, but that's a good sign, right?"

Lucian shrugged. "Maybe there's no need for a warning when the threat is obvious."

"I liked my theory better," Effie murmured, feeling a little light-headed.

Her Guardian gave her shoulder a warm squeeze then turned back to the rest of their group.

"Let's go," Lucian called.

Kael was the first to step through the portal, Kieran right on his heels. Ronan and Reyna were next, followed by Effie and Lucian.

The jungle was eerily silent as Effie crossed the portal's threshold. Not even those that called the jungle home were making their presence known. This was not the place she'd become used to.

The waterfall was to the far west of Bael, although portal travel turned the three-hour hike into a quick ten-minute walk. Due to its remote location, this part of the jungle was practically untouched by any external factors. There were no marked paths and no clearings of any kind. Nature had claimed this area as its own, concealing its treasure behind thick vines and sprawling trees.

Mist rolled along the jungle floor, the humidity of the day solidifying as the temperature rapidly dropped. Feeling like something was watching her, Effie cast her eyes around the shadowed ground, but it was useless. The sun had already set, casting them in almost perfect darkness. If the moon was up, the treetops were blocking its light.

"What time is it?" she whispered, the totality of the dark seemingly more attuned to the middle of the night instead of early evening.

"Can't be more than an hour after sunset," Kael replied, his voice low as he moved ahead.

"This way," Lucian whispered.

Effie flinched at the sharp crackle of leaves under her boots as she crept forward. It was overly loud with no other noise to muffle it, and she worried she just announced their location to whatever might be lying in wait.

The roar of the water was the first sign they were getting close. The scent of blood was the second.

Effie gagged on the heavy metallic tang. For the stench to be that strong . . . many must have died.

Her suspicions were confirmed less than a minute later.

Through a small break in the trees, Effie could make out the spray of water in the moonlight. Water tinged red. She froze, the horror of the image—of a waterfall spurting blood—momentarily stunning her. It was macabre in a way not even a battlefield could match.

"You alright?" Lucian asked, turning back to her.

Blinking rapidly, Effie nodded, finally seeing what had already drawn the others' attention.

The floor was littered with the corpses of well over two dozen jungle cats, all of which were predators in their own right. Effie struggled to classify them, but with their fur matted and stained with gore, it was nearly impossible to say. The graceful bodies were lying at awkward angles, the soft flesh of their bellies ripped open.

"The kills are fresh, perhaps an hour at most," Ronan said from where he knelt beside one of the beasts.

"That would have placed the attack right around sundown," Lucian replied.

Kieran's voice shook slightly. "That's in keeping with what I Saw. The sky was still painted orange in my dream."

Ronan coated a stick in the blood and held it up to his nose, lurching back in disgust after giving it a sniff. "Rancid," he declared.

Lucian and Kael exchanged frowns.

Kieran was staring at the bodies in confusion. "How is that possible if they've only been dead an hour?"

"It's the corruption," Kael announced, his eyes turning a glittering emerald as he accessed his power.

"What could have done something like this?" Effie asked, the scene before her not making sense.

"It looks like they turned on each other," Reyna murmured as she moved carefully around the bodies.

"No, look," Kael said, pointing to one of the creature's sheathed claws. "They didn't even have a chance to defend themselves. Whatever did this attacked before they had a chance to fight back."

"How could it have caught this many of them unaware?" Effie asked.

"Magic," Lucian answered.

Understanding dawned. "They were asleep when they died," Effie gasped.

Lucian nodded. "It seems so."

Completing her circuit, Reyna returned to Ronan's side. "So, they were put to sleep, dragged here, and then slaughtered . . . but why? That level of calculation suggests a greater purpose than mere murder."

The shimmer in the air was their answer. Effie's eyes snapped to the water churning beside them.

Lucian's jaw ticked as he arrived at the same conclusion. "They wanted to poison the water supply."

"What better way to ensure the corruption spreads far and wide," Ronan growled.

Shock had leeched Kieran's skin of all color. For someone who had Seen this, he looked more horrified by the implication than the rest of them.

"Is there any way to stop it?" Effie asked.

"We can burn the corpses, but if it's already in the water . . ." Kael trailed off, his unspoken words ringing loudly in her ears.

Too late. If it was already in the water, it was too late.

Defeat made her shoulders sag. Until they found a cure, they were going to continue to run into this problem. The damage that would result in the meantime would be catastrophic.

"Burn them," Lucian ordered, his deep voice edged with fury.

Ronan called upon Fire, a smoldering ball of red flame swirling in his hand. Before he could release it, shrill cries filled the air.

The hair on the back of Effie's arms and neck lifted, an overwhelming pressure settling hard and fast in her chest. Lifting her head, Effie's eyes landed on a furred face half obscured behind a massive leaf.

That couldn't be what set her warning off. The lajhár were peaceful creatures; even the black markings on their brown and gray fur granted them a perpetual smile. Notoriously slow, they spent the majority of their time sleeping high in the trees, far away from other predators. The only thing remotely threatening about them were the needle-like claws jutting out from their paws.

The lajhár crawled forward on the branch, and Effie's heart started to race. There was nothing peaceful about the feral snarl on its round face, or the blood that dripped from its claws.

"Lucian."

His name was the only warning she could give before death began to rain from the trees. Faster than she could count, furred bodies dropped from the branches, their cries filling the air.

Around her the others unsheathed their weapons.

"I never liked these little fucks," Ronan bit out as he swung his ax and sliced one of the lajhár in half. "Cute and cuddly, my ass."

Reyna snickered darkly as she hurled her blades into the air, killing the creatures before they could reach the ground.

Kieran was busy stabbing and kicking the small animals, his moves so frantic he appeared to be doing some kind of bizarre dance.

Blood dripped down Kael's arm where his flesh had been shredded by one of the lajhár's claws. The creature was still clinging to his shoulder, shrieking as it tried to go for his eyes. Kael ripped it off and threw it hard at the base of a tree. The lajhár bounced with a screech and scrambled across the floor, heading right toward her.

Effie flung her dagger, pinning its body to the ground. It was an instinctive move, but not her smartest. She was now down one weapon.

"Move!" Lucian roared, swinging his sword whose edges had turned to dark smoke.

Effie jumped out of the way as he decapitated the creature before taking out three more in one fell swoop.

No matter how fast they moved, or how many they took out, the creatures continued to come at them. Effie's hands were slick with sweat and blood as she worked her way through the ones closest to her.

Pausing only long enough to shove her curls out of her eyes, Effie's eyes flew wide as two of the creatures flung themselves at Reyna. She had her back turned and had no clue of the danger coming her way.

"Reyna!" Effie screamed, her throat burning with the intensity of her cry.

The Night Stalker spun at the sound of her name. Ronan was already moving, his ax spinning through the air as he took out one of the insidious beasts. The other one landed, its claws raking across her face and throat, before Reyna was able to tear him free and kill him. Ruby streaks dripped down her face, but she didn't stop, continuing to battle the next wave.

Sharp pain tore through Effie as one of the lajhár sliced through her leg. She'd been standing in place too long. Furious with herself, Effie stabbed the creature with more ferocity than she knew she possessed.

"They're still coming," Kieran gasped in warning, his hair matted to his face and neck.

Effie lost track of time as the battle raged. She panted, her lungs burning. This should have been an easy battle for them. The lajhár were hardly a threat against so many battle-tested warriors. But their sheer numbers were overwhelming, and those knife-like claws were coated with some kind of poison. She was starting to lose feeling in her leg.

"How many of these little fucks are there?" Ronan asked.

"Too many," Kael growled, stomping on the head of a nearby lajhár with a wet squelching sound.

Lucian looked torn, his desire to fight warring against the need to keep them safe.

The jungle floor started to vibrate as a roar came from the east.

"All this blood is attracting something far more deadly," Ronan cautioned, sparing a glance in that direction.

The lajhár, whose protective instincts should have sent them fleeing at the sound of approaching danger, only grew more frenzied.

"Lucian, we've got to get out of here. We can't fight the whole damn jungle on our own," Kael insisted, his right arm hanging limply at his side.

The vibrations grew more intense as whatever was coming for them moved in closer. It didn't take more than a passing glance to tell that their group was in no state to take on the unknown monster. At least three of them were injured, the lajhár's poison starting to slow their movements down as it worked its way through their bodies.

With a savage roar, Lucian killed two more of the lajhár. "Fall back! Get to the portal!"

Kael led the way as they followed Lucian's bellowed order without hesitation, but even as they tore through the forest, the bloodthirsty creatures gave chase. They were relentless in their pursuit.

The numbness was climbing higher up Effie's leg, making her strides awkward and lurching. Each step was agony, and soon Effie was falling behind the others, a fiery burn starting to replace the numb ache.

"Don't you dare," Lucian snarled, swinging her up into his arms.

He was running, holding onto her with one arm while swinging his sword in the other. Effie soon gave up trying to do anything more than hold onto him as she bounced and slipped in his hold.

It felt like a lifetime before they reached the portal, but finally, they were back in the clearing they'd arrived in.

Effie let out a relieved cry as the infuriated creatures shrieked when they slammed into an invisible barrier. Whatever magic worked to conceal the portal was keepings the lajhár from getting close enough to follow them.

"Why didn't we think about that sooner?" Ronan asked once Lucian and Effie came through the portal.

"Because no one thought they would actually get the better of us," Lucian grunted, his frustration unmistakable. "I'm not used to having to retreat from something the size of a damn puppy."

Lucian carefully set Effie onto her feet, but her knee buckled, unable to support her weight. It was only her Guardian's impeccable reflexes that kept her from sliding onto the floor.

"What just happened?" Effie asked, her knuckles white where she gripped Lucian's tunic.

Ronan let out a mirthless laugh. "Didn't you hear? We just lost a battle against a pack of demented rodents."

Kael scrubbed his good hand over his face, slumping against the wall. "The lajhár must have drank the water. It's the only explanation for a total temperament shift like that."

"The corruption was able to work that fast?" Kieran asked, his throat bobbing like he was about to be sick.

"Apparently," Lucian muttered darkly.

"It's not the only thing that works fast," Reyna said, her usually sultry voice thin and frail.

Ronan snapped his attention to her. "What do you mean?"

Reyna winced in pain as she gingerly poked at the deep scratches along the left side of her face. "I can't seem to see out of this eye."

"Their claws were poisonous," Effie interjected. "I didn't notice at first, but it explains the severity of our injuries. I shouldn't be having this much trouble walking from just a couple scratches."

"You too?" Lucian asked Kael, who gave a weak nod.

Ronan bit off a curse. "Come on, let's get you to the healers."

Reyna slapped Ronan's hands away as he tried to lift her. "My legs are perfectly fine, Shield."

"Shut up and accept the help, woman," Ronan growled.

"I still have one dagger left. Are you volunteering to be my target?" she panted in a saccharinely sweet voice.

"Mother's tits, Reyna. You can be a cold bitch."

"Just help me stand and lead the way. I'll be fine," the Night Stalker assured him.

Ronan looked ready to fight her over it, but was gentle when he helped her stand. "Come on, then."

Reyna wove her arm through his and leaned heavily against him.

Effie started to limp behind them.

"Where do you think you're going?" Lucian asked, stopping her with a hand on the arm.

"To the healers?" she said, thinking it obvious.

Lucian rolled his eyes. "As if I'd let you walk there on your own in that condition."

Not too injured to feel annoyed, Effie scowled at him. "You don't *let me* do anything, Guardian."

Kael snorted. "Not the time, little warrior."

Lucian gave her a tight-lipped smile and swept her back up in his arms. "It's either this or ass-first over my shoulder, fledgling."

"Fine," she snapped, inwardly relieved she wouldn't have to walk. It was getting hard to think straight with the shooting pain climbing ever higher up her body.

"Kael, will you be alright there until I get back?" Lucian asked.

The other Guardian gave a weak nod.

"I can help him," Kieran said, straightening.

Lucian shot Kieran a look so filled with vitriol Effie couldn't help but remember the night he'd made the man in the tavern piss himself. Not even she was immune to the promise of violence in her Guardian's eyes.

"And why should anyone trust you to be helpful, princeling?"

Kieran's pale cheeks turned crimson. "I'm more than capable of helping him walk down a few hallways."

"Are you? Only this morning you abandoned us in that cave. I still haven't quite figured that out, by the way. Were you scared or simply throwing a tantrum?" Lucian laughed, but it was a sound devoid of humor. "Either way is hardly a point in your favor, is it? In fact, I can't recall the last time you did anything remotely selfless."

"I warned you about my dream!" Kieran sputtered.

Lucian's eyes narrowed, and his voice dropped dangerously. "And I'm still working out what your play was. When I do—"

"Enough, Luc. Let the poor bastard help me."

Lucian's nostrils flared, his temper sinking its claws in deeper, before he released a breath and shrugged. "Suit yourself."

Wordlessly, Kael slung his good arm around Kieran's shoulder and leaned heavily into him. Kieran grunted under the weight but remained upright.

Lucian waited only long enough to ensure that the two men were moving before he set off in the direction Ronan had taken. From her perch in his arms, Effie glanced over Lucian's shoulder and studied Kieran.

Out of all of them, he seemed the most undone by the attack. He looked haunted as he stared at the ground. While disturbing, today's fight was hardly the worst thing they'd faced recently, and all of them were still conscious. That was a vast improvement from their last bout in the jungle.

So why then did Kieran look like they'd just suffered a massive defeat?

As if he could hear her silent question, Kieran lifted his eyes.

A shudder slid down Effie's spine at the emptiness she found there.

Kieran blinked, finally seeming to notice her, and his expression softened infinitesimally. There was a flicker of something in those green orbs, a warmth Effie hadn't seen since she'd stumbled into his room on a drunken mission.

Then Lucian spoke, shattering the moment. "Just a bit further," he murmured.

Kieran's jaw clenched and his eyes darkened, turning his handsome face into something that frightened Effie more than anything else she'd seen that day.

She let out a soft gasp as a shiver of premonition buzzed through her.

Lucian tightened his arms around her, mistaking the sound for pain. "It's going to be okay. You're safe now."

Effie might be in Lucian's arms, but the last thing she felt was safe.

CHAPTER 15

*F*or the first time since arriving in the citadel, Effie wasn't the only one to sustain an injury during one of their missions. It was a relief in the sense she didn't feel singled out as the weakest amongst them, but it also meant her friends were spread thin while visiting the others.

That left Effie with a lot of free time on her hands—time where all she could do was think. Being stuck with only her thoughts for company was Effie's idea of hell. Her mind was a dark place filled with ghosts. Only a masochist would want to spend any amount of time wandering around in there.

Although, some of the darkness inside her had quieted since coming to the citadel. Effie's new purpose gave her something to focus on besides the past. Well, that and a certain Guardian's intense gaze, but thinking of him filled her with a different kind of restless ache, so Effie avoided that as well.

The only reason she was still in the healing wing at all was because the healers had threatened to chain her to the bed if she tried to escape before they released her . . . again. Lucian's smug grin when they issued the ultimatum told her he'd help them do it.

Grunting, Effie plucked at the bandage wrapped around the bottom half of her leg. Her injury itself was minor once the poison was removed from her blood stream. The issue—and the reason she was currently trapped in this bed—was that no one knew if the poison would have any lingering effects due to the corruption.

After a restless night trying to sleep in the unfamiliar bed, and a half day spent failing to keep her mind occupied, Effie was fairly certain she was in the clear. If only one of the healers would come check on her so she could convince them of the same.

The door creaked opened and Effie sat up, her flicker of hope guttering at the sign of the scarlet robe. She hoped her face didn't convey her disappointment.

"Why is it you only seem to seek me out when you know I can't run away?" she muttered dryly, settling back into her pillows.

Smoke paused in the doorway. *"Would you rather I leave?"*

"No! I was joking." Effie sighed. "We really need to work on your sense of humor."

"Perhaps you need to work on the quality of your jokes."

Effie gaped. "Are you *teasing* me? Are you even allowed to do that?"

Smoke's answer was to move closer to her bed, although Effie supposed there really was no point answering such a question. He was part of the Triumvirate; he could do whatever he wanted.

"You aren't here with happy tidings, are you?" she asked when he sat at the end of her bed. *If he's getting comfortable, this definitely isn't an all-is-well kind of chat.*

"How are you feeling?" Smoke asked.

Effie gave an exasperated sigh. "I'm bored."

"Better than the alternative."

"You mean death? Leave me in here staring at the ceiling a few more hours and I'm not so sure I'd agree."

"Restless, Daughter?"

Effie opened her mouth to disagree, but thought better of it. Restless was one way of describing the feeling of unease that hadn't abated since their venture into the jungle. It was certainly the easiest explanation.

"How are the others?" she asked instead.

"They're worse patients than you."

Effie snorted. "I didn't know that was possible."

"Neither did I."

Unexpected laughter bubbled up in response to his sarcasm. "I had no idea you could be so witty."

Smoke shrugged as if to say there was a lot she didn't know.

"So if you aren't here to tell me something I want to hear, why did you come?" Effie asked.

Smoke's hood dipped as his voice filled her mind. *"What you said about your most recent vision concerns me."*

"That I seem to be the main focus?"

He nodded. *"I would like to work with you personally until we get to the bottom of it."*

Effie threw up her hands. "Finally!"

"That pleases you?"

"It's only the one thing I've been asking you to do since I got here."

Smoke cocked his head, reminding Effie of an inquisitive bird. If he had been anyone else, Effie would have guessed he was genuinely surprised by her reaction.

"Did you really think I would object?"

"It has been your tendency since you arrived."

Her cheeks grew hot. "Not recently," she said softly, picking at her blanket.

"You didn't want to share your vision with us."

Effie glanced up. "That didn't have anything to do with *you*."

"We are one in the same."

"Not even remotely," Effie said with a snort.

She could feel the weight of his stare even hidden behind his hood. For once, Effie was glad Smoke didn't have a human face. It would be impossible to look directly at that kind of intensity.

Effie chewed on her cheek, trying to find the words she needed to explain what she meant because it was clear he expected her to.

"I trust you, Smoke, because you have proven yourself worthy of that trust. You are the only one who has shown any interest in getting to know me. Not just as your newest Keeper, but as an actual person. You were the only one to drop the mask of your title and use your actual voice to speak to me. You were the one that came, time and again, to check and see if I was okay. Just you." Effie shrugged, not sure what else to say except, "You were the one that told me respect must be earned."

"So I did."

"It's not that I have anything against the Mirrors, but if I have to make myself vulnerable, I'd rather do it with someone who's proven they aren't going to use it against me." She gave him a wry smile. "I learned that lesson quite early on."

A low howl whipped around the room, and Effie jolted before she realized it came from him. If the sound of rustling leaves was a sign of the Triumvirate's amusement, then this was surely a sign of their rage.

"I Saw."

Effie's mouth went dry. She never knew two words could be so filled with anger.

"Well," she said once she finally recovered, "then you understand."

Effie half-expected an answer, but there was none.

When she'd first met the Triumvirate, she'd thought them unfeeling, like they'd sacrificed their humanity when becoming the beings that were responsible for overseeing the fate of the realms. Now she wasn't so sure.

Perhaps it was not a lack of feelings at all. Maybe the Triumvirate closed themselves off to keep from feeling too much. Centuries of prophecies depicting countless paths, most filled with death and destruction, had to enact a terrible toll. Perhaps shutting themselves down was the only way to keep from going completely mad.

"Would you like to See my vision now?" Effie asked.

"If you're up for it."

Effie rolled her eyes. "I have a scratch on my leg. I do worse to myself stumbling around the citadel."

Smoke stood and moved to the other end of the bed so that he was

118

standing next to her. Effie didn't flinch when his hand lifted, the dark blue rune in his palm filling her vision.

"What does it mean?" Effie asked, darting her eyes from his hand up to his hood.

"There is no translation."

"So what purpose does it serve then?"

"The runes focus our power."

"Like amplifiers? They make your power stronger?"

"More like the opposite."

Effie's brows scrunched together. "Why would you willingly make yourself weaker?"

"Not weaker necessarily. It's about control. Our runes are the physical manifestation of the spell we used to bind our power to our will. Without them, our power would be unchecked."

Effie wasn't sure she fully understood, but if the Triumvirate believed their power was safer under symbolic lock and key, she was not about to argue.

"So, for instance, without the runes you wouldn't need to touch someone to see inside their minds?" she guessed, glancing back at his hand.

Smoke dipped his head.

"That would get . . . overwhelming."

"Indeed."

Realizing that was all he was going to say on the matter, Effie closed her eyes. "Ready when you are."

The brush of his skin against her forehead was gentle. If she hadn't been waiting for it, she might not have felt it at all. There was a flare of heat where they were connected and then the sense of tumbling into herself.

The crash of glass rang loudly in her ears before the only sound she could hear was the rasp of her breath. Effie's vision came back to her between one stuttered heartbeat and the next, but this time she felt like she was seeing it from a different angle instead of actually reliving it.

Somehow Smoke had taken control of the vision, manipulating it as needed to allow himself the ability to see every nuanced detail. This included freezing the vision and then enlarging each individual shard of glass in the sky. One by one, he magnified them in order to focus on the reflection they contained—even the ones Effie herself hadn't noticed when experiencing it.

Time lost all meaning as Smoke moved from one image to the next. Some were so terrifying that Effie's heart began to race, but before she could give in to her fear, Smoke took it away.

Here in her mind his voice resonated so loudly it was all she knew. It wrapped itself around her like a caress, buoying her with its strength. *"What you see before you are only echoes. Nothing here can hurt you."*

Memories can still cut, she thought, not taking into consideration that connected as they were Smoke would be able to hear her.

"Only if you let them."

But the reflections . . .

"Show you every possible outcome. The dark as well as the light," Smoke pointed out, enlarging one image she hadn't Seen that revealed her beaming face. Releasing it, and letting the vision resume, he added, *"You cannot fear what might come to be."*

Isn't that exactly what we've been doing the last few days?

Smoke didn't answer her. Instead, he finished watching her vision, his presence helping numb her terror once the unseen monsters started ripping her apart. Even though there was nothing to explicitly see during that portion of the vision, the feeling of the ghostly hands tearing at her was still there. Effie could feel them as clearly as she felt Smoke's hand pressed against her head.

Vision complete, Smoke started to retract his conscious from hers. But not before unsummoned thoughts started to rise to the surface.

Lucian's heated gaze took center stage, the bronze flecks surrounding his pupils burning brightly as he lost his iron-clad grasp on his control. Effie could feel the rough scrape of his beard scratching her as he kissed her like a drowning man searching for air.

Then a different Lucian, this one barely holding himself together as he stood in the middle of her room. His chest rising and falling rapidly, his eyes holding a savagery she'd never seen in a man before. He had been more wild animal than human in that moment, the need to protect her shredding his sanity.

Next was his voice, a deep rasp that filled her body with molten heat. "Don't ever think I didn't want you."

Effie's cheeks burned as she opened her eyes and sucked in a shallow breath. "Enough!" she stammered, pushing herself out of Smoke's hold.

She stared into the darkness that hid Smoke's face, her heart hammering wildly as she waited for him to tell her that she could never be with Lucian.

Her mind was wild with all of the imagined reasons he would give her. That Lucian's duty was to the Triumvirate and she'd only get in the way. That he was immortal and she very much was not. That Lucian's heart had already been claimed by another.

When Smoke didn't speak, Effie went on the defensive. "The polite thing to do would be to forget you ever saw that. Those are private moments that do not concern you."

"You have feelings for the Guardian?"

"What if I do?" she asked, jutting her chin out.

"It is not my place to tell you who you are allowed to care about."

Effie opened and closed her mouth, stunned. "It's not?"

A soft rustling sound filled her room. *"You seem to have a few misguided notions about the Triumvirate's purpose."*

She didn't know what to say to that. The entire conversation had taken a turn she did not see coming.

"Your grandmother loved once. She even raised a family. Being a Keeper is not mutually exclusive with having a life. Why would you assume it would be different for you?"

Effie shrugged. "I hadn't really thought about it at all, to be honest. I'm just so used to being told I can't have something that I must have just assumed you would find fault with it. Or with me for wanting someone so far above me." The last words came out more bitterly than she meant them to.

"You think the Guardian above you?"

"Isn't he?" Effie snorted, shifting uncomfortably in her bed. "He's part of the Brotherhood, an immortal being with a sworn duty to serve you. How could I ever . . ." Effie trailed off; the words too painful to say out loud.

Lucian had never done anything to even suggest these fears were founded. He had a way of looking at her like he truly saw who she was, and he not only accepted her for it, he liked what he found there. She knew that these were old fears, ones that she had held onto for the better part of her life. They stemmed from the taunts of others, the hateful words spoken so often that when they replayed in her memory now they were in her own voice.

Smoke was silent for so long that Effie was afraid he was about to agree with her.

"Daughter."

Effie forced herself to look up.

"The Guardian's heart is his own. No one, not even duty, can dictate who he gives it to."

She let out a breath she hadn't known she'd been holding. "So you don't object?"

"Would it matter if I did?"

Effie didn't even need to think about her answer. "Not to me, but then I don't follow stupid rules."

More rustling filled the small room and a bit more of Effie's tension receded. *Who knew getting advice about love from Smoke could be so cathartic?* Her feelings for Lucian were still very new, and largely unexplored, she hadn't even been consciously aware of these worries until Smoke had quite literally pulled them to the surface.

"I think it might matter to Lucian, though," she murmured, recalling their earlier conversation about protocol.

Smoke went unnaturally still beside her. *"You aren't giving your Guardian enough credit."*

Effie shrugged. "Part of what makes Lucian so special is his honor. If it came down to having to choose between me or you . . ."

"Who says it has to be a choice?"

A part of her didn't believe it would be quite that simple, but another part, the one that was starting to believe in a future where they could be together, held onto that hope with both hands and refused to let go.

"That's probably not quite what you were expecting when you asked to see my vision," she said with a little laugh, embarrassed that their conversation had become so personal.

"That's always the risk with what we do. Although, it was certainly enlightening."

Effie blushed. "You really have to pretend you never saw any of that. It's like being caught in bed by your parents. Worse even—I actually care what you think about me."

There was an odd sucking sound, and Smoke visibly jolted.

She squinted up at him. "Are you laughing?"

"No," he said vehemently. *"I find I do not like being compared to your parents."*

"I did say I actually care what you think," she pointed out, laughing a little at his obvious discomfort.

"Yes, well. Anyone who abandons their child in such a heinous manner deserves to rot in hell."

Baffled, Effie shook her head. "Smoke, I'm sorry. It was just an off-handed comment. I never meant to imply you were anything like my parents."

"A woman who punishes her daughter by cutting into her flesh and a man who stands by and laughs while it happens are not parents."

She flinched, although that particular memory had lost its power to hurt her a long time ago. "Yes, well, I was a constant disappointment to them. At least the feeling is mutual."

Another howl tore through the room, spurring her into action. Leaning forward, Effie placed her hand on his arm. "Smoke, I'm fine. Please, there's no need to be upset about something that occurred decades ago."

If anyone ever told her one day she would offer comfort to someone because of what had happened to *her* when she'd been a child . . . Effie would have fallen to the floor laughing.

"It was not decades for me," he said finally, his smoky voice an uneven rasp.

"I appreciate your concern on my behalf, honestly I do, but I don't understand why it's upsetting you so much. Surely you've Seen far worse things during your lifetime."

Smoke lurched away from her and started to pace, the gracelessness of his movements doing much to emphasize his current distress.

"Rarely do I know the ones impacted by what I See."

"Oh," she said softly, finally understanding.

"I have suffered through your pain, experienced these inexplicable cruelties as if they were my own . . ."

Effie swung her legs off the side of the bed and stood.

Smoke spun to face her. *"You're supposed to stay in bed."*

"Shut up and come here," she demanded.

Smoke remained frozen in place.

"Fine, then. I'll come to you." Effie closed the distance between them and wrapped her arms around Smoke's middle, squeezing tightly.

He stood awkwardly at first, his arms raised to the sides as if he was unsure what to do with them.

"It's called a hug. You must be familiar with it," she murmured.

"You are . . . offering me comfort?"

"You're in pain," she said simply. "This is what a friend does when someone they care about is in pain."

A shudder traversed the length of his tall frame, so Effie held on tighter.

"But it is your pain I feel."

"Then hug me back," she challenged.

So he did.

CHAPTER 16

"*A*lright, Ms. Effie. You are free to go."

Effie was already up and moving toward the door before the healer finished speaking.

"In a hurry to be somewhere?" the woman, whose name Effie thought was Vesta, asked with a chuckle.

She paused long enough to shoot Vesta a harried grin. "I need to make sure I haven't missed anything while I've been locked up—I mean recovering."

Vesta winked. "In case it helps narrow your search, I heard the Guardians mention wanting to settle a score while they were waiting for answers. I'm not sure what they meant, but maybe it means something to you?"

"Settle a score?" Effie repeated, her brows dropping. *Who among us has a score to settle? Is Lucian having some kind of showdown with Kieran?* Head snapping up, Effie started running. If he was, she wasn't about to miss it.

"At least pretend you're going to take it easy!" the healer shouted after her.

Heart racing, Effie sprinted down the corridors, narrowly avoiding crashing into Kait in her hurry to get to the training room.

"Oof, sorry!" Effie called, barely slowing.

"Hey, Effie! Have you seen Tess or Jo? I can't find them."

"No, sorry. Not in a few days," Effie said over her shoulder, making the final turn.

Pushing open the double doors, she staggered to a halt. As expected, men were sparring, but neither Lucian nor Kieran were in the ring. The former was standing against the far wall, his arms folded across his chest as he watched Ronan and Kael circle each other. The latter was nowhere to be found.

Now that she was thinking about it, Effie hadn't seen Kieran at all since their return from the jungle. He hadn't even made a point to visit her while she'd been confined to the healing wing, which was highly unusual. While it was true she'd asked him to give her space, Effie hadn't actually expected him to respect her wishes. Not when he'd made a point of blatantly disregarding them up until now.

So where was he?

The sound of masculine grunts pulled her attention, and Effie moved to sit along the benches set in the far back of the room, her curiosity piqued. Ronan was one of the best warriors she'd ever known, but the Guardian had been fighting since long before he was born. This was a match worth watching.

Both men were shirtless, sweat dripping down their heavily muscled bodies. Ronan's red hair was tied up in a sloppy knot, strands sticking to his forehead and neck as he swung a fist at Kael's face.

Kael dropped and spun, his own arm pulling back to strike Ronan in the ribs, but the Shield anticipated the move and was dropping his elbow into Kael's back, just above his kidney. Kael grunted and staggered, his knee dropping to the mat.

"That's a point and the match," Ronan whooped.

"I'm still recovering," Kael muttered, rising. "Don't think this was a fair fight."

Ronan grinned, his blue eyes glittering like shards of ice. "Anytime you want a rematch, just let me know."

"Count on it," Kael said as they grasped forearms.

"My turn," Lucian said, pushing away from the wall and striding to the center of the room.

"I was hoping you'd step up," Ronan said with a dangerous grin.

Effie's brows flew up. Only a man with a death wish—or Ronan—would willingly face off against Lucian's brute strength.

Her Guardian pulled off his tunic and tossed it to the floor. Effie's stomach swooped as she greedily drank in the sight of all that tanned skin on display. He'd always been an imposing figure due to his sheer size, but she'd had no idea what he had been hiding beneath his clothes.

Lucian's body looked like it had been sculpted from granite, each part of him perfectly cut and defined. The muscles in his upper arms were twice the size of Ronan's, which didn't seem like it should even be possible. As it was, both of her hands could span just one of his pecs.

Effie shook her head. Lucian couldn't possibly be human. He was a giant.

Eyes dropping lower, she started to count the bunches of muscles stacked down the center of his stomach, following each ripple until her eyes reached the defined vee that trailed down into the dark leather covering his hips.

"Mother's tits," she whispered, feeling light-headed.

"I think you mean Lucian's dick," Kael snickered, plopping down beside her.

Effie blinked and shook her head, not even pretending she wasn't shamelessly ogling her Guardian. "Mother have mercy, I've forgotten my name."

Kael laughed harder. "One would think you'd never seen a shirtless man the way you're carrying on."

She'd dropped her eyes to Kael's bared torso. "There's shirtless men, and then there's *that*," she said, purposefully returning her gaze to Lucian.

"I'm going to tell him you said so."

"You're going to give him an even bigger ego than he already has if you do."

"Fair point," Kael murmured as Lucian and Ronan moved into their starting stances.

Effie's breath caught as she waited for the first strike. She'd seen Lucian fight before, but it had always been while she was in the middle of trying not to die. Seeing him now, with nothing to distract her, was like watching art in motion. Each move was flawlessly executed with a grace and speed that was unmatched.

Ronan quickly lost his smug smile as he had to work hard to defend himself from the blows Lucian was raining down with incredible precision.

Thank the Mother they were fighting without weapons. Even with a blunted blade, Effie didn't think Ronan would walk away without a series of new scars. Lucian was brutal; striking hard and fast while Ronan was unable to successfully land a single blow of his own.

Beside her Kael was chuckling.

Effie's eyes cut to him briefly before returning to the fight. "What's so funny?"

"Lucian's toying with him."

"He looks like he's about two seconds away from murdering him," Effie said, her heart rate increasing as Lucian landed another strike.

"You haven't seen anything yet," Kael said. "Just watch."

Ronan shuffled back, narrowly missing a kick to the side of his head, but Lucian was unfazed. As soon as his foot landed on the floor, Lucian leaped into the air, practically flying as he drew back his arm and landed a strike to Ronan's chest with the flat of his hand.

Ronan flew back, hitting the ground with a resounding thud.

"One," Lucian said, landing and holding out a hand to help Ronan back up off of the mat. He didn't even look winded.

Wincing, Ronan rubbed his chest. "I thought we agreed not to use our power . . ."

Lucian's smile grew. "I'm not."

Grunting, Ronan moved back into position. "Again."

Effie squirmed, watching Lucian in action was doing something to her. She could feel the flush of desire heating her cheeks, and a dull ache was growing deep within her. *Is it normal to get so turned on watching men fight?*

Missing none of her discomfort, Kael continued to snicker beside her. "I had no idea your bloodlust was so strong, little warrior."

"You can go sit somewhere else," she bit out. "Preferably on top of your sword."

Kael threw his head back and laughed, causing Lucian to look toward them, one of his brows raised.

It was the opening Ronan needed, and he didn't waste it. He tackled Lucian to the ground.

"One!" he crowed.

Lucian bucked, and in one fluid move he threw Ronan from his body before flipping to a crouch and pinning Ronan with a knee on the chest. It happened so fast Effie wasn't sure she was even tracking all of the men's movements. One second Lucian was on his back, the next he was on top of Ronan.

"Two," Lucian smirked.

"Fuck you, Guardian," Ronan scowled.

"Think I'll pass, Shield."

Effie let out a soft moan, her eyes glued to Lucian's ass as the leather-clad muscles flexed, giving her all sorts of delightful thoughts. Sweat trickled down her back and Effie's mouth went dry. *Mother save me.* She was going to combust then and there if she didn't get ahold of herself.

Kael tossed his towel at her head, momentarily obscuring her vision.

"Jerk," she muttered.

"Sorry, looks like you needed it. You're leaving a puddle beneath you."

In horror, Effie checked her seat. There was no puddle.

Kael was howling with laughter.

She hit him, hard, her fist slamming into his shoulder.

"I'll bet if it was two topless women grinding on each other over there, you'd be the one requiring a towel."

"Without a doubt," Kael agreed, his dimples flashing. "Doesn't mean I'm going to miss this opportunity. I don't think I've ever seen this side of you."

"What side is that?"

"Horn—"

Effie bared her teeth at him. "You keep laughing and my next punch is going somewhere much lower."

Kael's green eyes were twinkling, but he mimed buttoning his lips.

While they'd been bickering, Lucian and Ronan had finished their match. Her Guardian was helping Ronan stand.

Ronan shook his head. "You'll have to show me some of those moves after I've nursed my wounds."

Lucian slapped his back. "It would be my pleasure."

"You ever get tired of working for those robed fuckers, you're always welcome to serve with me."

"I'll keep that in mind," Lucian murmured.

Ronan and Lucian continued their chat, but Effie was too distracted by Lucian's body to pay attention. She tracked a bead of sweat as it rolled down his chest and over the planes of his stomach, her legs squeezing together to try and relieve some of the ache building in the core of her. Never had she had this kind of reaction to a man before, and certainly not just from watching him spar. *What is wrong with me?*

"Who's next?" Lucian asked, a towel slung around his shoulders.

Effie licked her lips, ready to volunteer for damn near anything that would get her under him.

As if he could read her thoughts, Kael pinched her and Effie flew up, shooting him a dark look.

"I think our little warrior wants a go," Kael said with a grin.

"Is that so, fledgling?" Lucian asked, his own lips lifting.

"I-I," she stammered, her mind emptying of all thoughts except a sweaty Lucian pressed up against her.

Her body's response was immediate. There was no way she could try and fight Lucian right now. On her best day she would lose in two seconds flat, but today she was way too distracted to even try. With her luck, she'd forget people were watching them and start rubbing herself against him like some kind of cat in heat.

"Gotta go," she mumbled, turning and heading for the door.

Kael's laughter chased her as she fled.

"Effie!" Lucian called after her, but she didn't stop.

Whatever was going on with her, whether it was her recent chat with Smoke putting ideas in her head, or simply just a woman's natural response to a desirable man, one thing was clear: until she cooled off—and Lucian was covered up again—Effie couldn't trust herself to be anywhere near her Guardian.

CHAPTER 17

*E*ffie stormed out of the room, her heart still beating frantically. Once she was well away from the training room, and the men it contained, she stopped. Her hand came up to rest against her chest as her eyes fluttered closed.

"Effie? Are you okay?"

She jumped, the unexpected voice making her feel like she'd been caught doing something inappropriate. "Kieran," she murmured. "What are you up to?"

He cocked his head, studying her. "I was just about to ask you the same thing."

"I was watching them practice," she said, gesturing vaguely behind her.

Kieran's expression hardened. "I see."

They hadn't been alone since Sylverlands, and Effie started to feel uncomfortable as the silence stretched between them. She missed the easy friendship they'd shared, even though she was still hurt by his cruelty. Not having had many friends, she cherished each one of them. She and Kieran may never be able to go back to the way things were before, but maybe they could find a new path.

"Kieran—"

"Effie—"

They both broke off, laughing at the absurdity of the moment.

Effie gestured for Kieran to go first.

"When would you like to resume our training sessions?" Kieran asked.

Effie's heart dropped. The Triumvirate hadn't told him he'd been replaced yet. *So much for trying to keep it friendly.*

"Um, well . . ." Effie stumbled over her words, trying to find a gentle way to break the news. "After my last vision—"

"The one in the cave?" Kieran asked, his voice holding a slight edge.

She nodded. "Yes."

"We should get to work on deciphering it. We've already lost valuable time."

"Well, you see, the Triumvirate decided that I should start working with them directly."

A muscle twitched in Kieran's jaw. "When did they decide this?"

"A couple of days ago."

"Why?"

"Because of what the vision contained."

As she'd answered his questions, Kieran's eyes had darkened and his golden skin turned a deep, mottled red.

"So you decided to cut me out completely, is that it?" he asked, his voice ugly.

Any empathy she might have had vanished at the accusation. "It was their decision."

"But you didn't fight them on it."

"Why would I? It is an incredible opportunity for me to learn. And besides, it's ultimately their call. We answer to them."

"Oh, come on, Effie. Spare me the good girl act. You do what you want and you damn well know it. No one has been able to talk any amount of sense into your entitled ass since you arrived."

Effie's hands curled into fists at her sides. She knew he was still hurt that she changed her mind that night, but that didn't mean she had to listen to him insult her.

"Kieran," she said, his name a warning.

"No. I'm done listening to your excuses. All you do is make a mockery of my feelings by throwing yourself at the first man who shows you any modicum of attention. First the Guardian and now the Triumvirate. Don't you know that they are only using you? You are a means to an end. None of them truly care for you. Not like I do."

It was a low blow. One that poked at every dark fear coiled in the recesses of her mind.

"For someone who keeps claiming to *love* me, you sure seem to make a habit of calling me a whore," she gritted out, anger churning within her.

Kieran shrugged, his eyes glittering. "You know what they say, if she spreads her legs like a whore . . ."

"How dare you!" She could barely see past her rage, the familiar taunt disarming her completely. "I am not any man's whore!" she spat as she threw herself at him, her hands curled into claws as she aimed for his face.

Kieran caught her wrists in a vice-like grip, roughly yanking her arms down before she could make contact. "Oh no? That's not what it looked like in the cave when you let him put his hands all over you."

Effie struggled in his grasp, her hatred for Kieran growing with each spiteful word he uttered.

"Has he made any promises to you? Claimed to feel anything for you?" Kieran's voice dropped to a sneer. "Your grandmother would be so disappointed if she could see what a little slut you've turned into."

Effie brought her knee up, slamming it into his groin. Kieran dropped like a stone, his moans filling the hallway.

"If you ever lay a hand on me again, I will gut you and not feel an ounce of remorse. Consider this your only warning." Effie barely recognized the deep growl of her voice.

She was shaking as she stalked away, a dark, violent part of her still demanding Kieran's blood. It took more than it should have to keep moving forward and not go back and finish what she started.

It was a good thing she didn't have her blades; she very well may have stabbed him. Unfortunately for Kieran, with the way he'd been acting lately, Effie didn't think anyone would mind if she had.

~

KIERAN CURSED himself as he hobbled down the hallway. His anger had gotten the better of him, but it couldn't be helped. Being Effie's tutor was the last claim he'd had to her. Without the position to force her to spend time with him, Kieran was out of opportunities to convince her to reconsider.

An empty void opened up inside of him, claiming any last shred of his sanity. Effie was all he had left. He'd given up everything—his family, his title, his home—to find her. He couldn't lose her now.

Which meant there was only one avenue left to him. It was time to move to phase two.

Kieran barreled through another hallway, seeking out the forbidden room that had become his sanctuary. He needed to find the book containing the reference to the TMJ prophecy.

His last attempt at forging a marker had backfired spectacularly. He never got his opportunity to play the hero—by dragging out the mangled corpse of a caebris he'd hidden under a nearby bush. His plan to "slay" it while the others were distracted investigating the corpses had been foiled by those damn flying cats.

Kieran had never seen anything like them before. Their arrival had been a total coincidence. How they'd managed to show up in the exact location of his trap, he had no clue. Given that they came from above, it stood to reason that they could move widely unhindered through the treetops. Kieran could only assume they'd come from the part of the jungle that had already fallen to the corruption.

He had been starting to worry that the others were onto him when they'd pointed out how the animals appeared to have been slaughtered in their sleep. So if nothing else, the presence of the furred creatures had given his massacre authenticity, even if he hadn't planned on their ambush.

But that was the least of his worries.

People were supposed to be in a panic at the arrival of the next marker. As far as he could tell, no one had even realized he'd recreated one. Either the Triumvirate hadn't been familiar with the passage containing the bit of prophecy he'd staged, or—and perhaps more likely—he'd missed an important component.

Kieran let out a snarl of frustration, his anger beginning to simmer once more.

His father always said revenge was essential; it taught your enemies not to repeat their trespasses. But this wasn't mere revenge; it was retribution. A justified act of vengeance to help him reclaim what rightfully belonged to him.

No one would stand in his way. Not Effie with her misguided notions and certainly not some immortal bastard who was trying to steal what was his.

The next time Kieran laid a trap the only one saving the day would be him, and if that meant removing the Guardian from the playing field permanently . . . so be it.

CHAPTER 18

*E*ffie was still fuming when she left the bathing chamber. Originally she'd thought a long soak might be a way to temper her unexpected ardor, but after her run-in with Kieran in the hall, she just hoped it would help her relax.

She'd gone so far as to make the water as cold as she could stand, hoping the near-freezing bath would cool her residual anger, but Kieran's words had burrowed deep and she was struggling to shake their hold.

"Why do you let him get to you?" she chided, opening the door to her room and coming to a stumbling halt.

Lucian was sitting on her bed, his elbows resting on his thighs and his head bowed. He looked up at her entrance, his eyes moving from the tips of her bare toes, up her equally bare legs, and coming to rest on the hand clutching the towel closed at her chest.

Effie's heart lurched, the sight of her Guardian momentarily distracting her. He looked damn good on her bed. For a second, Effie entertained the idea of letting her towel drop and crossing the room to join him.

Her Guardian cleared his throat and looked up at her with stormy eyes. The heat she saw there seared her, and the cold water dripping down her arms and back was suddenly refreshing.

"Do you often walk around the citadel in your towel?"

Effie shook her head, sending icy drops flying.

Because her visit to the bathing chamber had been unplanned, she hadn't brought a spare set of clothes. She'd left the ones she'd been wearing behind to be laundered, and risked returning to her room in a towel, not expecting to run into anyone in the hallway. Effie hadn't counted on someone waiting for her inside her room.

"That's a shame," he murmured, his lips twitching.

"What are you doing here?" she asked, fighting to keep her voice steady. The effect he had on her was absolute, and he wasn't even touching her. *What will it be like when he finally gives in?*

"I came to find out why you bolted from our training session. When you weren't here, I decided to repay your snooping with a little of my own."

Effie glanced around the tidy suite, not seeing anything out of place. "Find anything good?"

Lucian shrugged. "You going to tell me what you were ranting about when you walked in here?

"You going to turn around like a gentleman while I get dressed?" she countered.

A flicker of bronze burned in his eyes as Lucian slowly pushed to his feet. He held her gaze for one long heartbeat before purposefully turning around and staring at the ceiling.

Effie stared at Lucian's back, something warm unfurling within her and breaking through her lust-filled daze. She knew he craved her; she could see it plainly enough when he looked at her. But no matter the depth of his desire, Lucian made it clear with each thoughtful action that he wasn't about to take advantage of her.

The revelation only made Effie want him more. For most of her life, Effie had been at the mercy of people who didn't bother to consider her or her wishes. She'd had no idea how potent it could be to be treated as an equal. As a person whose thoughts and feelings held value. She was as drawn to Lucian's thoughtfulness as she was his strength. He was the kind of man she would never have to fear.

Not with her body, and not with her heart.

Lucian was a man she could love without having to hold anything back.

Effie knew then that being with Lucian would not be as simple as falling into bed. Being his would demand everything. It would simultaneously destroy and rebuild her. She would never be the same again.

The thought should have terrified her, but it didn't. Effie couldn't recall a single thing she'd ever looked forward to more in her entire life.

Blinking rapidly, trying to clear her mind, Effie moved to her trunk and selected a random pair of pants and a tunic. She turned away from Lucian and quickly pulled on the garments.

"Why do I get the feeling you weren't talking about me?" Lucian surprised her by asking.

"Because I wasn't," she said, fastening the last of her laces and turning back to him. "You can turn around now."

Lucian did, crossing his arms and leaning back against the wall. "So, what happened?"

"*Who* happened," she corrected.

"Kieran," he answered darkly, every ounce of playfulness draining away.

Effie dipped her chin in a nod.

"Did he lay a finger on you?" Lucian asked, his voice savage.

Effie made a show of inspecting her fingernails. "More like the other way around."

Lucian was not soothed by her confession. If anything, his anger swelled, filling the room with its force.

"What did he do?"

"What he does best," she answered evasively.

"Effie . . ."

Her eyes snapped up to his face. If she hadn't spent so much time with him, she might have missed the subtle details signaling Lucian's descent into that feral part of himself. She'd recognized the visceral, untamed part of his soul when he'd faced off with Ronan, and she saw hints of it again now. A sort of madness swirling within the depths of his eyes.

Knowing the only way to defuse him was to tell him the truth, Effie sighed. "He said ugly things. Nothing he hasn't said before."

A vein throbbed in Lucian's neck, the only outward sign that he'd heard her. "What did he say?" His words were measured, soft. He could have been talking about the weather for all the emotion they contained.

Effie wasn't fooled.

"He found out Smoke had replaced him as my tutor. As you might expect, it set him off. He told me I was being used, by both of you. That I willingly spread my legs for the first man to show me any sign of attention. That I was your whore."

Effie braced herself for Lucian's wrath, but it never came. She could feel it, the undercurrent of danger pulsing through the air, which caused the hairs along her neck and arms to stand on end, but he did not give into it.

Instead, Lucian moved into the center of the room until he was standing directly in front of her. He lifted a hand and ran his knuckles down her cheek.

Effie shivered, feeling the barely there touch in every part of her body.

"You are no man's whore." His voice was a deep growl; its intensity a sharp contrast to the gentleness of his touch.

"That's what I said," she murmured, her heart fluttering like a trapped bird within her chest.

Lucian ran a calloused thumb across her bottom lip in the ghost of a kiss. It was the only place he touched her, and she ached for more.

More pressure.

More contact.

More Lucian.

"Effie, you should know . . . if that's all I wanted, if that was all this was, I'd have had you beneath me five times over by now."

His eyes flicked up to hers then, the raw need shining there robbing her of breath and sending a flood of heat into her core.

"I'm afraid I won't be satisfied with anything less than all of you." His voice was a deep rasp, his emotion laid bare before her.

If there were any walls she'd still been clinging to, they crumbled. Decimated by his tender declaration. Of every reaction she could have foreseen, this hadn't even been a remote possibility.

"I'm not going to settle for only getting to taste your body." He leaned closer, his breath washing over her burning face. "Nor your heart."

"What else is there?" she whispered, her body swaying closer to his as her tongue darted out to wet her lips.

Lucian tipped her chin up, his eyes never once leaving hers. "Mortals believe that love can only be known once. If that is true, it is only because their lifespans rarely allow them to experience it more than once. As such, they mistakenly believe that this is all there is. That love is the deepest connection they can experience with another.

"Immortals know better. There is something more; a sharing of self so total that once experienced, it can never be undone. We refer to it as the *fuj d'âme*. A merging of souls."

Effie was speechless. Lucian was generally a man of few words, but Mother's tits did he know how to use them to devastating effect. Of course it would be all or nothing with him. He would hold nothing back, and he'd expect the same out of his partner—out of her.

Mother help her, but after hearing Lucian explain it, that's what Effie wanted too. She wanted to know what it would be like to be with someone that completely. Not just loved by them, but a core part of who they were, as essential to them as the air they breathed. For Lucian to be that man—to be the one asking to have that kind of claim to her —it was more than she ever dreamed.

If the woman in her was drawn to him, so was the timid little girl. Lucian wouldn't walk away; wouldn't leave her behind because of some perceived fault. Not only would his honor never allow for that kind of betrayal, he could never be that cruelly dismissive of someone he claimed as his. Lucian would be hers just as much as she was his.

To belong to someone in that way . . . it was the ultimate lure to the broken, scared girl locked away inside of her.

"Okay," she whispered, the word feeling inadequate, but it was all she was capable of.

Lifting on her tiptoes, Effie cupped his face and pulled it down so that she could brush her lips over his, hoping she could tell him with her kiss what she had no way of articulating with her words.

Lucian's response was immediate, his lips sealing over hers as a low growl rumbled in his chest.

She expected urgency, but there was none of the frantic desperation of their kisses in the cave. He was savoring her; exploring her mouth as if he had nothing but time. His lips rubbed over hers as he nibbled and sucked—in no hurry to go further.

He might not be, but her need was an inferno inside her. It had been steadily building throughout the day, taking a brief hiatus after her confrontation with Kieran, but back now with a vengeance.

Lucian ran his hands through her hair, tangling his fingers in her curls and gripping just enough that she could feel the tug all along her spine and in that pulsing heat between her legs. He pressed another kiss against her tingling lips and pulled back just enough to meet her hooded gaze. Her heart was thundering so wildly she was certain he could hear it.

"You want to get out of here?"

Effie blinked, her mind muddled from his kisses. She wasn't certain she'd heard him correctly. "What?"

"Do you want to get out of here and go somewhere with me?" he repeated, a small smirk playing about his mouth.

She glanced at the bed not more than three feet away from them. Clearly, it wasn't privacy he had in mind.

"Are you celibate?" she blurted, momentarily horrified by the thought she might have just tied herself to some kind of warrior monk.

Lucian's eyes flared wide, and he roared with laughter, tears swimming in his umber eyes. "No! Mother, no, Effie," he said between spurts of laughter. Still chuckling, he pressed another hot kiss to her mouth. "I just want to spend a night with you. One night where we can make the kind of memories that true intimacy is built on."

Her disappointment evaporated as her heart somersaulted in her chest. That might be the only answer he could have given her that would allow her to forgive him for making her wait. Again.

A bit of coherency returned as she shifted her focus away from Lucian and her in bed. "That sounds wonderful, but can we afford to do that? With everything else going on, is it wise to take the afternoon off?"

"It's not that much different than what you had in mind," he teased, the bronze in his eyes glittering.

Effie blushed. "At least we'd be in the citadel if someone needed us."

"Would you really want Kael to rush in while you're crying out my name?" he purred, nipping her earlobe.

Her heart stuttered at the erotic image he painted in her mind. She could vividly imagine her nails raking over his back while he thrust deeply inside her, her back arching off the bed as she climaxed around every throbbing inch of him. Then she imagined Smoke rushing in and shuddered. Lucian had a point.

"You're trying to kill me," she muttered. "Aren't you? This is some kind of sadistic game where you see just how far you can push me before I lose it completely?"

Lucian shifted to look at her once more, a smile softening the harsh lines of his face. "No. Not a game. I just want one night with you where the fate of the world isn't hanging in the balance."

She sighed, begrudgingly agreeing that it would be nice to spend that kind of time with Lucian.

"If it makes you feel better, our little trip serves the dual purpose of allowing me to perform a task for the Triumvirate, so it wouldn't *really* be selfish or an afternoon off."

Effie laughed and shook her head. "Fine. Where are we going?"

He gave her one of his enigmatic grins. "Do you want to come with me or not?"

"You know I do."

"Then stop asking me questions and grab your boots."

Rolling her eyes, she grumbled, "So bossy." As she turned to obey, there was a loud *thwack*. Effie jumped, her hands covering her ass as she gaped at Lucian. "Did you just *spank* me?"

"Want me to do it again?" Lucian winked, sending a surge of liquid heat through her.

Mother help me, I do. She couldn't even fling a comeback at him, her mind lost to the idea. Effie's cheeks burned as she struggled to stay focused on finding and lacing her boots. Lucian's smoldering stare was doing little to help her.

"Need help?" he offered with feigned innocence when she dropped her lace for the second time.

She pointed a shaking finger at him. "You just stay over there, Monk. Not all of us have the same infernal control over our baser instincts as you do."

Lucian smothered his laughter by covering his mouth with his hand.

She finished tying her boots and stood. "Alright, I'm ready."

Lucian reached for her, and Effie danced out of his grasp. "Oh no, if I have to keep my hands to myself, so do you."

Her Guardian scowled and dropped his hand.

Effie grinned with wicked glee. Finally, she wasn't the only one battling her desire. This should be an interesting excursion.

I wonder which one of us will give in first.

CHAPTER 19

*L*ucian walked beside her down the twisted streets of the town, his hands clasped behind his back. Effie hadn't had a reason to come back here since her unfortunate incident in the tavern.

"Does this place have a name?" she asked.

"*Vil d'lume*, the city of light," Lucian answered.

Effie's eyes roamed the silvery sheen of the buildings, loving how they sparkled in the afternoon sun. It was a fitting name. A feeling of peace settled in her chest, the contentment something she hadn't experienced more than a handful of times in her life.

"It really is beautiful here," she said with a sigh.

Lucian nodded. "In all my travels I've yet to find anything quite like the Keepers' city. It's a well-guarded secret."

"I can understand why."

As they moved further away from the citadel and into the actual heart of the city, the streets began to swell with people. All along the main street, shops were open, colorful items on display in their windows. The air was filled with the mouth-watering scents of freshly baked breads and fragrant spices.

Effie couldn't help but notice the townsfolk giving her and Lucian a wide berth.

Lucian caught her slight frown. "It's not their fault. I've acquired a bit of a reputation."

She was used to being on the receiving end of sideways looks and thoughtless hatred. She'd had no choice but to learn how to ignore those who condemned anything different. So her reaction now, seeing that same ignorance thrown at Lucian, shocked her.

Her anger was swift, rising like a tidal wave ready to come crashing down on everything in its wake. She expected more of these people. How dare they condemn a man who'd spent his life protecting them.

Jaw clenched, she took a step toward a woman who had grabbed her son by the hand and pulled him across the street, making a sign to ward off evil with her other hand.

Lucian stopped Effie with a hand on her shoulder. "It's okay," he said.

"No, it's not," she insisted, giving the woman a dark look.

The woman blanched, tugging her son into a stumbling run behind her as she raced down the street.

"You deserve better than their ambivalence and definitely more than outright disrespect."

Lucian rested his rough palm against her cheek. "So did you."

Effie sucked in a harsh breath, his words soothing a decades-old ache.

"I'm lucky I have one as fierce as you ready to defend me," he added with a slight smile.

She laughed at the absurdity of it. "As if you need anyone to defend you."

"Need? Perhaps not, but it makes the gesture all the more meaningful. I cannot remember the last time someone was offended on my behalf. Especially over so slight a snub."

"Yeah, well," she said with a shrug, "I've learned from the best."

Lucian chuckled, lowering his hand and holding it out to her. Effie wasted no time before weaving her fingers through his. Her earlier insistence had no place here. A public show of acceptance, of pride at walking beside the Guardian, was more important than any silly game she'd been playing. Let the others hold on to their ignorance. She'd defy them by openly flaunting her joy at being with him. They could choose hate, but she would choose love.

Every time.

Effie surprised him by pressing a kiss to the back of his scarred hand.

Lucian's eyes were unreadable as he stared down at her, a subtle smile curving his lips. The moment stretched until a light breeze sent her curls flying into her eyes, breaking it.

"So, what do Smoke and the Mirrors want you to do while we're here? Is there some dark and musty shop where a nondescript package will be waiting for us?" she asked.

"Nothing that exciting."

"Why send you, then? I got the impression they only sent their Guardians on the most important tasks."

Lucian lifted an amused brow. "Why can't a perimeter check of the city be important?"

"Is that what we're doing?" she asked, feeling a little letdown.

"More or less. These folks are under the Triumvirate's care just as much as those dwelling in the citadel. I'm here to get a general feel for the city, ensure that the people are happy and things are continuing to run smoothly despite the chaos outside these metaphorical gates."

"I still don't see why you are the one given this task. Seems simple enough."

Lucian shrugged. "Only a Guardian can see past the surface."

"Ah, yes. That would be handy."

He squeezed her hand. "Routine checks are essential. They can be the difference in whether we have warning of impending issues or not. It's always better to be prepared."

"I can't imagine there are too many major crises that arise here," she murmured, her eyes scanning the unguarded faces of people going about their day.

"Suppose it would depend on who you ask. People are people, everywhere you go. Petty crimes, domestic disputes . . ." Lucian trailed off to give her a pointed stare, "drunken debauchery."

Effie's cheeks warmed remembering her first night in the Pickled Piper. "There's something to be said for knowing how to unwind," she answered primly.

Lucian chuckled. "Does this mean you intend to continue your gambling career?"

Grimacing, she shook her head. "I don't think I have what it takes to make a true go of it."

He ran his thumb along the back of her hand, sending tingles racing along her skin. "Ah, I don't know about that. Something tells me you are better at hiding your thoughts than most."

"Maybe that was true once."

"It's not a skill easily forgotten."

"Is it a skill?" she asked, looking up at him.

"Absolutely. Especially during negotiations or on a battlefield. The less your opponent can predict what you're thinking, the longer you hold the upper hand."

"Who knew?" she murmured, finding it ironic that a life of servitude and trying not to draw the attention of others would be such good practice.

Effie's steps slowed to a crawl as her attention snagged on a painting in the window beside her.

It depicted a battle between three creatures Effie had only heard about in stories. In the center, a woman surged up out of the water, the bottom half of her tail coiling beneath her as water whipped around her like a cyclone. In the air, to her left, a dragon with blood-red scales spewed white-hot flames, turning the top of her water into mist. And on the land, to the right of them both, was a beast—his body both man and horse—his muscles bunched as he aimed his arrow at the dragon above.

The artist had managed to capture the intensity of the moment so perfectly, Effie could feel the tension in the bowstring, the heat of the flame, the bite of the water. It was stunning.

"We can go inside," Lucian drawled, when she had craned her neck back to keep looking as they started to pass it.

Giving him a wide grin, Effie rushed into the little shop. The walls were filled with similar paintings, the afternoon light glinting off them and making them come alive. Blinding seascapes, crumbling castles, a city in ruins—each painting was more achingly beautiful than the last. The artist's attention to detail was unmatched. As her eyes darted hungrily from one to the next, she felt like she was stepping foot into a new world.

"Can I help you?" a sweet rasping voice called from the back of the shop.

So focused on a painting of the night sky, Effie jolted, lurching into the table behind her and sending the small odds and ends flying.

Wincing, she turned toward the shopkeeper in the back with an apology on her lips.

The older woman's hands were raised. "There's no need. My Angus does worse when he comes to visit. No harm done."

Noting the paint stains on the lady's fingers, Effie asked, "Are these your paintings?"

The shopkeeper let out a startled laugh, her eyes darting to Lucian who was hovering near the door. "Goodness, no."

"You will have to pass on my love for the artist's work, then. These paintings are exquisite, truly."

Still looking at Lucian, a sly smile grew on the woman's face. "Consider it done. Have you seen the rest of his work? Painting is the least of what he can do with his hands."

Lucian let out a strangled cough, and Effie shot him a curious glance.

"No, I haven't. I've been too distracted to get much further than these."

"I don't blame you, dear. He's got raw talent, that one."

Effie nodded her agreement, stooping to pick up a few hand-painted cards that had fallen to the floor. Each one was the size of her palm, the thick cardstock cool in her hand. The back of the cards were the same; each a deep green that brought to mind the forest floor, with metallic gold embellishments curling along the edges like flowering vines.

They glittered as she moved them in her hand, lifting them into the light to better make out their details. A hint of color along the bottom caught her eye, and she flipped the first card over. It was a snarling wolf; its eyes narrowed in red slits, saliva dripping from its yellowed fangs.

Effie shivered, shuffling to the bottom and lifting the next.

This one was swirls of blue and white. It took her a second to realize it was a pool of rippling water, sunlight glinting off its surface. The last card finally clued her in to what she was holding. A woman surrounded by five pillars, runes emblazed in their surface. She was stunningly beautiful; her chestnut curls flying around her, smoldering flames at the tips. Her dress was the palest lilac at the top, blending into a deep eggplant at the hem, and a sparkling pendant glittered at the base of her throat.

Effie knew this woman. It was Helena, as perfectly rendered as if she'd posed for the portrait.

"It's a castle deck," she murmured, a low buzz of premonition zinging through her. What were the odds she and Lucian would stumble across a deck of cards after just talking about the game?

Effie twisted to the table beside her, more of the playing cards strewn across its top, the wooden box that held them laying open on its side. Her breath caught in her chest as she picked up more familiar faces, each so achingly familiar that a pang of homesickness overtook her.

There was the Palace; its circular towers standing proud against a sunny blue sky. A Talyrian in flight; her obsidian wings flung wide as molten fire spewed across the horizon. But the five that caught her eye were the ones with the symbols from the pillars in the Kiri card—Helena's card. The men they contained were as familiar to her as her own reflection. Kragen, the Sword. Ronan, the Shield. Timmins, the Advisor. Joquil, the Master. And the last, with silver eyes and a dark brow scowling up at her, was Von, the Mate.

"Would you like it?" Lucian asked, moving to stand beside her.

"Oh, I couldn't possibly afford something so beautiful," Effie protested, tearing her gaze away from Ronan's mocking grin.

"My dear, you must have the deck. It was clearly made for you," the shopkeeper insisted, startling Effie with how close she was standing.

Jumping, one of the cards slipped, slicing open the tip of her finger with its edge. She hissed at the sting of pain and dropped her gaze to the bead of scarlet as it dripped.

"Oh," she cried, trying to shove the cards below to the side, not wanting to ruin them with her blood.

She wasn't fast enough. Her blood splashed over one of the images, obscuring it and sending the buzzing inside of her to a full-blown alarm. Gasping, she toppled to the side, barely managing to cling to Lucian before hitting the floor. Eyes rolling back in her head, Effie's vision pulled her under.

SHE COULD TELL *before the images even appeared that something was different about this vision. It was as if her senses had been heightened, but also blocked.*

Blurred faces surrounded her as inhuman wails filled her ears. Effie spun, trying to find the source of the screaming, but the faces moved with her, not letting her out of their sight.

She tried to focus, but none of the features that should have been present were visible and things were spinning too fast around her to focus on any one picture for long. She could feel the frantic pulse of her power spiraling within and tugging on her inner awareness. It felt almost desperate as it tried to relay its message, but her brain struggled to make sense of what she was Seeing. The harder she struggled, the more disjointed the sensations became.

Fire licked up her legs, but ice ran down her spine.

Laughter replaced the screams; keening and filled with malice. It was more terrifying than anything else. The booming laughs grew so loud the sky shattered, raining ash down upon her skin. When she tried to brush the ash away, it caught on her fingers, sticky like blood.

Her stomach swooped, bile burning her throat as tears fell from her eyes and made the ash bloat and swell. Images formed on its mottled surface, turning once more into the blurred faces that surrounded her.

Again and again the images looped. Fire, ice, ash, screams.

But nothing was more terrifying than the laughter.

EFFIE CAME BACK to herself and immediately rolled to her knees, her stomach heaving. The images had been so frantic, so disjointed, it hurt to try and follow them. Between the spinning and swooping, she felt like she had been flung about like a feather caught in a storm.

"I'm sorry," she gasped, tears still streaming from her eyes as her stomach convulsed.

Lucian pressed a cool cloth to the back of her neck, the shopkeeper standing to the side with a concerned frown.

"What did you See?" Lucian asked in a low voice, his other hand running over her back in soothing circles.

Effie shook her head. "I-I don't know. I couldn't really make sense of anything."

Lucian frowned. "Nothing?"

Gulping, Effie shook her head. "Faces with no features. Laughter. Ash. Tears." She was struggling to pluck out any concrete moments from the vision, but they were blending together. The harder she tried to focus, the more confused she became.

"Laughter?" Lucian repeated.

"Could it have been her own laughter she was hearing?" the shopkeeper whispered, her dark eyes shooting to Lucian.

"*M-my* laughter?" Effie stammered, her eyes bouncing between the two of them.

She looked up at Lucian, waiting for his answer. He was staring at her, his expression drawn, bronze fire flashing in his eyes.

"What's wrong?" he demanded, his hand snaking out and covering hers, halting its frenzied movement.

Effie glanced down, surprised to see that she'd been scratching at her arms hard enough to draw blood. The buzzing still raged inside of her, her skin feeling too tight, like she was going to burst from the vibrations inside of her.

Panic set it. Something was very, very wrong.

"I need Smoke."

Something shifted in Lucian's eyes, but she was too jumbled to make sense of anything else. Distantly, she heard the rustling of cloth and a low murmur of voices before her mind shut down, trying to protect her from the overwhelming assault of sensations.

Effie had no memory of returning to the citadel, nor of Lucian leaving her. By the time she was aware again, hours could have passed. It was the sound of fire crackling in a hearth that finally cut through the void, the sizzling pops providing her with an anchor to focus on as she pulled herself out of the darkness.

It didn't take more than a cursory glance to tell that Lucian had brought her back to the Hall of Guardians. She was sitting in one of the high-backed chairs, a thick blanket that smelled faintly of him wrapped around her shoulders.

Kneeling before her was Smoke, his scarlet hood pushed back and her pale hand clasped between his.

"Welcome back, Daughter."

CHAPTER 20

"Smoke." His name left her lips in a warble.

She wasn't sure why the sight of him brought such swift relief, or why she felt like she was on the verge of tears—except that he might be the only person to understand what just happened to her.

"Where's Lucian?"

Smoke rose up from his knees, letting her hand fall limply into her lap. *"I had to send him away."*

"Why?"

"So he could do what needed to be done."

Effie couldn't imagine he'd left her willingly. Lucian was too fiercely protective to leave her in a vulnerable state. Although, waiting around while she stared vacantly into the distance probably hadn't been easy on him either. Her Guardian might have relished the opportunity to do something useful since he was incapable of doing anything to help her.

Either way, she harbored no ill will at his absence. It would be easier to discuss her mess of a vision with someone who could experience it himself and not have to worry about sounding like she'd lost her marbles.

"Are you ready to speak about what happened?"

Taking a deep breath, Effie tucked the blanket more tightly around her body as if she could absorb some of Lucian's strength through the garment.

"I know that our prophecies are trapped in metaphors, but the images that came to me were . . . chaotic. Blurred faces, ash, tears, the sense of being on fire . . . laughter." Effie shuddered, the cruel mocking sound echoing in her mind. Forcing herself to focus, she added, "There was no sense or reason to anything I Saw. Everything swirled together until it was all one jumbled mess. Even the pieces I could make out remained mostly out of focus or transformed into something else."

"Do you feel that what you Saw was about yourself?"

Effie bit her lip, considering the question. "It's hard to say, really."

Smoke lifted up his hand. *"Would you like me to—"*

Before he could finish the question, Effie flinched away from him, quickly shaking her head. "No, I don't think that's a good idea."

"Premonition?"

"No..." she responded slowly, checking herself for signs of the familiar buzz or tension.

He tilted his head and studied her. *"Then why?"*

Effie didn't fully understand the answer to that question herself. It was just a gut reaction. Not having a better explanation, she settled for a different truth. "I guess I just don't want to have to experience it again. It was awful enough the first time."

"Very well."

"That's it? You aren't going to insist?"

"I will always respect your privacy, Daughter. Your visions are your own; to share or not as you will. If what you Saw suggests imminent danger I would ask you to reconsider, but barring that," he spread his arms and shrugged, *"a verbal retelling works almost as well."*

"You aren't upset with me?" she asked, more than a little relieved he wasn't going to press the issue.

"Of course not."

Feeling a little more settled, Effie asked a question that had been bothering her. "Smoke, what's happening to my visions? Why are they . . . devolving?"

She didn't voice the real concern: that if her visions were no longer trustworthy, then she was no good to anyone. She wasn't ready to hear that without her gift, there was no place for her with the Keepers.

"Who says they are?"

"What?" she blurted in surprise.

"Just as the symptoms of visions change with time, so do the visions themselves. It is not uncommon for the future to appear fragmented or abstract. The more in flux the outcome, the more chaotic the vision. It is simply the nature of your gift."

"You mean . . . this is . . . normal?"

"What is ever normal about prophecy?"

He was so matter-of-fact, so damn unaffected by what felt like a cataclysmic shift to her, that she couldn't stop the incredulous laughter from bubbling up. Nothing got beneath that rune-covered skin of his. *Except your past*, she reminded herself, sobering slightly. If Smoke said this wasn't unusual, all she could do was trust that he would not lie to her about something so important.

"So, you're not worried about it?"

"Should I be?"

This was her chance to ask him. To give voice to the secret fear lurking within her. Effie opened her mouth, the words crowding on the tip of her tongue.

Smoke tilted his head, waiting for her to speak.

Heart racing, Effie closed her mouth and shook her head. She couldn't do it. Not yet.

"No, I guess not," she murmured finally. "I just didn't realize it wasn't unusual for visions to change. I'd become sort of used to them making more sense." She frowned. "Well, okay, maybe not sense, per se, but at least being a little less fragmented."

"Understandable."

"So, what now?" she asked, looking up from the silver embroidery on his sleeve.

"Since you do not feel prepared to show me, I need you to describe

your vision as best you can. Even fragmented, your vision contains a warning. With a second marker having passed—"

Effie jolted as if he'd burnt her. "A second marker? How? When?"

"The massacre in the jungle—"

"And you're just now telling me!" she shouted.

Smoke held up his hands to stop her angry tirade. *"You knew it was a possibility, but we only managed to confirm it today."*

"How could you not have realized it sooner?" she sputtered. "This seems like something you three should know. I mean, isn't that what you do?"

Smoke used silence like other men issued threats. Her accusation displeased him, and he was making sure she knew she'd overstepped.

Effie lifted her chin, refusing to give in. The Triumvirate were their leaders. They were the ones with access to every Keepers' prophecy ever made. Surely, something as important as a marker of the Shadow Years would be readily recognizable.

"Well?" she demanded.

"I think you misunderstand how the prophecies are stored. There are thousands of them, stored in our archives as well as our memories, but the nature of prophecy is patently obscure. There is rarely one specific outcome a prophecy could refer to, and more than one way for a prophecy to come true. We are not infallible. Miscategorization does occur."

There was nothing worse than a logical explanation when you were in the middle of a deeply emotional reaction. Effie didn't want logic. She wanted the Triumvirate to be all-knowing. Learning that they weren't attacked the sense of safety she felt being near them. Safety she hadn't recognized for what it was until it was threatened.

Effie didn't want the occurrence of a marker to be a surprise. Smoke and the Mirrors were supposed to know what was coming and give the rest of them a heads-up so they could stop it.

Frustration leaked into her voice as she asked, "So what makes you so sure you're right about this being a marker? If it's that easy to mislead you, how can you ever be sure about anything?"

"Why don't you tell me?" Smoke's voice swelled in her mind, sending chills cascading down her body. *"'And beasts will fall, the docile becoming fiends in their quest for blood. Peaceful no more, the prey become the hunters; upon the threshold of day, where life and death meet, converging into one. Let it be a mark of the end, a herald of destruction. None will be safe when the gentlest amongst us are lost.'"*

"Yeah, that sounds like a marker," Effie muttered, numb with the realization they were that much closer to annihilation.

Hearing the prophecy, seeing how vague the phrasing could be, she better understood why it could have been overlooked, or simply forgotten. But there was no doubting that this was tied to what happened in the jungle. The lajhár were obviously the docile creatures fiending for blood, and the attack's timing at sunset matched the reference to the death of day and birth of night.

No matter how many sites they searched looking for answers, until they could find a way to stop the corruption from spreading, they were dead in the water. The Chosen needed their Kiri. The Mother's Vessel was the only one powerful enough to put an end to this.

So, where is she? Why haven't Ronan's notes reached her by now?

Trying not to let the feeling of helplessness send her spiraling into despair, Effie looked back at Smoke. "What can we do? What are the other markers?"

"There are hundreds of possible scenarios. The only marker known with certainty was the first because it was the shepherd of the rest."

Effie's blood turned to ice and her heart pounded loudly in her ears. "If we aren't sure when and where the markers could potentially occur, how can we protect ourselves?"

"We decipher our visions. We look for the clues contained within and use them to point us to warnings from the past. If there's a way to stop this, we will find it."

"And in the meantime? Until then? You're putting a lot of hope into something that might not be the answer."

"We do what we have always done, Daughter."

161

"Stand back and watch while everything goes to shit?"

Smoke rested his hand on her shoulder. *"We do the best we can with what we are given."*

Effie closed her eyes as tears threatened. Smoke might be right, but it wasn't nearly good enough. The Mother blessed them with this gift for a reason, surely she couldn't mean to leave them without a means of salvation.

"How is so little known about this?" she whispered, her lashes wet with unshed tears when she opened her eyes.

"Do not give into your fear. You will find no answers there."

Effie scowled at Smoke. "I'm allowed to be upset."

"I didn't say you weren't."

"Smoke, there has to be something more that we can do than sit around waiting for the three of you to look through old books. Maybe if we help you—"

"You have been helping. More than you probably realize. What we need right now is information, not just that contained in the archives, but insights about the corruption that you and the others have gathered in your investigations. You can travel where we cannot. Each new detail you bring back could be the difference in uncovering the answers we seek."

"You want us to go back out there," she surmised.

Smoke nodded. *"Until a new attack is reported, we will monitor the jungle, track the spread of the corruption, fight the infected beasts, and learn what we can."*

Something was still bothering her. "What's the point of knowing about the markers if we can't prevent them?"

"The purpose was never to prevent the marker—not specifically. The markers are a warning of what's coming. The goal is to recognize them for what they are, and change the behavior that is causing them in the first place."

"But the Chosen aren't doing anything truly terrible, are they? Helena defeated the Corruptor. So why is this happening? Why now?"

"I wish I held the answers you seek, Daughter."

Effie chewed on the inside of her cheek, her thoughts churning. "Could it be as simple as dealing with the remnants of Rowena's false reign? Defeating the Shadows that escaped and preventing them from spreading their corruption?"

"Even if it's not the answer, it's what needs to be done."

Sighing, Effie nodded. "Then we need a better way of tracking the Shadows so they can be dealt with. We only hear about them once it's too late."

"Our Guardians said the same thing."

Effie's lips twitched. She might not be the one coming up with the big ideas, but at least she was thinking along the right lines. Either that or her time spent with Lucian was starting to rub off on her.

"So, what you're telling me is we're already doing everything we can."

Smoke was kind enough not to mention that's what he'd been trying to get her to understand this entire time. Sometimes the only way to accept something was to come to the conclusion on your own.

Feeling slightly mollified now that she knew they truly were doing everything in their combined power, Effie readjusted the blanket and glanced back at her mentor. Idly, she wondered when she'd stopped being afraid of his face. She hardly noticed his pitted eyes or scarred lips anymore. Maybe there were just other things that frightened her far worse than he ever could.

"Are you ready to return to our discussion about what you Saw?"

"Why do I feel like you're really asking me if I'm ready to be reasonable?"

The sound of rustling leaves filled the air. *"I know better now than to imply you are ever anything but reasonable."*

"Even when you compliment me it's tinged with smugness," Effie griped, certain his words didn't mean he actually believed what he was saying. It was all an attempt to pacify her and manipulate her into doing what he wanted. Chuckling, she shook her head. "We've come a long way from my hurling daggers at you in the forest."

"Indeed we have."

"I don't know how much help I'm going to be. I pretty much told you everything I remember."

"Close your eyes. Start at the beginning."

With one last centering breath, Effie did as she was told and descended back into the madness.

CHAPTER 21

*E*ffie flipped through the pages of her journal, reading and re-reading the same handful of passages until she could probably recite them verbatim, including punctuation. She didn't know what she was looking for—well, she did; she wanted answers. There was nothing new to be found within those cream-colored pages.

"Never did see the point of reading for pleasure," Ronan said, startling her.

Effie blinked up at him as the lines of text from her journal momentarily superimposed themselves over his handsome face. *Mother, how long have I been here?*

"Perhaps that's because you've never read anything worth reading. Although, I would hardly say this is a pleasure read."

Ronan grinned. "I'll admit, after learning my letters, I had little interest in anything that kept me indoors. Unless it was going to get me beneath sweet Hannah's skirts." Ronan let out a soft sigh. "Alas, it was never meant to be. I never did learn the answer to that particular riddle."

Effie snorted and tossed a pillow at him. "Brute."

Ronan shrugged, easily catching the pillow and dropping it onto the empty chair beside him. "I was a teenage boy. You can't honestly expect more of me than that."

"Yes, I can. I didn't know you when you were a teenager, so my expectations are colored by the man I see before me."

He leaned against the table, making her cup of tea rattle in its delicate saucer. "It's called growing up for a reason, darlin'."

She may have no interest in Ronan, but the term of endearment combined with his roguish half-grin still had the power to make her blush.

Clearing her throat, she nodded. "I suppose you're right."

Effie was more than familiar with the adage herself. She'd done her fair share of growing up in these past few months, certainly enough to know that growing pains were emotional more often than not.

Lifting a hand, she made to brush away a curl that had fallen free of the braid she'd made along the crown of her head.

"What happened?" Ronan snarled, shifting from playful friend back to attentive warrior instantly.

Effie froze, her hand still half-raised. Eyes wide, she stared up at his thunderous expression. "What do you mean?"

He was close enough that he barely had to move to reach out and gently grasp her wrist in his hand, turning it up until a smattering of purple bruises were clearly visible.

"Who did this?" he asked in a low, dangerous voice.

Effie knew better than to lie to him, but she also knew if she gave him a name, Ronan would tear out of here intent on repaying each mark on her body seven-fold.

"I dealt with it myself," she answered with just enough bite in her voice that Ronan's eyebrows lifted.

"Is that so?"

She gave him a dark smile. "He's lucky I didn't have my blades."

Ronan gave an approving grunt. "See that he does not have a chance to repeat the mistake."

"He won't." Effie meant it. She would not hesitate to take Kieran down if he tried to touch her again. Thankfully, Kieran had made himself scarce the last few days, so she hadn't had to deal with him, one way or the other.

Ronan studied her carefully, his thumb brushing over the worst of the bruises. "That he lives at all is a kindness he doesn't deserve."

"It's a few bruises, Ronan. Not nearly serious enough to concern yourself with."

"I'll be the one to make that decision."

Effie rolled her eyes and bit back a smile. She may not need him to defend her honor, but it meant a lot to her that he was willing to do so. Especially after a childhood where the only person who would have done the same was rarely around.

"Does Lucian know about this?" Ronan asked, his head tilting as he released his hold on her.

Effie shook her head, pulling her sleeve back down over the bruises. They hadn't appeared until the morning after her run-in with Kieran, and Effie had barely spent more than a handful of minutes with her Guardian since their outing a few days ago. She knew Ronan's reaction would be mild in comparison to Lucian's if he found out.

"Do I know about what?" Lucian asked, choosing that moment to walk into the room.

Effie scowled up at Ronan before looking back at Lucian. "Nothing."

His lips tightened, and he narrowed his eyes. "I don't believe you." Shifting his intense gaze from her face to Ronan's, he asked, "What isn't she telling me?"

Effie kicked Ronan in the shin, which only made the red-headed warrior laugh. "Oh, now I'm definitely telling him."

"Don't you dare!" she said, jumping out of her chair. A moment of inspiration made her blurt out, "You'll ruin the surprise."

Lucian gave her a look filled with suspicion. "What surprise?"

Beside her Ronan's shoulders shook with laughter. He knew she'd just talked herself into a corner and was happily going to stand by and watch her struggle to get out.

"I can't very well tell you, now can I? That's the very nature of a surprise."

MEG ANNE

"I don't like surprises," Lucian growled. "Tell me what you're up to, fledgling."

Effie scrambled to come up with a plausible answer, her wide grin genuine as she recalled the carefully wrapped deck of cards that had been in her room. "I wanted to thank you for the gift you left for me."

Her Guardian's expression cleared slightly. "I wasn't sure if you'd still want them after what happened."

"Of course, I do. They're the most beautiful thing I own," she added, her eyes drifting to the journal still open on the table. "Well, one of . . ." A warm heat blossomed in her chest as she realized her two most prized possessions had both been gifted to her by Lucian.

She looked back over to him, confused by the almost shy expression on his face. Shy and Lucian were not two things that went together. Before she could ask about it, his expression shifted, returning to its usual impassive mask.

"Don't worry about surprising me with anything. Your thanks are gift enough."

Effie lifted a brow. Now that the idea had taken root, there was no way she was going to let his generosity go unreturned. How she was going to do so was a problem for another day.

Wanting to keep the focus away from her and her bruises, she said, "We'll have to break the deck in together sometime. Are you familiar with the game?"

Lucian's eyes heated, and he gave her a slow grin. "Are we going to be playing for the same stakes you used in the tavern?"

There was no mistaking his meaning. She went crimson, her heart rate escalating at the thought of them taking turns peeling off layers of clothing. Desire pooled within her belly as she realized that she would likely be the only one standing naked at the end. Somehow that was even more erotic. Effie squeezed her legs together, shaking her head slightly as she tried to return to their conversation.

"If you wish."

Lucian's eyes blazed, the bronze flickering as his smile turned wolfish. "Oh, I'm going to have to insist on it."

168

Ronan cleared his throat. "Would you two mind toning it down a bit? I'm still standing right here."

Effie tore her eyes away from Lucian and gave Ronan a sheepish grin. "Sorry."

He smirked. "No, you aren't."

"I'm definitely not," Lucian said, making Effie laugh.

"I think this is my cue," Ronan said, shaking his head as he started for the door.

"Wait," Lucian said, "I actually came in here for a reason. The Triumvirate have called another meeting. We're to meet them in the sanctum."

Effie sobered. "Has something happened?"

Shrugging, Lucian said, "I guess we'll find out."

Ronan sighed. "I'll check and see if Reyna is feeling up to attending."

A pang of surprise rang through Effie as she realized she hadn't even once thought about the Night Stalker or the injuries she sustained in the jungle since they returned.

"She's been asking about you and if you might visit. She's worried that you haven't forgiven her for what happened in the cave," Ronan added, giving Effie a pointed look.

Tinka. To be honest, Effie hadn't given it a second thought after they returned to the citadel. In the end, it was what needed to be done. She couldn't blame the woman for being the one to hold the sword that dealt the final blow.

Effie shrugged. *Let them believe that for now.* It was certainly the easiest explanation. There was no way for her to express the sheer lack of concern she was feeling about the Night Stalker. If anything, she was more worried about *why* she didn't care in the first place.

"I've just been busy," she murmured.

Ronan's eyes were clouded as they met hers, like he could sense the lie behind her words. His look was not judgmental exactly, but filled with something . . . disappointment, maybe.

Giving her a slight nod, he slipped out of the room.

"That's not like you," Lucian said once they were alone.

"I know," she said. Her eyes lifted to his, expecting to see the same disappointment there, but there was none. Only concern.

"Do not be so hard on yourself," Lucian said softly. "The woman's death was difficult for you. It's not unreasonable that you need some time to come to terms with it. You will find forgiveness once your grief has passed."

Effie pressed her lips together and nodded. "I suppose you're right. I just need more time."

The lie settled uncomfortably in her stomach, but she couldn't bear to see Lucian's reaction when he learned that she simply didn't care. Not about Reyna's injuries or about Tinka's death. She was too twisted up in knots about everything that was happening, maybe there just wasn't room left for anyone else. Maybe?

Not even she bought the excuse.

A skitter of warning crawled down her spine, but before she could explore it, Lucian distracted her with a brush of his thumb over her cheek.

His eyes were warm, his lips lifted in a small smile when she peered up at him.

"As for wanting to thank me for the gift, the only thanks I'll accept is a kiss."

"I think I can manage that," she murmured, the warmth of his hand on her skin helping ease the feeling of apprehension that had settled in her chest.

Lifting up on her toes, she molded her lips to his, fire igniting within her as he pulled her body flush to his with a low groan.

"I should have waited until later to take my thanks," he muttered against her lips, punctuating the statement by trailing feather-soft kisses along her jaw. "One taste of you is never enough."

"Why stop at one?" she asked, the scrape of his stubble sending shivers along her skin.

"Duty calls," he said in a husky voice, pulling away.

"Damn your control," she said without any heat, opening her eyes to smile up at him.

"Never has anyone tested it as much as you."

"I take that as a compliment." She smirked at him as she dropped her voice, "And a personal challenge. I look forward to the day I shatter it entirely."

Without waiting for his reply, she started to move past him, squealing when one of his arms banded around her and pulled her back against his chest, the evidence of his desire pressing into her back.

"Not nearly as much as I do," he growled low in her ear, before lifting and twisting her in one smooth move.

"What happened to duty?" she asked a bit breathlessly as he pressed her against the wall, her legs winding around his waist.

"Fuck it. They can wait a few more minutes," he muttered, slanting his mouth back down on hers.

CHAPTER 22

The best thing about Lucian's kisses, Effie thought fifteen minutes later as they walked down the hall hand in hand, was that they vanquished all of the darkness that had tried to take up residence within her. With the mere brush of his sinfully soft lips, he'd entirely dispelled the unease and replaced it with a giddy sort of happiness.

Whatever was growing between them gave her hope for a future free of bloodshed. One where she'd wake up surrounded by his strong arms and sleepy kisses, and the most difficult decision they'd have to face was whether they would be leaving their bed.

As he pushed through the sanctum's doors and they crossed the threshold into the blood-red room, Effie watched that future slip further away.

Grim faces turned to meet her as they moved inside. Ronan stood to the side, his arms crossed and his expression thoughtful. Reyna was nowhere in sight. Kael's dark skin looked ashen, his dimpled smile notably absent. Kieran was pale and practically vibrating with tension as his blazing eyes found hers.

"What did we miss?" Lucian asked.

"Keepers are missing." The lone, hooded figure in the center of the room answered.

Effie stiffened, ice running through her veins. "Who?"

Lucian's hand flinched in hers. He really hadn't known why they'd been called to meet, Effie realized. Otherwise he never would have let them linger.

"When?" he snapped.

"We know of two for sure—Jo and Tess—but there may be others. We're still waiting for about thirty to report in."

Effie remembered stumbling into Kait, who had been searching for them. She'd been in too much of a hurry at the time, but had the other women looked stricken, or was that just how Effie imagined it now that she knew the other two were actually missing?

Effie struggled to remember the last time she'd seen the two women. She recalled speaking to Jo during the party in the citadel, after Rowena had been killed. For Tess, it had been even longer. *Has it really been that long?*

She knew she'd been distracted with her own assignments from the Triumvirate, in addition to other, more personal matters, but how had she not realized they were missing?

"How long have they been gone?" she asked, the floor feeling like it shifted beneath her feet as a low hum started beneath her skin.

"It could have been days or weeks. There's no way to know at this point."

"They were told to stay within the citadel," Lucian ground out.

Effie could feel the anger rolling off of him. People he was supposed to protect were missing. There was no way he'd forgive himself until they were found.

"Apparently, they felt compelled to travel."

Lucian bit off a curse. "Do we have any clue where they might have gone?"

Smoke, or perhaps one of the Mirrors, lifted a hand to gesture at Kieran. *"The Dreamer is the one who notified us of their disappearance. He's had another vision."*

Lucian twisted to Kieran, his eyes bottomless. "Where?"

"I will take you there," Kieran said, his voice filled with barely veiled disdain.

Effie knew that he hated that Lucian was touching her. Even now, in the midst of a crisis, he was still hung up on perceived slights.

"You will stay, Dreamer, and go over the details of your vision."

"What?" Kieran snapped, turning to the man on the dais. "I'm the only one that knows where to go."

"Lucian and Kael know the jungle better than anyone. Tell them where to go. They will know what to look for. You will stay and review the vision in detail. The last one you had turned out to be a marker. We cannot afford to miss a single clue."

"I've already told you what I Saw—"

"If you'd rather, I can take the vision from you . . ." the robed figure trailed off, lifting his runed hand higher.

Kieran stiffened, his hands balling into fists. "You will not."

Effie knew better than the others how much Kieran hated the possibility of the Triumvirate stealing his other thoughts. To him, it was the worst kind of violation. He'd shamed her for allowing them to do the same to her.

"Then you stay. Now tell the others where to go so that we do not waste any more time."

"Fine," he snarled, his fury palpable. He was visibly shaking when he said, "East side of the jungle by the river, near the border to the Broken Vale. That's where I Saw them last."

Kael and Lucian exchanged a look.

"The nearest portal is an hour walk from the border. We will need to leave now," Kael said.

"What about a stone?" Ronan asked.

"They're all spent," Kael replied with a shake of his head.

"We go on foot," Lucian said. "Everyone grab what you need. We leave immediately."

EFFIE COULDN'T HELP but notice how their group had diminished. It'd been small to begin with, but less than a week ago there'd been six of them, plus Zane and Xander, investigating Sylverlands and now they were down to four.

It made the jungle feel ominous. As if the threat of what was waiting for them alone was enough to pick them off.

Not that it was necessarily true. Only one person of the initial eight was willingly staying behind due to her slow recovery, and the two Sylvanese men weren't even in the same territory at present. But still . . . the feeling lingered, causing Effie to keep glancing back over her shoulder to peer into the shadowed areas between the trees.

Something was out there, but would they find it before it found them?

With each step, she grew less certain of the answer.

Effie was with three of the strongest warriors in history, and it wasn't exactly like they were stepping onto the battlefield. But she couldn't shake the feeling that they alone wouldn't be enough.

"Do you know what's waiting for us?" Effie asked Ronan, keeping pace with him just behind Lucian and Kael.

He shook his head; his face set in hard lines. "No. Whatever Kieran shared with the Triumvirate, he did before we arrived. Clearly, they didn't think the information was pertinent."

Effie mulled it over, trying to follow the thread of logic in why they'd hold back information. "Maybe there was nothing specific to share," she said eventually, with a little shake of her head.

"How do you figure?" Ronan asked, pushing a bowed branch up so it wouldn't smack him in the face.

"Well . . . if his dream was about Jo and Tess before they went missing, it's possible there was nothing specifically amiss. The dream could have just shown them and nothing more . . . sinister."

"Hmm," Ronan said, picking up the thought. "So, then we'd be looking for a sign of capture instead of corruption."

Effie nodded. "Although the two things aren't necessarily unrelated. Not with the Triumvirate thinking this has the potential to be another marker."

Ronan's expression darkened. "Let us both pray to the Mother it is not. The last thing we need is a third marker to pass without any sign of Helena."

"Still?" Effie asked, a tendril of fear snaking through her.

He gave a terse shake of his head. "She never would have left if she had any doubt that we'd be safe in her absence."

"Should we send for the rest of the Circle?" Effie asked.

"Kragen and Joquil are off searching for Von and Helena. Timmins remains at the Palace in case she sends word, and to ensure that things continue to run as smoothly as possible."

"Do they have any idea where she might be?"

"Our best guess is she went to visit the pride in Talyria. It's the only realm that is closed to us."

Effie's heart sank. "It's been weeks. Surely she'll come home soon?"

Ronan gave her a smile that didn't quite reach his eyes. "I'm sure she will."

But would it be in time?

Determination solidified within her, and Effie stood a little straighter. "If we have to face this without Helena, then it's time we plan for that eventuality. I never was one for sitting around and waiting for someone to come rescue me," Effie said, pulling not just Ronan's attention, but also her Guardian's.

She gave Lucian a small smile, and he gave her an inscrutable look in return before turning away.

"We're hardly sitting," Ronan said, gesturing to the jungle.

"No, but we're not coming up with ways to fight the corruption either. Without a plan, one of these days, we're going to walk straight into something we won't walk away from."

"Is that what you See?" Ronan asked, his blue eyes spearing her with their intensity.

"I don't need a prophecy to show me that."

Ronan fell silent as they continued forward, his voice soft when he finally spoke. "What do you suggest?"

"Helena cleansed the land before. That means it can be done. We just need to find a way to replicate it without her."

"Without Spirit magic, you mean?"

Effie let out a frustrated sigh. This was the exact thing that had been weighing on her. Chewing on her bottom lip, her eyes fell back to the Guardians in front of her.

"The Chosen aren't the only ones with magic. Maybe the answer lies elsewhere."

Ronan followed her gaze, his brows lifting. "What are you hinting at?"

"The Guardians have the ability to manipulate the essence of any living thing. Surely they can do *something* about the corruption."

"Don't you think they would have by now if it was that easy?"

Effie shrugged. "They might not know how without being tainted themselves, but that doesn't mean they can't. We just need to help them figure out how."

"You don't give up once you set your mind to something, do you?" Ronan asked with a small chuckle.

Her answering grin was feral. "I wouldn't be alive today if I gave in easily."

His expression shifted, eyes darting back to her bruised wrists. "No, I don't suppose you would be."

Eyes still on Ronan, Effie didn't notice the odd pile of branches until the sharp crack rent the air. With a yelp, she flew up, her ankle supporting her full weight as she flipped upside down and into the trees.

Three distinct voices screamed her name, sending birds fleeing their perches.

She watched, pain ratcheting through her leg, as Ronan reached for her. Effie's arm strained as she tried to grasp either of his proffered hands, but she was moving too fast, and soon all there was in every direction was a sea of green.

Now having a better idea about how Tess and Jo were taken, Effie knew there wasn't a second to spare. She struggled to pull herself upright, clawing her way up her ensnared leg until her upper body was parallel with it. Not sure what to do with her other leg, she settled for keeping it curled into her chest.

Banding both arms around her extended leg, she used her arms to hold her in place and fought to catch her breath. The rush of blood to her head made her stomach roll, and she quickly started to shake, the position awkward and adding pressure to the place where the rope coiled around her ankle.

Searing pain lashed through her ankle, and she let out a low gasp. A quick check with one hand told her it wouldn't be as easy as untangling the rope from her leg. There were jagged metal teeth woven through the coarse strands. Two of which had already dug deep into her skin, hot blood dripping down her leg and coating her fingers.

With a grunt, Effie glanced around. If she didn't find another handhold, fast, she would soon be too slick with her blood to maintain her grip. The nearest branch was above her, not a far reach if she could manage to swing herself up a bit more, but tricky with the barbed pieces of metal jutting out from the rope.

Or she could risk dropping down.

Effie craned her neck, seeing the thick branch about a body's length beneath her. If she could cut through the rope, she should be able to drop down onto the branch and perhaps scramble down the rest of the way.

Fingers trembling, she ran them along her leg, letting out a scream of frustration to find that her dagger had fallen free. Patting around to the other side of her body, Effie could have wept when her fingers ran over the sharp blade of her second one.

"Thank you," she muttered, quickly working to free it from its sheath. The dagger slipped in her wet hand, and her breath caught as gravity tried to pry it out of her slippery grasp.

"Oh no, you don't," she growled, tightening her hand around the dagger's hilt.

Effie's relief was short-lived, however, as a new problem presented itself. To cut through the rope at her ankle, she had to find something besides her leg to hold onto. As it was, her fingers were already starting to slip along the leather of her pants. It was hardly an ideal handle. Furthermore, if she didn't, she wouldn't be able to properly plan her drop down to the branch, and would be just as likely to crash all the way back down to the jungle floor below.

"Elder's rotting rod," she snarled, not immediately finding anything she could use.

The snap of a branch had her eyes darting to the left, but the shivering leaves were the only evidence that something—or someone—was coming for her.

"Hello?" she called, hoping that maybe it was one of the men coming to free her. It was a futile hope, and she knew it since they would come from below—not above—but it sprang forth all the same.

When there was no answer, Effie shifted her grip on the dagger, her decision made for her. There was no time to waste. A fall through the trees it would be. Hopefully she'd manage to grab hold of something on her way down. It was that or stay hanging here trussed up like some holiday goose. Neither was a great option, but of the two she preferred the former.

Grunting, she began sawing at the barbed rope in earnest. Its cords were tougher than she realized, the sharp blade of her dagger barely cutting through the first of the fibers when two more distinct cracks sounded just above her.

A heavy pressure settled in her chest, robbing her of breath. Effie didn't dare look up as goosebumps erupted along her arms.

She was out of time.

Her moves grew frantic, blood dripping down her hand as more of the jagged metal pieces snagged into her soft flesh. Effie bit back a cry of pain, the surge of adrenaline spiking through her, helping her maintain her focus.

A low chittering sounded, and Effie grit her teeth.

It was here.

The rope was as thick as three of her fingers, she'd barely managed to cut through a third of it. She was completely and utterly fucked.

Heart pounding, Effie lifted her chin, her eyes scanning the leaves above her. She sucked in a ragged breath, her eyes widening as two faces pushed through the leaves, peering down at her with snaking eyes, their blood-stained teeth bared in savage smiles.

"Lookie what I caught for us, Tess. A plump little mousie."

What had once been Tess licked her lips. "Delicious."

Effie screamed, the sight of her missing friends so unexpected she lost her hold and fell back, her only weapon joining its twin in the jungle below. There was a sharp tug on her ankle as the metal dug in deeper and the rope once more held the entirety of her weight. Pain exploded behind her eyes.

"Look at the mousie dance," Jo cackled as Effie swung from the rope.

"Stop playing with our food," Tess snapped, her hoarse voice a sibilant hiss.

Another garbled scream was torn from Effie's throat as the rope surged up, sending shooting pain all along her leg. Black fog swam at the edge of her vision, threatening to pull her under, but she fought against it. Freedom from the pain was a lovely thought, but unconsciousness would be the death of her.

More branches batted at her as she was pulled up through the trees until her bottom half was being dragged against a splintered wood floor. She could feel the creatures' hands on her legs as they pulled the rest of her body into their treetop lair.

Bile burned in the back of her throat as Effie braced herself for what came next. This might be her last opportunity to even the playing field. Especially without a weapon.

Flexing her stomach muscles, Effie arced up, snapping the rest of her body into the darkness and using the momentum to crack her head into something that felt like stone.

There was a satisfying *crunch* and the spurt of something warm across her forehead as her head flew back. She wasn't sure who or what she hit, but she hoped like hell it hurt them half as much as it hurt her.

"Mousie's a bad girl," a voice thick with blood sneered somewhere to her right.

Still disoriented from bashing her head into what she fervently hoped was a skull, Effie didn't move before the second creature scuttled over her body, pinning her arms down on either side of her.

The smell of decay and rotting flesh filled her nose as the Shadow formerly known as Jo opened her mouth in a snarl.

Saliva dripped from her mouth and splashed onto Effie's face as she hissed, "Bad girl, mousie."

Thankful for the sparring lessons with Kael where he'd forced her to get herself out of similar positions, Effie used her good leg to shift her weight and toss the creature off her body.

Crouched against the wall, Effie quickly took in her surroundings. The wooden building was small, built for children perhaps, and had clearly seen better days. The wood was rotten and damp, a few moldy blankets tossed along the floor. It was wider than it was tall, and there was barely enough room for an adult to stand upright. At least one of average size. For once, her small stature would work to her advantage.

That might be the only thing currently in her favor.

Two against one were rarely good odds. Add to that the lack of weapon and a shredded ankle, and things were looking decidedly grim. The odds may be stacked against her, but she was not about to die in this Mother-forsaken treehouse.

Fueled by a feral need to survive, Effie scanned the dim room and eyed the two Shadows crawling toward her. There was nothing she could use against them, save her hands.

Hand-to-hand combat it is, then. Effie pushed to her feet and curled her hands into fists, angling her body so that her injured ankle was behind her and not bearing any of her weight. It was an awkward position, but it was the best she could manage given the circumstances.

"Mother as my witness, if I get out of this alive, Lucian owes me a damned arsenal of weapons. I'm tired of finding myself without one when it matters most," Effie said in a bland tone, feigning a casualness she did not remotely feel.

"Oh, you won't be leaving, mousie," Tess said, spitting out a mouthful of blood.

"Not alive," Jo crooned.

"What are you waiting for?" Effie taunted, bringing her fists up the way Kael had taught her.

Everything faded, her vision tunneling until all she was aware of were the two women lurching toward her.

Alright, Effie, you can do this. Get them on their backs. You can't use your legs so you need to get them on the floor. They aren't full Shadows—otherwise their blood would run black—so you should be able to stun them with a few well-aimed blows. The head would be best. You need to get one of them out of the picture quick so you can try and fight them one at a time.

She continued to feed herself directions, her mental voice as steady as if she was Kael or Ronan talking her through drills.

The women broke apart, choosing to come at her from either side. It was a smart move, as it would split her focus, but Effie anticipated it. She threw up her left elbow, striking Jo in the nose and then twisting and following it up with a punch to the throat. Jo stumbled back.

Tess grabbed at her waist, and Effie hopped to the side, using all of her strength to push the woman off of her. Tess went flying, and Effie blinked in surprise. She knew she'd been getting stronger due to all of her morning training sessions, but there was no way she should have had the power to do that. Especially not to someone infused with a Shadow's innate strength.

The distraction cost her. Jo was back, her broken nails slicing into Effie's skin as she reached to fist her hand in Effie's curls.

Effie growled low in her throat and shoved both her fisted hands into the other woman's stomach. There was a sickening crunch as ribs snapped in half and Jo bent over with a keening cry.

A quick check revealed that Tess was still on the other side of the room, so Effie launched herself at Jo, tackling the woman to the ground.

It was a graceless move at best. More a throwing of her body than a well-aimed blow, but it was effective nonetheless. Barely bothering to take a breath, Effie straddled Jo's narrow hips and began throwing punches at her face. She could feel the crunch of bones beneath her fists, and the spray of blood as she continued to strike.

The Shadow was screaming beneath her, trying to buck her off, but Effie was only focused on making each hit land. She aimed for the center of the creature's head, seeing nothing of the woman who'd tried to be her friend. All she saw was an enemy. One that needed to be put down.

Effie let out a savage cry, pulling back her arms again and again. Never satisfied, never pausing. She continued to rain down blows one after the other, until it was no longer clear whose blood coated her hands.

Fury fueled her, spurring her on. A dark voice whispered in her ear that it was her or them. There was no choice. She was not dying today.

These. Things. Would. Not. Win.

Each word was punctuated with another wet strike.

The body beneath her had long since stilled, but still, Effie didn't stop. Not until the thing no longer resembled anything remotely human —and even then she continued to punch into the pulpy mess.

Effie didn't know what finally made her stop. Only that something not wholly sane within her calmed, settling back into its cage. She was shaking, her knuckles raw, and her body painted in blood.

Chest heaving, Effie sat back on her heels, immediately shifting her weight to the left and off of her injured ankle as she searched for the second Shadow.

How come she hadn't made her move by now? Effie had certainly been distracted enough to make an easy target for the other woman.

But Tess was nowhere to be found. What could she have possibly done to cause a Shadow to flee from *her*?

Taking a shuddering breath, Effie glanced back down, and finally *saw* what had become of Jo. A horrified whimper escaped her as she processed what she'd done, the level of brutality she'd been capable of unleashing.

No wonder Tess fled.

Scrambling off of the body, Effie crawled to the corner of the room and threw up.

CHAPTER 23

"She's in here!"

Effie lifted her head up just enough for her eyes to peek up over her arms. Much of the afternoon light had faded, leaving the treehouse mostly in shadow. She could just make out Lucian's dark head in the soft light that still fell through what passed for a window.

She had no idea how long she'd been curled into a ball in the corner. Everything after when she'd gotten sick was a blur. Although she must have snagged one of the blankets off the floor at some point, because one of the moldy scraps of fabric was flung over the top half of the corpse in a desperate attempt to cover up what laid beneath.

If only it was as easy to hide the image permanently seared into her mind.

Lucian took one look at her and then glanced at the body beside her.

"It would seem that we're too late for a proper rescue."

She couldn't even muster a smile.

Lucian frowned. "Effie?"

Tears filled her eyes, and she squeezed her arms tighter around her trembling body. How was she supposed to explain what happened when she barely understood it herself?

A muscle ticked in Lucian's jaw, and he eyed the wooden structure, his frown deepening as he did. "Effie, I'm going to need you to come to me. I'm too big to move about in here. Can you do that?"

Apparently, she took too long to respond because Lucian started to push his shoulders through the small opening in the floor anyway. A shiver raced along her skin as she realized it was the same one that Jo and Tess had used to pull her up by the legs. Effie shoved the thought away, she didn't want to think about either woman right now. Or what was left of them.

"No! Don't!" Effie cried, holding out a hand to stop him. "I'll come to you."

She didn't want Lucian to come anywhere near the shrouded corpse. He might be tempted to lift the blanket. She didn't want him to see proof of what she was capable of. How could he look at her with anything but disgust again if he did?

It was more difficult than she'd thought to unfurl her body, her overworked muscles cramped and unwilling to budge. With a low groan, she managed to move to her knees and crawl to Lucian.

He sucked in a breath when she made it into the light.

"Effie."

"It's not mine," she managed, referring to the blood she knew covered her.

His eyes shifted from her battered hands up to the matted hair hanging in clumps around her face.

"I know what happened to Jo—" she broke off, choking on the name.

Lucian's eyes darted back to the corpse behind her and gave her a grim nod. "We'll save the storytelling for later. For now, let's worry about getting you home."

She nodded, a tear slipping free as she sucked in another breath. "Okay."

"Can you slide forward a bit more? If you swing your legs down the latch, I can grasp you around the waist and help you down. There's a ladder alongside the trunk of this tree that leads to another platform below. There's an entire series of houses up here. It took us a while to find the one you were in."

Lucian kept talking, his voice warm and unhurried as she tried to follow his commands. He only stopped when her swollen foot came into view. It was an angry purple, her skin shredded from the rope and barbs, and more than twice its normal size.

"Here, I've got you," he murmured, no longer waiting for her to try and navigate getting out of the little house on her own.

Effie was more than willing to let him take over. Wrapping her arms around his neck and her legs around his waist, she buried her face into his shoulder and breathed him in.

"We're coming down!" he shouted over her head. In a quieter voice, he added, "Hold on to me."

Lucian began climbing down a ladder she hadn't noticed. Effie didn't once worry about falling. Lucian wouldn't let her.

"I'll take her," Kael said, holding out his arms for her as they neared the landing.

"No, it's fine," Lucian said, the sound of his voice rumbling against her cheek.

Peering through her hair, Effie watched Kael nod and step back.

"Mother's tits," Ronan whispered from somewhere out of view.

Effie held onto Lucian tighter, attempting to hide as much of her gore-spattered body as possible.

"Effie, look at me," he ordered.

She shook her head.

"Look at me, fledgling," he said again, this time in a voice coated in steel. He wasn't taking no for an answer.

Loosening her grip, she lifted her chin. A tremor ran down Lucian's body as his eyes roamed over her face.

Not knowing what else to say, Effie blurted the first thing that came to mind. "You owe me a new weapon. Lots of them. Something more substantial than a fucking dagger."

Lucian's eyes widened, and his mouth curled into a smile. "Is that so?" He tilted his head. "Seems like you managed well enough."

Some of the horror of what happened must have shone in her eyes because Lucian's smile faltered.

"I'll get you whatever you want," he said gruffly. "If you don't know how to use it, we'll train you until you do."

Effie nodded, relieved that much, at least, would be settled. She started to lower her face back to his shoulder, preferring to stay out of sight as much as possible.

"Wait," Lucian said, halting the movement. "I need to set you down for a second so I can get a better hold on you. It's a long walk back to the portal from here."

"Should we try and make her a litter?" Kael asked from behind her. "It might be more comfortable."

"Effie?" Lucian asked, looking down at her.

She dug her nails into his back and shook her head.

The only place she wanted to be right now was in Lucian's arms. She hated that it made her appear weak, but he was the only thing keeping the panic at bay, and she didn't want to risk it coming back. Some combination of his strength, scent, or maybe just the steady sound of his heartbeat had managed to make her feel more like herself than she had since ending up in the treehouse.

Effie didn't recognize the savage creature she'd turned into up there, and she never wanted to be that thing again. She didn't care that it might have just been her sense of self-preservation taking over. She'd been scared of a lot of things in her life, but nothing so much as who—what—she'd turned into when facing off with Jo and Tess. That other Effie was beyond terrifying.

Especially since she could still feel the echoes of pleasure she'd experience when destroying Jo.

Revulsion made her stomach roll, and Effie squeezed her eyes shut. *No. I would* never *take pleasure in killing anyone.*

She repeated the mantra over and over. It was one thing to kill for survival, but another to revel in it. Effie didn't want to be the kind of person that enjoyed another person's pain. Not even if they deserved it.

"I'll carry her," Lucian said. Dipping his chin to whisper in her ear, he added, "I won't let you go."

"Thank you."

After wrapping up her ankle in a makeshift bandage, and a quick bit of strategizing, the men worked out the fastest way to get out of the trees and back to the portal. Effie leaned against Lucian, barely hearing any of it. She was numb. Numb to the pain and to her surroundings.

"She's shutting down," Kael said, sounding like he was speaking from a great distance.

"It's battle fatigue," Ronan said. "I recognize the symptoms."

It wasn't until Lucian spoke that she snapped back to the conversation.

"We need to get her to a healer."

"Not the healing wing," Effie protested weakly as Lucian lifted her back up, cradling her in his arms.

"You need to get your wounds tended to," Lucian insisted.

"I'm tired of waking up in that cold, sterile room. Can't they tend to me in my suite? If not, they may as well just put my damn name on the door and let me redecorate considering how much time I've spent in there."

Lucian's lips flattened. "We'll go to the healers, so as not to inconvenience them, but you can stay with me."

"Okay," she said, letting her eyes fall closed as Lucian started walking.

"I fucking hate it when you agree with me that easily," he muttered darkly, lengthening his strides.

Effie's lips twitched, but her eyes remained closed. "Why's that?"

"Because it means something's seriously wrong."

189

CHAPTER 24

*I*n the end, Lucian didn't end up taking her to the healing wing first. He started down the hall that would take them there and didn't make it more than two steps before noticing the way Effie was cringing away from the others' curious stares.

"I don't want them to see me like this," she whispered.

He recognized the shame and guilt in her voice. Every warrior knew what it was like to walk off the battlefield feeling like you'd left some part of your humanity behind.

Lucian felt her pain like a knife to the heart. Effie shouldn't have to know what that was like. He was supposed to protect her. Not that she couldn't fight her own battles, but she shouldn't have to. Why should she bloody her hands when his were more than stained enough for the both of them?

"I'm going to help her clean up first. You guys report in," he said, sending Kael and Ronan away.

He'd been carrying Effie for over an hour, but barely felt her slight weight as he took her to his room. The way he was feeling right now, he might never let her go again. That was twice in the span of a week he'd thought he lost her. Lucian didn't think he'd survive a third.

Not without burning down the world around him.

"Where are we going?" she asked, lifting her head and looking around.

"To get you washed up."

"In your room?" she asked as he kicked open the door to the Guardians' shared chamber.

"Would you prefer somewhere else?"

Her eyes were a brilliant blue as they blinked up at him from her blood-smeared face. "This is probably a bad time to try and get me naked, Guardian."

Lucian snorted. "Trust me, fledgling, if that was my intent, I'm sure you'd be more than willing."

Effie's lips lifted in the barest hint of a smile, and some of the weight in Lucian's chest lifted. If she was smiling, then she would come back to him. Maybe not tonight, or even tomorrow, but she would recover from the horrors of the day.

"You're probably right," she muttered as he carried her through his room and into his black tiled bathing chamber.

"Just to be safe, we'll leave the clothes on," he whispered, earning another rasping chuckle.

Lucian smacked the silver tile that allowed the warm water to flow from the ceiling.

"You're going to get wet," Effie protested when Lucian stepped beneath the spray with her still cradled in his arms.

"So are you."

It wasn't long before the water that fell to the floor was tinged red. Needing to distract himself from the possibility that more of that blood was hers than she let on, Lucian set Effie down on a bench set back into the wall of the shower.

"Isn't the point of your shower that you're supposed to remain standing?" Effie asked with a laugh, lifting a hand to brush her hair off of her face.

Lucian pressed another small disk in the wall, dispersing a white cream. "If I recall correctly, you weren't so good at the standing part even without an injured ankle."

Effie stuck her tongue out, and Lucian's heart clenched. With each fresh wave of gore that ran down the drain, the more of the woman he knew returned to him. Distantly, Lucian realized that caring for her like this might have been just as much for him as it was for her.

Rubbing his hands together, Lucian began to lather the soap.

"Shift a bit to your left," he instructed.

Eyeing him suspiciously, Effie did as she was told.

Lucian began to run his hands through her hair, detangling the matted strands as carefully as he could, while still massaging the soap into her scalp and using his thumbs to press into the knotted muscles along her neck.

Effie let out a little moan that he felt straight in his groin.

Not the time.

"That feels amazing, Lucian."

The rest of his blood flowed south as he struggled to focus on washing the soap from her hair. She might be making the sweetest noises he'd ever heard, but this was hardly a seduction.

She's injured, you ass. Lucian forced himself to pay attention to the cuts and scrapes covering most of her skin to help alleviate the sudden tightness in his pants.

He couldn't tell which of them was breathing harder by the time he was done and Effie was clean once more.

Turning off the flow of water, he said, "If you'd like, I can run you a bath so you can soak for a bit before we get that ankle taken care of. Or, if you're in a lot of pain, we'll dry you off and get it handled straight away."

Effie's eyes glowed as she peeked up at him with a small smile playing on her lips. "Would you be getting in with me?"

Lucian closed his eyes, more tempted than he'd ever been by the image of their bodies sliding against each other beneath the water. "That's probably not a good idea," he said in a strangled voice.

"I trust you," she said, reaching out and taking his hand.

"It's a good thing one of us does."

Her laugh was low and husky. "We'll both behave. I just want to be close to you, Lucian. You keep the darkness away."

His eyes snapped open and his desire ebbed at the haunted look in her crystalline eyes.

"Part of war is death, Effie. No one will blame you for doing what you had to do."

It killed him when Effie looked away from him, pain etched in every curve of her body. She was holding herself so carefully, as if one wrong move would see her falling apart.

"There's self-defense and then there's what happened today," she said, her voice hollow.

Needing to touch her, Lucian settled for pushing a few blonde curls away from her face, letting his fingers linger along her jaw. "Tell me what happened."

She shook her head. "Please don't make me."

"No one makes you do anything, remember? But, I do think it will make you feel better."

"I think you're wrong."

Lucian sighed, crouching down until his face was level with hers. "Effie, I know what it means to take a life. To recognize the person on the other end of your sword as you watch the light fade from their eyes. It's a bloody business, but it's inevitable."

"She was my friend," Effie said, her voice broken.

"She wasn't the person you knew anymore."

"You think I don't know that? That it makes it better? Lucian, I—" she broke off, pressing her lips together and shaking her head.

"You what?"

"I *destroyed* her," she whispered, the look in her eyes so devastated it hurt him to look at her. Effie's hands shook as she lifted them. "I destroyed her with my bare hands. I didn't stop, Lucian. Not even when she was dead. I-I couldn't stop."

She was crying openly now, her entire body shaking with the force of her sobs.

Lucian pulled her into his arms, sitting down on the shower floor and easily supporting Effie's weight as she fell against him. "You were protecting yourself."

"No—"

"Yes," he insisted. "Effie, neither her nor Tess would have hesitated to kill you. You've seen what the Shadow-touched can do. They aren't human."

"They still knew who I was, Lucian. It wasn't like with Tinka. They weren't mindless beasts."

"Not yet, but who's to say that's not where it was heading? We have no idea how quickly the corruption transforms its host."

"Tess is still out there somewhere."

"We'll find her."

Effie scrubbed at her face, hiding behind the palms of her hands.

"Hey," Lucian murmured, tugging gently on her wrist. "Don't hide from me."

"How can you even stand to look at me after what I did?"

"You think what you did today compares to the worst of what I've done in my lifetime? You want to talk about darkness, Effie, I can promise you my soul is blacker than yours will ever be."

Effie shook her head, her expression fierce. "Not possible."

"How can you be so sure?" he asked, lifting his brow.

She rested her hand over his chest. "I see who you are, Lucian. There might be darkness, but it is eclipsed by all that is good and honorable within you."

Her words gutted him. "Effie, if you can be certain, so can I," he finally managed.

She opened her mouth to argue, and he pressed a finger against her lips.

"Do you trust me?"

"With my life," she answered, without hesitation.

"Then believe me when I say, nothing you could do would ever change what I see when I look at you."

Her pulse fluttered in her neck, and then they were crashing together, their lips and tongues tangling in their desperation to get closer.

Earlier promises forgotten, Lucian ran his hands along the sides of her leather-clad body, pulling her more solidly astride him. The leather vest she wore over her tunic was water-logged, the fabric swollen and difficult to manipulate. Lucian quickly gave up bothering with the buckles, feeling little guilt about tapping into his power to deal with removing it. If ever there was a time to take advantage of the ability to transform matter, surely it was now.

Effie let out a soft chuckle as the garment fell free. Grasping a side of her vest, he flung it across the room, smiling when its wet slap caused her to laugh harder.

"Neat trick," she murmured, her thumbs feathering over his neck as she wove her hands into his hair and leaned in to kiss him.

"I'm full of them," he murmured against her mouth, biting down on her plump bottom lip.

Effie whimpered and shifted her weight above him.

"Am I hurting you?" Lucian asked, sliding his hands under her tunic and up her back, pulling the wet fabric with him.

"I'm going to hurt you if you stop," she hissed, trailing hot kisses along his jaw, before sitting back so that Lucian could pull off her tunic.

All that was left was a transparent scrap of fabric that left little to the imagination. But it was still a barrier between them, and he wanted none. Running his finger down the center of her chest, Lucian hooked it down into the flimsy band and pulled, the soft scrap giving way.

Effie peered at him shyly, her cheeks flushed and lips swollen from their kisses.

Lucian swallowed, his blood roaring in his ears as he tried to find the words to tell her how beautiful she was in that moment. Drops of water cascaded down her creamy skin, her wheat-colored hair looking like burnished gold where it clung to her neck. Her thick lashes were dark spikes framing glowing blue eyes.

Running his eyes down the column of her throat, Lucian paused in his exploration to brush his thumb over the raised, silvery crescent of her scar. The scar itself was horrific, thick and jagged, and running from the base of her neck to halfway across the top of her shoulder. But for Lucian, it was a testament to her fearless spirit. She'd earned it saving his life.

Leaning forward, he reverently pressed his lips to the mark.

Effie shivered, her head falling back as she moaned his name. "Lucian."

Letting his eyes dip down lower, he watched the rapid rise and fall of her chest as the rosy peaks pebbled, begging for him to take them in his mouth.

Her breath caught as she waited for his next move. "Touch me," she begged.

Curling his arm around her, Lucian pulled her closer until her breasts brushed against his chest.

She fit against him like a dream, her body built like it was made for him. Sliding his hands from her waist and down over her rounded ass, he flexed his hips up into her center.

Effie gasped and ground down on him, increasing the friction until Lucian was the one groaning.

He dipped his head, raining kisses along her velvety soft skin. She arched up into him, fisting her hands in his hair when he finally took one of her nipples into his mouth, sucking hard, palming her other breast with his free hand.

"Finally," she groaned.

Lucian scraped his teeth along the sensitive flesh and pulled back to look at her. "We're just getting started."

Effie let out a strangled breath, dropping her forehead to his. "Who said you could stop?"

Suddenly she froze in his arms, letting out a hiss that had nothing to do with pleasure and everything to do with pain.

"Effie?" Lucian asked, worried that he might have accidentally touched one of her injuries.

"Lucian . . ." His name was a strangled gasp, confusion and fear permeating the word.

"What's wrong?" he asked, his hands hovering over her skin, afraid to touch her.

"I—" she broke off with another cry, curling her right arm into her body. "Mother's tits, that hurts."

"What? What's going on?" Lucian was trying to keep his panic in check, not certain what was happening except that Effie was in a lot of pain. "Is it your ankle?"

Effie shook her head; the feverish desire he'd seen in her eyes only seconds before replaced with tears. "It's . . . agony," she hissed, her back arching as her thighs spasmed around him.

The veins in her neck jutted out, the muscles in her neck rigid. She gritted her teeth and dug her fingers into her arms as another tremor racked her body. It looked like she was having some kind of convulsion, almost like a slow-motioned imitation of what happened to her when she had a vision.

Lucian tried to take her in his arms, but Effie let out a low, keening wail as if his touch only caused greater pain.

He dropped his hands as if she burned him.

She cried out again, the sound burying itself inside of his chest. She was in pain, and there was *nothing* he could do to stop it. He couldn't even hold her.

Not knowing what other option was left to him, Lucian threw back his head and roared.

"KAEL!"

CHAPTER 25

*E*mbarrassed, frustrated, and more than a little scared, Effie pulled the blanket tighter around her bare shoulders, not ready to face the hooded gazes surrounding her.

What more could she tell them? It wasn't like she understood why her body felt like someone had shoved a white-hot rod straight into her bones. One second she'd been blissfully lost to the feel of Lucian's mouth on her, and the next it felt like she was being melted from the inside out. And not in a good way.

She'd been too overwhelmed by the searing pain working its way through her to pay much attention, but Kael had come tearing into Lucian's bathing chamber, only to take one look at them huddled on the floor of the shower to spin back out again.

By the time her fit had passed, two robed figures and a healer were waiting for her in Lucian's room.

The healer had taken care of the worst of her injuries, but there was little he could do about the deep ache in Effie's muscles. She'd likely be sore for a couple of days.

"Is there anything else I can do for you?" the elder gentleman asked in a low, soothing voice.

Effie attempted a smile and shook her head. "No, but my thanks to you."

With a little bow, he left the room, leaving Effie to the mercy of the three men surrounding her.

"What?" she snapped, needing to break the uncomfortable silence.

"What happened?" Lucian countered.

Effie shrugged. "I already told you."

"You haven't said shit," he said, crossing his arms and leaning against the wall. Lucian's tanned skin was pale, his eyes all but black as he stared at her. She'd scared him.

Trying to alleviate some of the tension, she glanced at the men wearing the scarlet robes and asked, "Are you going to let him get away with talking to me like that?"

"Answer the question."

She frowned. "I don't know what to tell you. Yes, my ankle hurt, but it wasn't anything I couldn't handle. Then, out of nowhere, this bone-deep ache started working its way through me. The ache turned into a burn, which turned into . . . *something*. I don't know where it came from, or why it happened."

"How do you feel now?"

"Fine."

Lucian scowled at her, and Effie flinched.

"Okay, I'm a little sore, but I'm *fine*. I swear. More embarrassed than anything."

And tired, she added to herself. After the day she'd had, all she wanted to do was curl up with Lucian and sleep for a year. Maybe two.

"What were you doing right before the pain started?"

Effie went crimson and risked a glance at Lucian. "Taking a shower."

"Has anything like this happened before?"

"No. Never."

The questions halted, and Effie wondered if they were talking amongst themselves. Her theory was confirmed when Lucian straightened. She's suspected for a while that the Triumvirate frequently communicated telepathically with their Guardians, but this was the first time she'd witnessed them doing so. Generally, they made a point to include everyone present in their conversations—at least she'd assumed they had.

"She'll stay with me tonight."

The two Triumvirate members bowed their heads in agreement.

"Let us know if anything else of note occurs during the night."

Effie looked back to Lucian and could tell from his expression that absolutely nothing of 'note' was going to happen between them tonight. He still looked pissed.

She let out a disappointed sigh. Things had been going so well.

"Rest well, Daughter."

"We'll see you in the morning."

"Goodnight," she called softly as they left.

The silence stretched, and Effie shifted uncomfortably on the bed when Lucian made no move to come closer to her.

Staring down at her lap, she wiggled a finger through a tiny hole in the black wool. "I'm sorry," she mumbled.

"Sorry? What the hell for?" Lucian asked, sounding truly baffled.

"For being a constant inconvenience. It seems like you are always having to *deal* with me."

"You are not an inconvenience."

She let out a bitter laugh. "Sure. And you're not currently plotting the fastest way you can get out of here."

Effie heard a rustle of fabric as Lucian crossed the room.

"You want to know what I'm thinking right now? I'm trying to figure out how to ask you if I can hold you, and knowing that it makes me a selfish bastard to ask anything of you right now."

"You-you what?" she asked, her head snapping up.

Tension was practically rolling off of Lucian. His muscles were tense, his eyes wild. Her Guardian was on the brink, but of what, Effie didn't know.

"Of course you can."

Lucian closed his eyes, his throat bobbing as he swallowed. He unclenched his hands, flexing the fingers as he sucked in a breath.

"Lay down," he demanded.

She pushed back from the edge of the bed and scooted back until she was on the other side, leaving room for him to sit down beside her.

Lucian was still wearing the same damp clothes he'd been wearing while showering with her, but he made no move to remove them. Instead, he unlaced his boots and tossed them on the floor and then swung his legs up and rolled to face her.

"Roll over."

She shifted until she was facing the wall, her back facing Lucian.

Without a word, he wrapped his arm around her and pulled her against him until her back was pressed against his chest.

Lifting a hand out from the blanket, she ran it along his fisted hand. He let out a breath that sounded suspiciously like a sob, his hand trembling beneath hers.

"Lucian . . ." She started to lift her head.

"Sleep, Effie. I'll watch over you."

Lacing her fingers through his, Effie snuggled into the pillow and closed her eyes. After what happened in the treehouse, she didn't expect to find sleep easily. But her body was exhausted, and it wasn't long before she drifted off, if not peacefully, at least with the certainty that nothing would dare come for her while Lucian stood guard.

CHAPTER 26

*K*ieran turned the corner and came to a complete stop when a door opened, side-stepping into an open room to remain hidden. He knew the Guardians resided in this particular wing of the citadel, but it was the quickest route to the Hall of Prophecy, and he had to get this book back before anyone discovered it was missing.

A soft giggle made him freeze.

Effie? What in the hell is she *doing over here?*

Craning his neck around the doorway, Kieran let out a low hiss as rage started to bubble up within him.

She took a step into the hallway, wearing a shirt that fell down to her knees. She'd belted it around the waist to try to make it fit better, but there was little to be done to conceal the fact that the garment did not belong to her.

A low growl sounded in the back of his throat. There's only one reason a woman would leave a man's bedroom in the morning wearing his shirt. Kieran didn't need anyone to tell him just whose shirt it was either.

His suspicion was confirmed when an arm snaked out of the room and pulled her back.

Tilting her head up, she gave Lucian a sweet smile, her cheeks a bright pink. "I thought you told me I needed to go eat."

Lucian looked down at her, lifting a hand to caress the side of her face. "Not without a proper goodbye."

Effie twisted in his arms so that she was resting against the doorframe and facing the shirtless Guardian. "Is that so?"

Kieran watched the sickening display unfold like a man watching his entire life burn down around him. His knuckles were white where they gripped the wall, his breathing uneven. *No. No. NO!*

"What did you have in mind?" she asked, her voice so soft Kieran could only just make it out from where he was hiding.

Lucian tilted Effie's chin up, leaning down to run his nose along hers.

"Tease," she said, placing her hands on his shoulders.

Bending slightly, Lucian wrapped an arm just underneath her butt and lifted her up so that her face was level with his. She wrapped her legs around his waist and gave the Guardian a look so heated that a piece of the doorframe broke off in Kieran's hand.

He looked down at it in shock, his hands shaking, his nails torn and bloody from digging into the wood.

Effie's soft moan had Kieran spinning around and storming down the hall.

That fucking. Traitorous. Bitch! She'd rather debase herself by spreading her legs for some immortal bastard than be loved by the son of a king? Fine.

The little slut was no longer worthy of his affections.

But that didn't mean Kieran was going to stand by and allow anyone else to have what was rightfully his.

If he couldn't have her, no one would.

Kieran was shaking, barely seeing anything except the image of Effie in Lucian's arms.

"You lost?" a deep voice asked.

Kieran blinked, Kael's face swimming into view. "Are you?"

Kael lifted a brow, his green eyes narrowing. "I'm not the one walking around where I don't belong."

"Piss off."

"You don't want to pick a fight with me, princeling."

"Maybe that's exactly what I want to do," Kieran snarled, moving until his face was inches away from the other man's.

"Stand down," Kael whispered, those weird flecks in his eyes glowing.

Kieran clenched his jaw. "You all think you're so much better than me. You have no idea. No. Idea."

"You need to calm down."

"Make me, Guardian!" Kieran shouted, his rage bubbling over as he swung his fist up.

Kael dodged, and Kieran's fist went slamming into the wall. He felt the crack of bone all the way up his arm, but the pain did little to dampen his temper. Pulling his fist back, Kieran moved to strike again.

The Guardian caught his arm before the blow could land. "What the fuck are you doing? Do you have a death wish, princeling? Is that it?"

"Maybe I'm just tired of looking at your fucking dimples."

Kael grinned, but there was nothing pleasant about the baring of teeth. "That's just too fucking bad." Leaning forward, he dropped his voice. "The others may have forgotten about your little trick in the cave, but I haven't. I'm watching you, princeling. You're up to something, and I'm going to figure it out."

Not until it's too late. "Good luck with that."

Kael shoved Kieran away with a palm to the chest. The blow was forceful enough that Kieran went staggering back.

"Go take a cold shower and cool off. If you're still like this when I find you again, you and I are going a few rounds in the ring. With weapons. Trust me, you don't want that."

Kieran snarled at Kael but didn't bother responding. He had no intention of cooling off. No intention of doing anything but what he should have done in the first place.

Fuck the markers. Fuck the sneaking around. The time for games was over.

Effie needed to pay for her treachery.

They were *all* going to pay.

It was time the Keepers learned what happened when you betrayed a royal son of Eatos.

CHAPTER 27

*E*ffie smiled softly to herself as she folded up Lucian's shirt and set it down carefully on her desk. She would never forget the wonder of waking up in his arms. Those first sleep-fogged moments when she couldn't remember anything outside of the man beside her. Not the horrors of yesterday's battle. Not the visions. Nothing but how peaceful he looked as he slept.

Unable to help herself, she'd traced the arches of his brows, and ran her finger gently over the space between them that was usually creased in some sort of scowl. Although lately, less of those broody glares had been leveled her way.

When he'd opened his eyes to find her staring at him, he'd smiled and reached out to cup her face.

Shivers ran through her as she replayed his husky growl as he'd looked at her. "Good morning, beautiful."

The quiet moment was likely the most intimate of her life. It was the first time she'd spent the entire night curled in a man's arms. She'd never slept better.

Effie could have happily spent the entire day there, pretending that they were the only two people in the world . . . but ever dutiful, Lucian reminded her that she was supposed to check in with both the healer and the Triumvirate after breakfast.

As much as she wanted to explore the hard planes of his chest and continue where they'd left off in the shower, the timing was wrong. Maybe once this was over, she and Lucian would have a chance to finish what they'd started.

Sighing wistfully, she picked up the shirt and brought it to her face, breathing in the scent of Lucian a final time. He wasn't getting it back anytime soon, she decided, carrying it over to her bed and stuffing it beneath her pillow.

She made it two steps out the door before realizing she'd left her journal on the desk. Smoke had requested she bring it with her for their sessions. He wanted to search for recurring images and track their appearance throughout her visions. Considering that all of her visions since arriving at the citadel seemed to be filled with blood and Shadows, she wasn't sure how helpful that was going to be, but he was the expert.

In the two months she'd been at the citadel, the only thing Effie knew with certainty about her visions was there was nothing certain about them. She was still suffering the same side effects and the warning hidden within the frightening images were no easier to decipher than when she'd gotten her first one.

If anything, they were worse now. Perhaps not the side effects, but definitely the complex nature of the visions themselves. Every time she started to believe she was getting a handle on them, they evolved.

An all-too-familiar buzzing started just beneath the surface of her skin, and Effie shivered. The feeling intensified as she moved down the hall. Usually, she could identify what sent off the warning, but this time it appeared without prompting.

Unease crawled through her, making her stomach tighten. Glancing around, Effie double checked that she was still alone.

Quickening her steps, Effie rushed on until she was practically running through the citadel.

Where is everybody?

As if the thought was the trigger she'd been waiting for, her vision went black, and Effie skidded to her knees.

COUGHS RACKED *her body and tears filled her eyes as she tried to See what was happening. She couldn't make out anything through the thick gray fog that surrounded her.*

Tendrils of smoke separated themselves from the haze and wrapped themselves around her ankles, turning into clawed hands as they crawled up her body.

She tried to run, but the hands held her in place while the swirling fog turned into row after row of faceless bodies.

Swinging her arms, Effie tried to push the army away from her when they—along with the acrid fog—vanished.

The space around her filled with books until hundreds of heavy tomes towered around her. Looking down, she was standing on a stack of books, each one easily the size of a table.

Peering closer, she noticed that the glowing title beneath her feet was written in runes. Across the room, a book flew open, the pages rapidly turning before tearing themselves free of the binding and taking flight.

All around her thousands of whispering voices filled the room. The words were indistinct, but their urgency grew with their volume until the indecipherable voices were screaming in her ear.

Stumbling down, hands over her ears, Effie fell from the tower of books, the page-birds circling above her as she tumbled into the darkness.

BREATHING HARD, Effie pushed herself up, cold sweat dripping down her neck. While the vision had passed, the harsh buzzing still raced through her veins.

"At least that one wasn't as bad as the last," she muttered, trying to get to her feet.

A wave of dizziness hit her, and she reached for the wall, using it to keep her upright as her eyes fell closed and she struggled to catch her breath.

The smell of smoke still filled her nose and she coughed, even though the hall was clear.

Worried now, Effie lurched forward, her steps still staggering. *Smoke. I need to get to Smoke.*

Ronan found her drunkenly weaving her way down the hall, her body taking longer than usual to recover from her vision.

She grasped his arm gratefully, not giving him a chance to speak before she sputtered, "I need to see Smoke."

Concern shot through his gaze, but Ronan didn't question her. "The Triumvirate are gathered in the archives. I was actually just coming to find you. They think they might have found something."

She gave him what she hoped passed for a grateful smile and started off in that direction, Ronan matching her pace and offering her an arm to help balance her steps.

"Thank you," she murmured, leaning on him more heavily than she would have liked.

Together, they made it to the central archive, Effie seeing nothing of the opulent room except the shelves filled with books. Her heart started to race as she moved deeper into the room.

Images from her vision started to take shape, and it was hard to tell the difference between what was real and imagined. Effie swatted at a paper bird diving at her head before she realized she was the only one who could see it. Embarrassed, she dropped her arm and focused on the three scarlet-robed men.

The central one turned his hooded face to her. *"Daughter?"* Smoke inquired, his usually soothing voice concerned.

Effie opened and closed her mouth, suddenly worried that her vision might have been a warning about the Keeper. Shaking her head, she shoved the thought away, refusing to accept the possibility.

"I had a vision," she said, pausing to lick her lips. "It was similar to the last. Well, slightly more coherent, but only just. There was fog, thick and acrid, it turned into bodies. An army. They marched upon me and then vanished. Then books—" she gestured around herself wildly

"—started to take flight. Well, pages from books. The titles were written in runes."

Effie stopped talking, her head pounding. It felt like the warning was just out of reach. Why would pages from books fly about the room?

Within her, the buzz of her premonition turned into a shriek. Effie bit back a cry, not wanting to call more attention to herself. The vision was what was important right now. They needed to focus on that, and then they could deal with whatever madness was inside her.

"A prophecy is coming true," Smoke said as if it was the most obvious thing in the world.

"Which prophecy?" Ronan bit out.

One of the Mirrors shook his head. *"It's too soon to say."*

"Is there a hint in my vision?" Effie asked, her hands balling into fists as another jolt of premonition raced through her.

"Perhaps."

"One of our books is missing."

"We believe it contains the answers we've been seeking."

"Missing? How?"

"Who else had access to your collection?" Ronan asked, perhaps more helpfully.

"This particular volume? No one. It was sealed off in the Hall of Prophecy."

A gasp escaped as dead weight sat heavy in Effie's neck and chest. Her gift was no longer warning her something was coming.

It was already here.

Effie tried to speak around the unexpected weight, but it was a struggle just to breathe.

"Daughter?" Smoke asked, the first to notice, as always, that something was happening to her.

Before she could try and answer, a loud boom rang out. Ears ringing, Effie couldn't hear anything as the swirling lights floating around the room flickered out.

Red runes sparked to life along the floor, casting the room in an unearthly glow. Ronan shoved Effie behind him, reaching for a weapon he didn't have.

Her hearing slowly returned, and she could make out bits of phrases, and the men made plans behind her, but Effie barely made note of them. She was more worried about the screams coming from another part of the building. They confirmed what she'd already known, what her gift had been shouting at her to recognize.

The citadel was under attack.

CHAPTER 28

"*H*ow did they breach the citadel?" Ronan demanded, the need for vengeance blazing in his eyes.

"Nothing is impenetrable if given the key."

"You think someone let them in?" Effie asked, spinning to face Smoke.

There was a shrug. *"It is the only plausible answer."*

"But who?" she sputtered, her thoughts immediately turning to Tess.

Effie gasped. *Is this my fault?* The Keeper would be familiar with the portals and other secrets of the citadel. It was not a far stretch that she would come seeking revenge. But the screaming . . . this was not the work of one Shadow-touched female.

The ground started to tremble and bits of stone fell from the ceiling.

A vicious growl sounded deep in Ronan's chest. "Where the fuck are your Guardians?"

"Doing their job."

Effie's heart seized at the thought of Lucian caught unaware. *If anyone can withstand a surprise attack, he can.* She knew that it was true. Lucian was the fiercest among them, but her heart could not help but worry.

More tremors shook the building and a beam snapped from the ceiling, narrowly missing them as it crashed to the floor.

Thunder that had nothing to do with the shaking building swelled in the room. The Triumvirate's anger was palpable, their emotional storm almost as frightening as the unexpected attack.

"Get her out of here. Quickly!"

"And take her where?" Ronan snapped. "This was supposed to be the safest place in Elysia."

Appalled, Effie shot an accusing glare at her mentor. "If you think I'm going to run away like a scared little mouse then you clearly do not know me at all. I will stay and fight with the rest of you."

She could feel the weight of Smoke's stare settle over her. *"Many were likely caught unarmed. Go to the armory. Gather what you can for them."*

"And what will you do?" Effie asked, her body already angled toward the hallway that would lead them to the room filled with weapons.

"Protect what is ours."

Effie had not seen the Triumvirate fight—it's what the Guardians were for—but a shiver of fear crept down her spine at the ominous words. She was glad they were on the same side.

Ronan was already running, Effie just behind him, when she stopped mid-flight to fling her arms around Smoke. "Stay safe," she said into his chest, squeezing tightly as she offered a quick prayer to the Mother to protect her friends.

"You as well, Daughter," he said, his voice oddly thick in her mind as he returned her embrace. *"Now, go."*

His hands burned where they wrapped around her wrists to pry her off of him. With a shaky breath and a little nod, Effie started to sprint for the door. She didn't dare to look back. Not when the loud slam of doors bursting open echoed down the hall or the sound of wet grunts filled the air.

With a choked cry, she pumped her legs faster. She was almost down the hall when there was another splintering crack. The sprinkling of dust on her arms was the only warning she needed. Effie flung herself forward, rolling awkwardly as she hit the floor.

Panting, heart lodged somewhere in her throat, Effie stared at the mountain of debris that was now filling the hallway. The ceiling had caved in. Two seconds more and she would have been trapped beneath it.

A large hand grasped her by the arm and pulled her up.

"No time to linger."

"Ronan," she gasped, "the kind of power necessary to do this—"

"Shadows, aye, I know. We've killed them before; we'll do it again."

"Yeah, with an entire army. Ronan, an attack of this magnitude—" Effie shook her head, unable to finish the sentence.

Placing both his hands on her shoulders, Ronan shook her slightly. "Look at me."

Stomach rolling, she obeyed.

"You cannot worry about the odds. One enemy at a time. That is how we'll win. Do you understand me?"

Effie nodded. "Yes, sir."

"Good. Now, we have orders—"

"Ronan!"

Reyna's shout had both their heads snapping toward her.

"Reyna?"

"RUN!" she screamed, bloodshot eyes wide with panic as she frantically raced toward them. She was only half-dressed, but already covered in blood and ichor, a lone curved blade her only weapon. For the Night Stalker to flee instead of fight . . . that could only mean one thing. She was badly outnumbered.

Behind her, three blue-robed healers followed suit, one tripping in his haste. He fell to the ground with a pitiful whimper, one of his friends skidding to a halt to turn and help him. It was the last thing they ever did.

Just behind them, four Shadows stalked forward, forming an evil sort of diamond as they chased those fleeing.

215

The central figure, more skeletal than anything animated with life had a right to be, held out its hands. The two healers began to gasp, clutching their throats as the Shadow pulled the air from their lungs.

Effie watched in growing horror, their strangled cries breaking her heart. Without weapons of their own, there was no way to fight back. Not even to distract the Shadow long enough for the suffocating healers to try and escape.

Ronan let out a savage roar, calling up his twin powers of Fire and Earth.

Effie gaped, remembering Ronan didn't need weapons to be deadly. He was Chosen. His power was more than enough to protect him.

Maybe they had a chance after all . . .

The Shadow grinned then, most of his teeth visible through the gaping hole in his cheek. His eyes focused on Effie as he curled his left hand into a fist, cutting off the healers' cries. The silence more horrifying than anything else as their lifeless bodies dropped to the floor.

Ronan threw his power into the ground. The effect was instant, the ground began to grow and swell, cresting like a wave.

"Let's go!" he shouted, not waiting to see the result of his efforts.

Reyna was already barreling past him, the last of the healers hot on her heels. With a final glance at the four Shadows, Effie watched the shock wave make contact, knocking the Shadows off of their feet and slamming them to the ground.

Knowing it wouldn't keep them occupied for long, Effie started running.

"In here!" Ronan called, slamming open the dining hall doors as he careened into the empty room.

"We need weapons," Effie reminded him. "How is hiding in here going to help us?"

Ronan lifted a brow, moving to the back of the room. "We'll never make it to the armory before they catch up. At least in here we have options."

She eyed the rows of wooden tables with their stacked dishes. "Are we planning on hurling plates at them?"

The Shield held open the door to the kitchen with a dark grin. "I find that chef knives can be quite deadly."

Of course.

Reyna was rifling through the knives, running her fingers along the blades and testing their balance. "These will work well for throwing," she murmured.

Effie's attention was seized by blades twice the size of her forearm. Hefting the meat cleavers, she gave a test swing, trying to get used to their weight in her hands.

Ronan let out a low whistle. "You'll have to get close with those."

It was Effie's turn to give him a savage grin. "Without fire, the only way to stop them for good is to remove the head. I was going to have to get close anyway. At least these will be faster than a dagger."

Ronan nodded, selecting a heavy-looking mallet and the longest knife as his own. "I can't risk using my Fire without burning the entire place down around us."

"Decapitation it is then," Reyna said, moving to stand beside him.

Reyna's dark hair was unbound and tangled, hanging to her waist in a mess of braids. Her skin was deathly pale and waxy, her lips cracked and her eyes feverish. She hardly looked well enough to stand, let alone fight. The lajhár poison had affected her far worse than the rest of them. Effie could only assume it had something to do with her being a Night Stalker, since she and Kael both seemed to have made full recoveries.

"Maybe you should sit this one out," Effie murmured.

Reyna's eyes went dark and dangerous. "The day I stop fighting is the day I die."

"What about you?" Ronan asked, talking to the healer curled up into a ball near the massive hearth.

"I-I don't fight, sir. It goes against everything I believe in to cause harm."

Tossing a blade at the shaking man's feet, Ronan said, "Perhaps you better learn how to get over that. It's them or you. Your choice."

217

Looking like he was about to be ill, the healer nodded, picking up the knife with trembling hands.

"You know which end to use, right?" Ronan added.

Effie would have thought Ronan was joking if his face hadn't been cast in such grim lines.

"Yes, sir."

"Good."

Even though Effie was waiting for it, the crash of wood smacking into stone made her jump.

"They're here," she said, tightening her grip around the heavy wooden handles.

CHAPTER 29

*E*ffie peered out the wide window, taking care to stay hidden.

The Shadows moved into the dining hall, looking like they were out for a leisurely stroll. There was no need for them to rush, the victory—in their minds—assured.

"Come out, come out, wherever you are," one of them crooned in a rasping voice.

"Be careful what you wish for," Reyna snarled, hurling the first of her knives.

It struck true, burying itself in the rightmost Shadow's eye.

"Now that wasn't very nice," it said, pulling the blade—and its eye —free with a disgusting pop.

"These are the same Shadows that killed the healers, so we know at least one of them controls Air," Ronan murmured, standing on the opposite side of the window as Effie.

"Should we assume there's one of each?" Effie whispered, thinking that a full set of corrupted elements was going to be damn near impossible to beat on their own.

"Mother, I hope not," Ronan said.

Effie closed her eyes. *Please don't let there be Fire.* Exhaling, she opened her eyes and waited for Ronan's signal.

Between them, Reyna threw another one of her knives.

The Air Shadow knocked it to the floor with a wave. "Is that the best you can do?"

Reyna bared her teeth, blades resting between each of her fingers. "Hardly," she snarled, unleashing a fan of knives so quickly that the Shadows didn't have time to react. The four blades finding homes in the throats of each of the Shadows.

"Now," Ronan said, diving through the opening running full speed at the one-eyed Shadow.

Effie opted for the door, as it provided a clearer path to the Shadow on the right. She was knocked back before she was halfway. *Earth*, she realized as the floor opened up before her. Struggling to her feet, she finally noticed what she'd missed before. All four of the Shadows wore familiar black robes.

The missing Keepers. Bile rose in her throat at the thought of more of her peers dying by her hand. *How could you let this happen?* she thought angrily, sending the accusation to the Mother. *You're supposed to protect your children.*

An all-too-familiar rage began to burn within her. *You don't get to condemn us.* With an angry bellow, Effie jumped across the chasm in the floor and hit the other side of the hall in a slide, her blade lodging itself into the Earth Shadow's shin and slicing clean through. Scrambling up, she twisted and swung her second blade at the fiend's neck.

A blast of Air knocked her sideways, making her miss her mark.

Effie let out a furious howl.

The Earth Shadow dropped to the floor, unable to support its weight with only one leg. In front of her, the Air Shadow lifted its hand, spittle flying from its mouth as it snarled at her.

Effie sucked in a ragged breath, her mind emptying as a vice clenched around her lungs.

No!

Nails scraped along her leg as the Earth Shadow pulled her to the floor. Stars exploded behind her eyes as the little bit of air she still had was knocked from her lungs.

Above her, she could hear Ronan roar. Reyna had joined them, but Effie couldn't see where she was, her vision going black at the edges. The healer was nowhere to be found.

It was getting hard to think as she struggled to breathe. Swinging blindly, Effie lodged one of her blades into the Shadow crawling over her. Hot ichor spurted over her face and neck.

Suddenly, the pressure on her chest lifted, and Effie sucked in breath after painful breath, her throat burning.

Spots still dancing, she could only just make out the Shadow above her as it licked its lips and leaned down to sniff her.

"So good," it groaned, running its tongue along her neck and across the scar where its brethren had marked her.

Disgust curled her lip, and Effie brought up both arms in a pale imitation of an embrace. With a loud grunt, she slid the blades through the back of the creature's neck, almost entirely severing the head from its body.

More of the foul liquid poured forth, but Effie didn't care. She was too focused on pushing herself free of the Shadow, shoving her knee into its squishy chest and swinging her blade down to complete the kill.

Her blood sang with fierce satisfaction as the severed head rolled away. Looking up, she saw that Ronan and Reyna had taken care of two of the beasts, leaving only one left. One that was no longer near them.

Following their gazes, she found the last Shadow—and the healer. Or what was left of him. His eyes bulged from his head, blood dripping from every visible orifice as the Shadow played with him.

She had no idea what element the creature might have controlled, never having seen anything like this before.

"Hey!" Effie shouted, thinking only to stop the torture.

It twisted its neck, turning to face her. It was practically bald, only a few wisps of hair clinging to its head as it sneered at her. "Wait your turn," it hissed.

Effie gagged as it used its perverted power once more, causing the healer's swollen eyes to pop. More blood bubbled from its lips and nose, even after the healer was clearly dead.

Body on fire with her fury, Effie launched herself at the Shadow with a hoarse cry.

Ronan's shouts sounded behind her, but Effie heard nothing over the sound of her racing heart.

She tackled the beast, losing one of her cleavers in the process. Knowing she had no defense if it had the chance to turn its power on her, Effie slammed the base of her weapon down into the creature's face. Bones crunched beneath her, and Effie roared, slashing and slamming the weapon down faster than she thought possible.

There was no coherent thought, only the need to destroy.

Again and again she brought her weapon down, seeing nothing in her bloodlust.

Feeling a hand on her shoulder, Effie spun, snarling, her weapon raised and ready to strike.

"Effie, Effie, it's me! It's dead. You can stop."

She blinked up at Ronan's shocked face, not really seeing him. Shaking, Effie glanced back down. Not only had she severed the head from the body, she'd mutilated it beyond recognition.

Instead of disgust, she felt a savage pride.

Let the fiends come. She would tear them apart.

If the Mother wouldn't save them, Effie would.

CHAPTER 30

*K*ieran dragged the last of his prisoners through the portal with a satisfied grunt. When he'd laid the traps to catch the Keepers, he never imagined it would work so well. At his last count, he'd had a dozen of them locked up throughout the jungle, although two were missing when he went to claim them.

Still, ten Shadow-touched were more than enough to cause a little chaos.

To be fair, it wasn't Keepers he'd intended to catch. Not at first. Unfamiliar with the way the corruption spread, he only guessed that trapping creatures in a contaminated area would cause them to turn.

It wasn't until he'd found the first poor bastard in his trap that he realized the potential. Corrupted animals were one thing, but to use their own members against them? There was a certain kind of poetic justice to that. It would land a much stronger, emotional blow against the Keepers.

Besides, it never hurt to have an army on standby.

Getting them out of their cages had been trickier than catching them. He may have played a part in creating these Shadow-touched, but they hardly saw him as any sort of leader. He was smart enough to know better than to go anywhere near them until they were restrained.

Thankfully, he'd been prepared and had brought enough of the *Bella Morte* powder to knock them all out. Once unconscious, tying them up and dragging them through the jungle had been relatively easy.

Tugging on the ropes he'd tied around the waists and wrists of his last three pets, Kieran pulled them through the empty hallway and shoved them into a nearby room. They'd deteriorated quickly since he'd seen them last. No longer capable of speech, the once revered Keepers were now little more than animals.

Savage, blood-thirsty animals.

The *Bella Morte* had just started to wear off, his last dose significantly weaker than the first couple. It was hard to know how much he'd have to use, and Kieran cursed himself for wasting too much of the drug on his first batch.

He'd need to hurry now; they were starting to regain consciousness. The first Shadow-touched opened its eyes and immediately growled at him, gnashing its teeth and struggling against its bindings. The others stirred. Kieran knew the ropes wouldn't contain them for long. Not once the drug wore off and they were no longer under its effects.

Not wanting to be anywhere near them when they managed to escape, Kieran dropped their ropes and slammed the door shut. His other pets should already be free by now. It was time to see how they were faring.

As he moved deeper into the citadel, he started to hear the screams.

Satisfaction settled deep in his belly. *Excellent.*

Turning the corner, Kieran came to a sudden halt. Where there had once been a spiraling staircase leading up to a series of bedrooms and meditation suites, there was now nothing. The entire section of the citadel was gutted, stone and wood piled in a series of tiny mountains, blocking his way. Weak afternoon light shone down and illuminated the tiny dust motes that continued to rain down from the area above.

"Elder's sagging sack," he murmured. *How in the hell had a handful of Shadow-touched managed this?*

Tingling started in the base of his spine, and Kieran glanced around, suddenly uneasy.

Doubling back, Kieran raced through a separate hallway, this one leading him to a courtyard that jutted off from one of the main archives. The deeper into the building he went, the more frequent the pile of bodies became.

He lost count after thirty.

Surely the Guardians should have been able to make short work of the Shadow-touched. It wasn't like they had the power of . . .

Kieran wasn't able to complete the thought as his eyes landed on two lumbering figures standing in the courtyard.

Shadows.

Where the fuck did they come from?

Kieran froze, his mouth opening and closing as he tried to make sense of what he was seeing.

As more Shadows joined their brethren in the courtyard, everything clicked into place. It all made sense. The destruction. The body count.

There was only one way this was possible.

The Shadows had been hiding in the jungle this whole time.

Watching.

Waiting.

These new sentient creatures were much more terrifying than their predecessors. Ever since shaking off the hold of their maker, they'd regained the ability to think and rationalize. As a result, they were now able to strategize and avoid detection by the Guardians—something that had never been possible before when their wills had been bound to another.

Kieran's thoughts were coming faster now. Each sickening puzzle piece falling into place as his blood turned to ice.

The only way any Shadow could have made it into the citadel, let alone a group of this magnitude, was if they'd followed Kieran through one of the portals. Portals they never would have been able to find, let alone access, without him showing them the way.

As he watched, one of the Shadows leaned down and bit into a fallen Keeper. The man let out a pathetic scream as he struggled weakly against the creatures hold. Around him, the other Shadows let out victorious cheer as they followed suit, tearing into as many of the fallen as they could get their hands on.

It was then that Kieran knew. Khouman's frantic story converged with what he was seeing before him. The Caederan scouting party had been attacked by Shadows. Even though they'd been healed, no one could save them in the end. One by one, the scouts had turned, irrevocably changed until nothing of the people they'd been remained.

Kieran had never been the one building an army. It had been *them* the whole time. The Shadows. They had found a way to turn others.

For weeks they'd been traveling throughout Elysia spreading their fucking plague, while the Chosen scratched their arses trying to figure out what was happening. And now it was too late.

How many more would turn before anyone was the wiser?

Kieran's stomach rolled, guilt and panic warring inside of him. He'd known his actions would have casualties, but he hadn't cared. He'd wanted to teach the smug bastards a lesson. But never, *never* had he meant for this to happen.

Not that anyone would believe him.

They would condemn him first and ask questions later.

He couldn't be here when they figured out what he'd done.

Heart pounding like a death knell, Kieran rushed back to the portal room. The screams of the dying chasing him the entire way.

The citadel was the only home he'd had left, and now it was little less than ruins. Soon it wouldn't be more than a pile of rubble.

Because of him.

He had nothing left. No home. No love. No future.

Heart heavy, Kieran raced through a portal, not caring where it led him and never once looking back.

CHAPTER 31

*R*onan grabbed Effie beneath her arm and heaved her up from the floor.

"Come, Effie. We need to help the others."

Wiping her face on her forearm, Effie adjusted her grasp on her weapon and turned away from the corpse below her.

"Let's go," she said, oddly calm despite the world falling down around them.

The walls continued to shake every few seconds, large cracks snaking down the walls and ceiling.

Screams continued to surround them as they pushed through the citadel. Closing her eyes, Effie let the sounds fuel her rage. So long as she stayed angry, she would be strong enough to do what needed to be done.

Ronan led the way, Reyna beside him. Effie trailed behind them, stepping carefully as the building continued to shake. It wasn't long before they started to see the bodies of the fallen, like gruesome mile markers leading them to the heart of the battle. Gritting her teeth, Effie stepped over them, trying not to let herself think about the fact that she couldn't recall their names.

"Ronan, look," Reyna said, pointing to a particularly grizzly mound of bodies. "Weapons."

Effie watched Reyna lift a quiver and bow from a puddle of thick blood and sling them over her shoulder. As her eyes roved over the desecrated remains of her peers, Effie should have been disgusted. As it was, she couldn't manage more than idle curiosity. Body parts that should have never seen the light of day were strewn across the floor, the bodies that once contained them no longer recognizable as anything but meat. What would a Shadow have to do to turn someone into *that*?

Still kneeling, Reyna grabbed two swords and a mace.

Ronan accepted all three, holding the shorter of the swords out to Effie. Without a word, she took it from him and wiped the blade clean on her pants.

"Ah, look, it's my favorite mousie."

The voice was barely human, but Effie recognized it all the same, her body going completely still as a surge of anticipation worked its way through her.

"Tess," she growled, twisting to the left to find the Shadow-touched woman flanked by two others.

"Keepers, retreat!"

The part of Effie that was still her, registered shock at the Triumvirate's order. The new, primal part of her ignored it, wholly intent on revenge. She stepped forward, both her blades raised.

"Effie! Effie, fall back, you heard the order," Ronan shouted, already turning to obey.

"No! This *bitch* is the reason for the attack. I'm not letting her get away again."

A manic cackle bounced off the walls at her words. "Is that what you believe? You didn't *let* me do anything, little mouse."

"The citadel has fallen."

Any remaining sanity fled with the words. Effie's sanctuary was gone. The Shadows stole it from her, and now they must die. Starting with this one.

Ronan grabbed her arm and pulled hard enough to bruise. "Effie. It's time to go. You heard the Triumvirate; the citadel is lost."

Effie whirled on Ronan, shoving her elbow into his stomach. "Get off me, unless you want to be next."

His eyes widened in surprise. "Effie—"

"Look at her, Ronan. She's not herself," Reyna murmured beside him, leaning against the wall for support. Her expression was pinched, her mouth a tight line. Her energy was rapidly diminishing, soon she wouldn't be able to remain standing.

"Better take care of your woman, Shield."

Torn, Ronan looked between them, his loyalties divided.

"If you want to run and hide, then go," Effie snarled. "I don't need you."

Ronan took a step toward her, looking determined. "I will drag you out if I have to. I'm not leaving you alone."

Behind her, the Shadow-touched laughed, the sound fraying her already thin patience.

"Try it and I'll geld you."

Ronan paled, but reached for her anyway.

Effie swung her blade down, twisting her wrist just before she made contact so the flat end smacked his arm. "Next time I won't miss, and it won't be you I'm aiming for." She purposefully let her eyes fall on Reyna, her voice low and laced with malice.

The Night Stalker's eyes widened and her throat bobbed.

Shaking his head, Ronan stepped back. "Effie," he tried a final time, his voice pleading. "Don't do this."

"Don't you see? This is all there is," she said, turning away from him and leveling her gaze on the trio before her.

"What about Lucian?" he asked, his voice sounding far away.

"What about him?"

There was a soft feminine gasp of pain and then Ronan grunted. "I'll be back for you."

Effie was past hearing, focused only on the three beings standing before her. A ball of flame hurled past her shoulder, setting two of the three alight. Ronan must have truly given up if he was willing to risk his Fire. But even that bit of help wasn't enough to redeem him in her mind. A true warrior never would have run from the fight.

Neither woman so much as flinched at the shrieks of pain coming from the smoldering bodies writhing on the floor. They'd be dead soon. No need to waste energy thinking about them when the true fight was before them.

Effie adjusted her grip on her weapons, her eyes never leaving Tess' cruel grin. She'd already taken down two Shadows today. A single, Shadow-touched woman would be no match for her.

They were in a small alcove, the area opening up where two hallways joined. There wasn't much space to maneuver, but there was enough. So long as Ronan's Fire continued to burn down the hallway behind Tess and not switch directions, Effie would have long enough to finish the kill without any other of Tess' Shadow friends joining the party.

Tess remained motionless, her hands splayed by either side of her body. "What are you waiting for?" she crooned.

"Just savoring the suspense," Effie replied, her voice a dark purr.

"Before you die, little mouse?" Tess asked, tilting her head as the black veins slithered obscenely in her eyes.

"Before I kill you."

Effie raised her sword, legs pumping as she raced forward, only to stop short with a startled cry as the muscles in her arm began to spasm. The pain ricocheted down the right side of her body, almost blinding her with its intensity. This was ten-times worse than what happened in the shower, the muscles in her arm tearing and snapping as if they were coming undone.

"What are you doing?" she gasped, eyes wide as she stared up at the Shadow-touched woman.

Tess didn't answer, but her smile widened. The sight of her joy bringing with it a fleeting moment of panic.

Looking down at her arm, Effie blinked rapidly. Something was *slithering* beneath her skin. The muscles and tendons in her arm shifted, trying to adjust to make room for whatever was moving inside of her.

The pain was absolute, Effie's eyes tearing as her body tried to rearrange itself.

Tess started to laugh, watching with a malicious glee. "Looks like I don't need to do anything."

"No!" Effie growled behind clenched teeth, refusing to let this abomination win.

Even though her arm felt like it was being torn from her body, Effie still had one good one. Letting the sword fall from limp fingers, she hefted her cleaver higher in her left hand.

Tess laughed harder, which only fueled Effie's rage.

Snarling, vision cloudy with pain, Effie pulled her left arm back, inhaling deeply. As she exhaled, she let the cleaver go, watching it spin through the air and wedge itself in the center of Tess' forehead.

The laughter abruptly stopped as ichor-tainted blood started to drip down the once beautiful face.

Heart still thundering, Effie stumbled forward, her right leg buckling as the stretching and tearing feeling from her arm worked its way down her body. Nothing was going to stop her, not when she was this close.

Limping forward, Effie tugged her weapon free from the woman who'd fallen to her knees, a wet gurgle bubbling forth from her mouth.

Large, milky-white eyes blinked up at her, and in them she could see her reflection. In that long, drawn-out moment, Effie was no longer sure which of them was the monster.

Nor did she care.

Grasping the woman by her hair, Effie tugged her head back, exposing her throat. Leaning forward so that her mouth brushed against Tess' ear, she whispered, "When you get to hell, tell them that I sent you."

The dead woman's head was already falling from her body before Effie finished speaking.

CHAPTER 32

*A*ll around him the Keepers and the citizens protected by the citadel fought for their homes and their families. It didn't take centuries of experience to see that it was a losing battle. More than half the buildings in the city were burning, thick smoke hanging heavy in the air and turning it a menacing, burnt orange. Those that weren't on fire were little more than dust with nothing left to show that they'd once existed at all.

Lucian felt the loss of the city like the loss of a limb. He'd called many places home throughout his life, but had always found a special kind of peace in the Vil d'lume. Now that it was destroyed, the survivors would try to rebuild, but they'd never capture what had been lost. That kind of magic only ever exists once.

Lungs burning, Lucian spun around, searching for his next target. He didn't have to look for long. The tainted beasts were everywhere. Drenched in blood and sweat, he no longer knew how much of it was his, but Lucian didn't stop swinging his blade and fighting for what was left of his home. For the people he considered his.

While the Guardian plowed through an endless stream of Shadows and their Shadow-touched minions, the Chosen used what powers they had to try and mitigate the damage. These were no seasoned warriors,

233

few if any had more than remedial control of their elements, but between them they'd been able to offer enough of a distraction that Lucian and his men could fight back.

"Keepers retreat!"

Lucian was not a sentimental man, but he was grateful for the quick thinking that had him grabbing the handful of items he'd tied around his waist before donning his armor. By the time the day was through, nothing within the citadel would remain.

Looking out over what had once been the central fountain, Lucian met Kael's eyes, his brother's grim expression matching his own.

"The citadel is lost."

There was nothing left they could do now but survive.

Lucian fought like a man possessed, his blade spinning around him so fast he was obscured by the blur. He hacked and slashed, showing no mercy for the monsters that stole the lives of the innocent. They deserved none.

No matter who they'd once been.

Dropping to his knees to dodge a bolt of sickly green acid, Lucian used his momentum to roll forward and cut the legs from the Shadow who'd flung it. A wet gurgle sounded above him, telling him Kael had completed the kill.

The two men didn't acknowledge each other. They didn't need to. Not when enemies still walked among them.

Dragging in a ragged breath, Lucian scanned the thinning crowd, seeking out his next target. The battle was starting to slow, the ground littered with corpses. So many familiar faces stared up at him with blank eyes, and more than he cared to admit had died by his blade. Dozens of Keepers had been turned—although one was too many.

How? How had this happened?

Frustration and grief simmered in his veins. All the prophecies and warning in the realm hadn't been able to stop this from coming to be.

Howling in rage, Lucian swung his blade, the tendrils of inky smoke wafting along the edges burned through rotting flesh and made quick work of a snarling Shadow. The fiends may have destroyed his city, but at least few, if any of them, would survive to celebrate the victory.

A flash of red caught his eye. Lucian stared hard at the crumbling stairway as Ronan stumbled down it with the Night Stalker leaned heavily on his arm. They were the first to step out of the building since the Triumvirate's order to fall back. Lucian didn't want to contemplate what that meant for the rest of the Keepers.

Heart pounding, he looked behind the warrior, searching for a head of familiar blonde curls.

Effie was nowhere to be found.

Lucian's heart stopped, and his eyes flew back to a guilty-looking Ronan. He was already moving, his voice barely human as he snarled, "Where is she?"

"She wouldn't leave. Somethi—"

Blinded with rage, Lucian shoved the man, sending him staggering back. "You *left* her?" he roared, disbelief and fear turning his blood to ice.

"She's not—"

Voice dropping low, Lucian looked Ronan dead in the eye, not wanting to leave any room for misinterpretation. "You better hope she's alive when I find her, Shield, because if something's happened to her, nowhere in any world will keep you safe from me. I will hunt you down and slit your throat in your sleep."

Ronan's nostrils flared and a flash of something burned in his eyes, but he only nodded.

Pushing past him, Lucian ran up the stairs and into the burning building, the shouts of his brothers lost in the wind.

LUCIAN LOST TRACK of the number of rooms he combed through, pausing only to turn over a body and ensure it was not the one he was looking for. The burst of relief each time it wasn't grew fainter as he ran out of places to search.

Entire wings of the citadel were gone, leaving Lucian with the option of trying to dig through the debris or climb over it. More often than not, he had to turn around and try to gain entry from a different direction.

One way or the other, he would find her. There was no other acceptable option.

Lucian knew that he should have been at her side as soon as the fighting was underway. Effie was *his* charge, his responsibility. But she'd been cut off from him, and the townsfolk were all but defenseless without him.

He'd justified his absence by telling himself that Effie was with Ronan. The Shield should have kept her safe. The bastard damn near flayed him alive when they met for Lucian failing to do the same. So how? How by all that was holy could he have just left her?

Lucian shook off the rage, needing his battle calm to stay focused. Emotion had no place here.

Taking the next turn at a run, Lucian skidded to a halt. Less than an arm's length before him, a small body was crouched over something on the ground.

"Effie?"

A wet growl was his only answer.

The hair along the back of his neck lifted. There was nothing human about that sound.

Suddenly, the answer to a question he hadn't wanted to face slammed into him.

Denial was a cruel mistress. She let you bury your head until the truth of a matter cut you to the core. When it would hurt you the most.

Lucian would have laughed if he wasn't so close to losing it entirely.

There had been so many clues, the truth begging him to notice. He'd missed it. *Him*. A fucking Guardian with the ability to see life's very essence. Never once did he think to use his power to check her. Not after Sylverlands, when he'd inadvertently done so, and she'd shone more brightly than twenty fucking suns.

Never, in all his years as a Guardian, had Lucian seen anyone shine as Effie had that day. There had been no doubt in his mind that her soul was pure. That she was untainted.

He'd never made a costlier mistake in his immortal life.

It was only now, when it was too late, that he finally understood his error. Her soul's radiance was the very reason he hadn't sensed the dissonance. The same must have been true for Tinka.

Khouman's broken words swam to the surface. *'Would never hurt a fly unless it was to save someone . . . but then I started to notice the changes in her. A savagery so out of place with her gentle heart . . . Surges of temper . . . A new proclivity toward violence.'*

Tinka had taken weeks to transform, then, just like now, no one realized what happened until it was too late. Until their loved ones were lost . . .

If Lucian had taken the time to search Effie's essence again, would he have found the microscopic stain? Would it have made a difference?

Or had Effie's days been numbered ever since that Shadow tore out a piece of her and contaminated her blood?

Lucian didn't need his power now to show him what should have been obvious as soon as the first of her symptoms started to appear.

Her sudden disregard for her friends.

Her muddied visions.

The unexplained bout of physical pain when he'd held her in the shower.

All things that had been explained away as something far less sinister than the truth.

In order for the corruption to fully spread inside its host, it must have to tear the person's soul apart first. No wonder it had taken so long for the changes to be revealed. The weaker and more prone to evil the person, the faster the corruption spread. But for Effie and Tinka, those who were truly good, the transition was much slower, but no less absolute.

Lucian's heart caught in his throat as the blonde head started to turn toward him. Even though he knew what he'd find, he almost dropped to his knees as reality stared him down. Years of training was the only thing keeping him upright.

"Hello, Guardian," Effie snarled, black lines slithering through milky white eyes. "I've been waiting for you."

Lucian's blade dropped to the ground with a dull clang.

Letting out a savage battle-cry, the woman who cradled Lucian's blackened heart in the palm of her hand launched herself at him, the promise of death shining in her mutilated eyes.

Effie and Lucian's journey concludes with The Keeper's Vow, coming November 2019. Order your copy now to be one of the first to know how it ends!

Can't wait for more Keepers? Check out Kieran's story, The Dreamer and see how the obsession begins.

FROM THE AUTHOR

If you enjoyed this book, please consider writing a short review and posting it on Amazon, Bookbub, Goodreads and/or anywhere else you share your love of books. Reviews are very helpful to other readers and are greatly appreciated by authors (especially this one!)
When you post a review, send me an email and let me know! I might feature part, or all, of it on my blog or social media sites.

XOXO

Meg Anne

meg@megannewrites.com

Want to know when I have a new release or get exclusive access to my newest works? Join my mailing list:

MegAnneWrites.com/Newsletter

ACKNOWLEDGMENTS

There are so many people that are responsible—in big and small ways —for the creation of this (and every) book. Most of them I try and thank regularly. They are the ones who celebrate the small victories with me, are there to listen or let me spam them when I come up with a piece of dialogue so good I just need to bask in it, and the same ones that help me talk through the writer's block. They are my tribe and I am so lucky to have them.

That said, there's one person that deserves extra special attention, so this time around he's the one I want to focus on. Not because all those other people aren't essential—they are—but because I *literally* could not do this without him.

Never has anyone supported me and my dreams so thoroughly. He's shouldered every burden to allow me to focus on living my dream. From making sure I take breaks to eat, to being my alpha reader and plot partner, to being my web developer and graphic designer, my PA, my partner in crime, my inspiration, my big spoon—he takes care of every need. I may write about soulmates and epic badass alpha's, but he's the real deal. The love of a lifetime. He's the reason I get to write full time, and I can never thank him enough for that.

To my husband, I love you with all of my heart. You are my safe space. You give me room to fly, but are the reason I'll always come back home. I am so thankful we are on this journey together and that you are just as excited about it as I am.

ALSO BY MEG ANNE

FANTASY ROMANCE

THE CHOSEN UNIVERSE

THE CHOSEN

MOTHER OF SHADOWS

REIGN OF ASH

CROWN OF EMBERS

QUEEN OF LIGHT

THE KEEPERS

THE DREAMER – A KEEPERS STORY

THE KEEPER'S LEGACY

THE KEEPER'S RETRIBUTION

THE KEEPER'S VOW

PARANORMAL ROMANCE

CURSED HEARTS

CO-WRITTEN WITH JESSICA WAYNE

STAR-CROSSED

AMRIA

SUPERNOVA

ABOUT MEG ANNE

Meg Anne has always had stories running on a loop in her head. They started off as daydreams about how the evil queen (aka Mom) had her slaving away doing chores; and more recently shifted into creating backgrounds about the people stuck beside her during rush hour. The stories have always been there; they were just waiting for her to tell them.

Like any true SoCal native, Meg enjoys staying inside curled up with a good book and her cat Henry . . . or maybe that's just her. You can convince Meg to buy just about anything if it's covered in glitter or rhinestones, or make her laugh by sharing your favorite bad joke. She also accepts bribes in the form of baked goods and Mexican food.

Meg loves to write about sassy heroines and the men that love them. She is best known for her adult fantasy romance series The Chosen, which can be found on Amazon.

Made in the USA
Monee, IL
27 August 2019